*A*GAINST THE *S*PREAD

Anna Dawson Book Two

MARA JACOBS

Published by Mara Jacobs
©Copyright 2012 Mara Jacobs

ISBN: 978-1-940993-97-3

For more information on the author and her works, please see www.marajacobs.com

Against The Spread

As I rounded the corner, seeing the brilliant lights of the betting boards ahead of me, my phone rang. I ducked into the lobby of the oyster bar and pulled my phone out of my pocket. Like whoever was on the line was going to see me heading to the book room. And what if they could? I hadn't told anybody but Vince that I wasn't betting.

"Hi, Jimmy," I said after looking at the caller ID.

"You near a TV?"

"I'm at The Orleans. I just finished playing, I'm heading home."

"Head to the bar there by the poker room," he said.

"I'm closer to the book," I said and left the oyster bar and headed to the far end of the book room where the televisions lined the wall.

Jimmy could have been calling me to watch a news story, I suppose, and that of course wouldn't be on the TVs in the sports book. But I knew that wasn't the case. This call had something to do with the sports world. It was too early for game results.

A feeling of dread seeped through my body, chasing all remnants of the Hummer away.

"What's up?" I asked cautiously.

"Your boy," was all he said.

The dread stopped seeping and started rushing. I'd never told Jimmy about JoJo and Raymond, but a few weeks back I did give him a tip to bet against CIU. Couple that with the fact that I'd been absent quite a bit over the past weeks, and Jimmy was no dummy.

"My boy?" I played dumb.

Jimmy snorted. "Just get to a screen."

"I'm there," I said as I reached the line of televisions. Most of the leather chairs were empty at this time of morning, but I remained standing.

On three of the screens I saw Raymond Joseph's face smiling out at me. It was the head shot of him in his Fighting Hogs jersey, his trademark corn rows neat and tidy. His grin huge.

There was no volume on any of the screens, but I didn't need it. I really didn't even need to see the scrawl at the bottom of the picture to confirm my fears, but I read it anyway.

Central Iowa University star accused in point-shaving scandal.

To my brothers—Tom, Tim and Tyler.
My favorite corporation.

One
❖

I LOOKED IN THE REARVIEW MIRROR *of the rented car for the third time in as many minutes. Nobody was following me. I hadn't thought so, but I still checked. The precautions on this trip were more relaxed than normal, but there was no need for sloppiness.*

I'd been doing this long enough to know that just when you let your guard down, something bad happened.

Of course, something bad had happened to put me in this position in the first place.

I checked my MapQuest directions again, and made the turn as printed. Another mile down the two-lane highway, amidst a sea of snow-covered cornfields, and then I saw the flashing neon light for Chuck's Place.

A few cars sat in the lot, but this place was off the beaten path and far enough away from the university that my nervousness started to ease.

A little.

This was a new thing for JoJo—my less than scrupulous alter ego. No disguise, no false voice to practice, the only difference in my appearance from this morning in Las Vegas was the Central Iowa Fighting Hogs cap and sweatshirt that I'd bought at the Dubuque airport.

I took off my leather jacket, placing it in the empty passenger seat. I bit off the price tag of the sweatshirt and pulled it over my head. I gathered my shoulder-length hair into a ponytail and put on the cap, threading the ponytail through the back hole. I adjusted the cap, looking in the rearview mirror. I pulled it as low as I could and still be able to see. *Typical college kid meeting up with a guy in a bar.*

Yeah, right.

I entered the bar, saw my guy wasn't there yet and took a seat in a booth in the back, facing the door.

The bartender came over right away—not too much for him to do with only five other people in the bar—and I ordered a pitcher of some light beer on tap and two glasses.

No fancy imported beer, no fruity drinks that were my housemate Lorelei's specialty.

No need to be remembered.

That was shot to hell ten minutes later when my guy walked in the door. Being a basketball star at CIU wasn't what did it. Just being black in this all-white bar (hell, nearly all-white state) was enough for everyone to turn their heads.

To be fair, everyone had turned their heads when I walked in too. Plain old, white, average me.

I wondered if this place was a good pick, if he'd be too memorable, but the others quickly turned back to the bar and their drinks.

"JoJo," Raymond Joseph, point guard for the Fighting Hogs, said to me. Sneered at me to be more accurate. He slid into the seat across from me. He, I noticed, had no Hogs regalia on at all.

"Raymond," I responded, cool, even, no hint of the attitude he'd given me. I didn't throw it in his face that he was the one who'd called me, setting up this meet. I knew what he was going through only too well, I wasn't going to throw salt in that wound.

He poured himself a beer, took a small sip and placed the glass on the table. "You got it?" he asked.

I nodded, looking around the bar. "You think this was a good place to meet? Maybe somewhere more crowded? Or outdoors? Or even your apartment again?"

I'd been to Raymond's apartment once. I'd left him my number in case he wanted to do business again and hoped like hell I wouldn't hear from him. Though I knew I would.

He'd called a few days ago.

"I've heard that people mind their business here," he said. I looked at the patrons again, now giving them imaginary nefarious traits. Truth was, Raymond and I were probably the lowest of the lowlifes in the place.

Or at least I was.

"Plus," he added. "It's too fucking cold to meet outside." I agreed with him there. "I'm too known on campus. And," he looked at me with loathing in his eyes, "I don't ever want you in my apartment again."

"Fair enough," I said.

"Besides, there won't be a next time. This is it."

I just nodded and handed him an envelope thick with hundred-dollar bills under the table.

I took a gulp of my drink, pulled out a ten and left it on the table for the beer. I stood up to leave. As I passed him, I stopped and turned to him, my back to the rest of the bar. "You'll be seven point favorites this Saturday," I said softly.

His hands were still under the table, clutching the envelope, but I could see his shoulders clench and I figured that envelope was going to be crushed by the time he pocketed it. That was okay, crinkled money was still accepted.

"No," he said. "That was the last time."

"Okay." I started to reach out to him, but I couldn't ease his pain. His disgust. Of himself and me.

I wanted to ask him how his sister was doing, but I didn't. He'd see that as strong-arm tactics or even a threat. But really I was just curious—and concerned—for how Raymond's little sister was doing in the drug rehab that his ill-gotten gains had paid for.

I kept quiet. I put my head down and left the bar.

At the airport, I put the Hogs hat and sweatshirt in the trash can in the ladies' room. Too bad, I liked them, but I didn't want anything that could tie me in any way to this trip, this school or to Raymond Joseph.

I hoped…I really hoped…that was the last I'd seen of Raymond and Dubuque.

But somehow I knew I'd be back.

MY NAME IS JOHANNA ELIZABETH DAWSON. I'm thirty-four years old and originally from Wisconsin, though I've lived in Vegas for the past thirteen years. After the first three years out west, I found myself in major gambling debt and in the hospital, recuperating from a broken foot, courtesy of said debt.

I met then seventy-something Ben Lowenstein in the hospital. He was recuperating from hip surgery. He calls me Hannah. I didn't correct him when I introduced myself as Anna—what everyone else calls me—since I never thought I'd see him again. I'm still not really sure if I became his keeper or he mine, but we've been sharing a home ever since. Lorelei joined us six years ago and basically runs the place. She's a forty-year-old dancer in a town not kind to dancers over thirty. She calls me Jo—short for Johanna, not JoJo.

Nobody in my "real life" knows me as JoJo.

I make a good living playing professional poker. Ben, Lor and I live in style. Until I mess up and need to turn into JoJo.

I PULLED INTO THE DRIVEWAY of my Summerlin home later that night. Which was really early the next morning, but that was not unusual. In fact, I'd planned the flights close together so that I wouldn't have to be gone for more than nine or ten hours, my usual time away from the house to play poker.

A regular working Joe. Nobody would need to know that I'd been across several states and time zones.

And broken umpteen laws.

Victimless crime. Helping a poor girl get the assistance she needed. Yeah, yeah, I could spin it anyway I wanted—and I did—but the truth was, sometimes I'd get into trouble with a money-lender (and not the kind insured by the FDIC) and JoJo would need to make an appearance.

That JoJo now knowingly involved a player—Raymond Joseph—was new and went against my, albeit limited, moral code. Usually I just slipped a star player something that made him unable to play the next day. He never knew what hit him, and my debt was wiped out. No harm, no foul.

Yeah, right.

I shut out the self-loathing voice in my head and entered the house. It was quiet and dark and I walked to Lorelei's bedroom on the opposite side of the house from my room.

I quietly peeked in her door and could see the moonlight illuminating her flaming red hair across her pillow. "Jo?" she croaked, lifting her head.

"Sorry, Lor, I didn't mean to wake you." I didn't normally come this way when I came home from playing, but the last few weeks had been anything but normal and I wanted to make sure my family—such as it was—was safe and sound.

"Isss okay," she slurred, still half asleep. "What time is it?"

"Late," I said. "Well, early."

She nodded, her eyes still closed. She laid her head back on the pillow. "You want me to take Ben and Gus to breakfast tomorrow? Today?"

"Nah, thanks. I got it," I answered. "I'll probably just stay up." It would only be a couple of hours before Ben, and his friend Gus who was staying with us, were due to meet their buddy Jimmy for their daily breakfast. I could catch a nap, but I'd probably just put on ESPN and watch the ticker of scores from the night's games.

"Okay," Lorelei said and burrowed deeper into her covers. As if an afterthought, she asked, "How'd you do?" She wanted to know how my night of poker playing went. If there would be a wad of cash on her dresser when she got up to put toward the family coffers.

In fact, it was a very successful night, but there'd be no money waiting for my oh-so efficient girl Friday.

"Busted out," I said.

"Mmmm," she said with no real concern. There was no reason; she knew I'd come through in the long run. I always had.

What she didn't know was that sometimes JoJo picked up the slack.

I walked down the hallway to Ben's room. He slept with the door open now. Had for the last few years so Lorelei could hear him if he had trouble getting around in the night. There was also a monitor that connected to my room, the kitchen and the family room, as well as a bell that sounded if he went out the glass door in his bedroom, onto the patio.

Ben was half snoring, half snuffling in his sleep. I walked quietly in, and sat down in the chair to watch him.

Ben was eighty-two years old, and other than his hip, which made walking slow, he was doing well for a man his age.

Or had been until he'd lost two of his closest friends. One being his best friend of seventy years. We'd recently buried Danny then Saul, and I think a part of Ben with them.

It's what brought me to his room each night. I sat in the chair across the room from my friend and watched as he slept.

Two hours later, he was gently tapping my shoulder as I slept awkwardly in the leather club chair. He was fully dressed. I must have been really zonked to not have heard him.

"Hannah, dear, it's time to go for breakfast." His brown eyes were full of concern as they took me in. "Would you like to just go to bed? I'm sure Lorelei could take us. Or Gus could drive us himself for that matter."

I rose from the chair, and stretched, my muscles sore from the tense night before and the cramped flights. "No, I'm good. Let me just splash some water on my face, and I'll be ready."

He looked at me for longer than I liked, as if trying to decide something about me. Finally, he nodded, his small, bony frame turned from me, and he pushed his walker in front of him out the doorway.

Two

❖

THE TABLE WE CHOSE for breakfast seated four. We used to need one for six. Well, actually, we never needed to worry about it. We'd had a table at the back of the Sourdough Café in the Arizona Charlie's, an off-the-Strip casino, with our name on it, because we ate breakfast there every morning. Even had the same waitress, Grace.

That was before we lost Danny and Saul.

In the days since, we'd been trying different places each morning, trying to find a new regular spot.

Trying to find a new life without The Corporation.

Jimmy Mancino, Gus Morgan, Ben Lowenstein, Danny O'Hern and Saul Greene had formed The Corporation, a group of retirees who had once ruled Vegas as sports odds setters. They'd worked at different casinos, had been rivals in their heyday. But since retiring, they met every morning for breakfast and had become close friends.

Until Danny and Saul had been killed.

I suppose Jimmy, Ben and Gus still made up The Corporation, but none of them had used the term lately.

And we sat in a different restaurant every morning.

Originally, we'd just set out to find someplace different, the memories at the Sourdough too fresh and raw. But the first day, Jimmy—huge, fat, never met a morsel he didn't like, Jimmy—

complained about the meal so we went somewhere different the next day. Then Ben, never one to eat a big breakfast anyway, didn't like the coffee. At the next place, silver-haired, silver-tongued Gus—who, with his Paul Newman good looks and devilish smile, hadn't met a waitress he couldn't charm out of her panties—was unhappy with the service.

And so began our mornings of revolving restaurants. Good thing every Vegas casino had a breakfast place as well as several other restaurants. We hadn't even had to venture beyond the Strip yet.

Which brought us this morning to the corner nook restaurant of the old Barbary Coast. It had been sold and renamed, but my nostalgic boys had rubbed off on me, and I still called it by its original name.

After breakfast, we pulled out our sporting events odds sheets from various casinos and started talking about today's games and whom we liked. I was drawing a circle around UCLA to cover the point spread against Stanford when something compelled me to look up and toward the entranceway.

There stood Detective Jack Schiller. Las Vegas Metro Police, homicide division.

"Oh, Christ," I mumbled to myself and quickly ducked my head, causing Ben, sitting on the same side of the table as me, to look up.

"Oh, it's Jack," he said cheerily. His wrinkled hand automatically rose up to get Jack's attention, but stopped midway. He turned to me, as if sensing his glee was not shared.

His hip was for shit, but Ben's brain was still sharp as a tack.

I hadn't seen Jack since he'd dumped me. No, that's not true. I'd seen him at Saul's funeral, but we hadn't spoken.

What was there to say? He had a drinking problem, I had a gambling problem. We'd spent a few weeks together trying to figure out who was killing The Corporation, having incredible sex and pretending that our issues wouldn't interfere with our burgeoning relationship.

He'd wised up first.

Jimmy and Gus turned around, totally negating my idea to pretend I hadn't seen Jack. Jack's eyes scanned the room and settled on the four of us, which wasn't hard as three of us were staring at him.

"Guys," I pleaded. "Be cool."

Jimmy snorted. Gus shrugged. Ben looked at me with compassion. And then that traitorous old man had a look of pleasure cross his face as Jack strolled toward our table.

He was wearing his usual work uniform of chinos, blue chambray work shirt, tie and leather jacket. As he got closer, I could see the haggard lines of his face, the dark circles under his eyes.

I couldn't even silently congratulate myself that he must be miserable without me; that was Jack's usual look.

Whether from the drinking or the things he must see on a daily basis, most likely both, the man always wore a look of bone-deep weariness.

It looked good on him.

Of course he'd come over to say hi. It would be fine to ignore me, but he'd bonded with the boys and to snub them was not Jack's style. I just hoped it would be a quick hello to the boys and then he'd move on to his own table or to whomever he was meeting here.

I admit it, the crazy female in me came out and I quickly scanned the restaurant to see if there were any women sitting alone, looking as if they were waiting.

Nope. None. I'm not even going to tell you the sick sense of relief that came over me.

"Ben. Mr. Mancino. Mr. Morgan," Jack said when he got to our table. He nodded to Jimmy and Gus then made his way around to Ben.

Recovering from a gunshot wound, Gus had been pretty

much out of it when Jack had been in my life, and Jimmy had never really warmed to Jack the cop, though he had a grudging respect for him.

But Ben and Jack. Well, there was something more with those two.

I watched them carefully as they shook hands, Ben placing his free one on top of their joined ones. Jack settled his other hand on Ben's shoulder. I took a weird sense of joy in the fact that two men that I held in such high esteem seemed to admire each other as well. Like it validated my choices or something.

And yes, even though he dumped me, and he probably had demons that could frighten Satan, I still thought of Jack Schiller as a good choice.

His judgment about me had been right on, hadn't it?

"Can you sit, Jack?" Ben asked motioning to an unused chair at the table next to us. "Have you eaten, yet?"

Jimmy started reaching for the chair Ben had pointed at, but a raised hand from Jack stopped him.

"Actually, this isn't a social call, Ben," Jack said. "Even though it is good to see you."

I waited to see if his gaze included me, but he was looking only at Ben.

"Then we won't keep you," I said, a bit too much bite in my voice. Damn. "If you're on duty and all," I added, trying to sound as if I only had Jack's business interests at heart.

He looked at me fully then, his brown eyes staring at me with the same compassion that Ben had flashed me moments ago.

God, how I hated that he knew how hard it was for me to see him.

"My business is with you," he said, still looking at me.

"I thought our business was done," I said tightly. Ben sighed beside me. He didn't often get to see his Hannah so…shrill, I guess was as good a word as any.

Or brittle, because that's exactly how I felt seeing Jack again. As if I'd snap if he touched me. And yet I was willing to venture it.

He ignored my taunt. "This is police business."

"You mean you came here purposely to see me about police business?" I said, slow to catch on. It had been a long night in Iowa last night, and it looked like it was going to be an even longer day today.

"Yes."

"How'd you find us?" Jimmy asked the question that was on the tip of my tongue.

Jack kept his eyes on me as he said, "It wasn't easy." He then looked up, and around the restaurant. He didn't ask what we were doing here instead of the Sourdough Café.

A good detective, Jack Schiller.

"What business?" Gus asked, again beating me to the punch.

Jack looked at the three men. I could tell he was deciding how much to tell them all. He'd probably prefer it if I rose and left so he could speak to me alone without having to ask me in front of my friends.

I stayed seated and waited for Jack to make up his mind. He scrubbed his hand across his tired face, a move I knew well and that never failed to endear him to me. I started to rise, to take the decision away from him, but he motioned for me to stay sitting. "Paul Coscarelli was killed last night."

He looked at me as if that should mean something but it didn't. I looked at Ben, who shook his head, then Gus, who shrugged. Jimmy had a sadistic smile on his face. "So, that SOB finally got what was coming to him."

"Who is Paul Coscarelli?" I asked Jimmy.

"Paulie Gonads," Jimmy and Jack said at the same time.

Oh. Him I knew. Only too well. My foot, the one Paulie had shattered years ago for an unpaid loan, ached under the table. In fact, it was for Paulie's boss, Vince Santini, that I'd been in Dubuque doing JoJo business. Paulie also ran Vince's back room, high-stakes poker games, which I regularly sat in on.

When JoJo had done her job correctly, Vince's games, and loans, were open to me.

"His name was Coscarelli?" I murmured, realizing that I'd talked to the man at least three times a week for the last thirteen years and I didn't even know his last name.

"Yes," Jack said.

"How was he killed?" I asked, although if Jack was standing here, I had a pretty good idea already.

"Murdered," Jack confirmed.

"How?"

"Bullet to the head," Jack said softly. He put his hand on Ben's shoulder, knowing...caring that Ben would automatically think of Danny and Saul.

I started to reach for Ben's hand, to give comfort, but Ben raised his hand closest to me and patted Jack's hand resting on his shoulder. I felt a childish hurt well inside me.

I looked across the table. Gus was deep in thought, probably also thinking of Danny and Saul. But Jimmy was watching me. Watching me watch Ben and Jack. He gave me a "fuck it" shrug, and I tried to do just that.

"You came to talk to me about Paulie?" I said to Jack, bringing him back to the point.

"Yes," he said. "Maybe we should go somewhere else?"

Ah, so he did care about me a little. Or at least on some level wanted to protect me.

Not sure how much the boys knew about my dealings with Paulie, he didn't want to ask about him in front of them. They knew some of the ugliness, but not all. Certainly not about JoJo. But then, Jack didn't know about JoJo either.

And the fact that I couldn't...wouldn't trust him enough to tell him was the main reason we weren't together.

I looked around the crowded restaurant. They did a good breakfast business here. They put a plate of fresh coffee cake on your table before you even got your coffee like Mexican restaurants did with chips and salsa. I was kind of hoping that we'd found a winner. "There are no empty tables. We could go out to the casino floor. It might not be that loud this early."

"I was thinking about the station," Jack said. "Maybe Jimmy could drive Gus and Ben home? I'd bring you back to your car later."

"I can drive us home," Gus said. "I got clearance from the doctor to drive."

Gus had been shot in the leg when The Corporation had been targeted. He'd moved in with Ben, Lorelei and me to recuperate. I knew he'd gone to the doctor, I'd driven him myself, but I hadn't realized he'd been given a green light to drive. I kind of hoped that maybe Gus would stay with us for awhile. It was good for Ben to have him around.

"Okay," I said, handing the car keys to Gus. I looked at Jack. "You'll bring me home?"

He nodded. "Whenever you're ready."

I packed up my odds sheets, embarrassed that Jack saw them. Not that betting on sporting events was illegal in Vegas, but he knew that was my weakness.

My heroin.

My bourbon. That was a term he'd understand.

I'd wanted to ask the boys what they thought about the UCLA game, but my pride wouldn't let me do it in front of Jack. I folded up my sheets, shoved them in my jacket pocket and rose from the table.

"Where we eating tomorrow?" Jimmy said as I stepped away.

"Same place?" I said hopefully. I liked this place, and I was starting to think the boys really needed to find a new home base. Needed to move forward. Put roots down with just the three of them.

Four of us.

The men looked at each other, waiting to see who brought up the reason we should find a new place. Nobody jumped in, and a tiredness seemed to pass amongst the three of them.

"Yeah, same place," Jimmy said and Ben and Gus nodded their agreement.

"Okay," I said. "See you tomorrow, Jimmy." He grunted at me, his nose stuck back in the odds sheets.

Ben and Jack shook hands again, Jack said his good-byes to Jimmy and Gus, gaining another grunt from Jimmy.

I crossed around the table and stood by Jack. "I won't be long," I said to Gus and Ben. Gus waved to me, and Ben smiled. He had a mischievous look on his face, and I wondered if he had put a hit out on Paulie just so Jack would have an excuse to come find me.

We were silent on the walk to Jack's car. I didn't say anything because this was Jack's play, and I was going to let him call the shots.

There were hundreds of people in Vegas who would have had dealings with Paulie, would have been able to answer the questions for Jack that he wanted answered. I was sure they were just the kinds of things that he could probably find out from his fellow police officers in the vice department. Who did Paulie work for? Vince Santini. Did he have any enemies? Too many to mention. Did I know of anyone who would want to harm Paulie? Again, too many to mention.

There must be another reason Jack had decided to find me. There were just too many other people that knew Paulie better than I did to go to for information. Maybe there was a personal reason why Jack wanted to see me, and he'd used Paulie's murder as an excuse. That's why I'd waited to get him alone to ask what was going on, and didn't bring it up in front of the boys.

Sitting beside him in his car, I let the foolish hope that I'd squashed earlier out of its tiny box. It blinked hard at the light, unaccustomed to the brightness. But it came to life quickly.

I looked at Jack, studied him while he weaved his way through the morning traffic. Even though we hadn't been together all that long, I still missed him.

His brownish hair hadn't been cut since we'd parted. He wore it short, but it looked good this tiny bit longer. I looked for signs that either he was still drinking or that he wasn't. His eyes seemed a little bloodshot, but they always did, just from the hours he kept. Lots more homicides committed in Vegas in the wee hours of the morning than at noon.

His hands were steady on the wheel, no shakes when he reached over to turn the radio on.

Apparently he wasn't ready to talk yet, either.

But he'd come for me.

I sat back in my seat and wished the ride would take forever.

THE SMALL INTEROGATION room looked very similar to the room Jack and Botz had used at the morgue when we'd worked on the Corporation case together. Was that what this was all about? Did Jack think I'd want to help with this case because of knowing Paulie?

I felt bad Paulie was dead and all, but men don't live long lives in Paulie's line of work. Being an enforcer for a loan shark put you on a lot of people's lists. Usually you were safe because said people were more afraid of being found by Paulie, but who knew, somebody could have gotten fed up with Paulie beating on them and put an end to it.

And Paulie meant nothing to me personally, certainly nothing like the boys did, so Jack couldn't have thought I'd want to be in on this case, could he?

Was it just an excuse to check up on me? Make sure I was

okay? That my gambling habit hadn't put me in a hole out in the desert?

God knows I'd thought about—and worried about—since we'd split up.

"You remember Detective Botz?" Jack said as we made our way through the maze of desks to the area that Jack and Frank Botz shared.

"Sure. Hi, Frank," I said.

Frank was Jack's partner, and I liked him. He always wore a goofy tie—today was Homer Simpson—and played the Columbo "just help me to understand" dimness, but he was a sharp one.

He also cared about Jack, and I appreciated that in him.

Frank nodded at me, but I noticed he didn't return my smile. "Ms. Dawson."

The last time he'd seen me, there'd been a smoking gun in my hand and a dead body at my feet, so maybe I wasn't Frank's favorite person. But I thought he'd liked me well enough when Jack and I were together.

Jack kept going past his desk area and I followed. Frank stepped in behind me, and I realized we were headed to the interrogation room.

So much for this all being a ruse about trying to get me back.

Apparently, after proving my worth on the Corporation case, I was to become the department snitch? Their in to all things gambling?

I'd almost consider it if it meant seeing Jack on a regular basis.

I wasn't sure I'd be able to help. They wanted to know what I knew about Paulie, who hated him enough to put a bullet through his brain. I wasn't the person who knew those details, though I might be the only person who would talk to them without a ton of attitude and hassle, which was probably the reason I was here.

We walked into the room. Jack motioned for me to sit. He didn't meet my eye, but looked over my head at his partner. They did some kind of silent thing between them. Jack must have won—or lost—because he was the one that sat down in the chair facing me. Frank remained standing against the closed door.

I looked at Jack. Waited for him to start. He ran his hand over his face then took a notebook and pen out of his jacket pocket. He flipped the notebook to a blank page and laid them both down on the table in front of him.

A feeling of unease washed over me.

I was wrong; this wasn't about seeing me. This wasn't even about getting information about Paulie.

I raised my hand to my neck, to my horseshoe pendant. I tapped three times then lowered my hand.

Jack watched the movement, seemed to register it, then he finally looked me in the eyes. His were cold, and all business.

"Ms. Dawson, where were you between midnight and three a.m. last evening?"

Three

❖❖

"YOU TOTALLY AMBUSHED ME," I said to Jack two hours later as he drove me home.

"That's the way questioning works," he said, still emotionless, eyes solely on the road.

When I'd realized that I was being treated as a suspect—after I got over the shock, and my stupidity for not seeing it sooner—I'd clammed up. We'd spent the next two hours with me refusing to answer any questions then finally asking to either be charged with something or be brought home.

Frank and Jack had looked at each other, done another invisible signal of some kind, and Jack had led me out to his car.

"That may be the way questioning regularly works," I said now. "But I'm not your regular...what do you call it...perp?" I got a small smile out of him at my attempt at cop-speak.

"You most definitely are not," he said with some warmth—finally!—in his voice.

"So why the dog and pony show?"

"You are someone who was a known associate of Paul Coscarelli. I personally have seen you interact with him, have seen him strong-arm you." His hands tightened on the steering wheel.

That had not been one of my prouder moments, Jack seeing Paulie take me away to answer for JoJo's only slip up.

He'd tried to intervene, but I'd stopped him, preferring to deal with Paulie—and my mess—on my own.

It'd been the beginning of the end for us.

"The back story of how he...collected...years ago from you is well known in gambling circles," Jack continued.

I unconsciously slid my bad foot underneath my good one. No sense in trying to deny it, Jack knew about Paulie's signature injury.

He had licked the damn scar.

"He put you in the hospital."

"I put myself in the hospital," I said, trying not to let the shame I felt come through.

He flexed his hands on the steering wheel, letting out a sigh. "Because of our past...relationship...I had to play this strictly by the book. Well, not strictly, I shouldn't have been in the questioning room at all. But..." He let the thought drift away.

"So you think I'm capable of murder?" I asked, then wished I hadn't. Jack had been standing next to me when I'd killed a man.

But that was different, I told myself, as my stomach clenched with remembered guilt.

"That was different," Jack said, reading my mind.

"Yeah, it was," I said quietly.

He reached over then, placed his hand on mine and squeezed. Before I could flip my hand over and squeeze back, his hand was gone.

"I think anyone is capable of killing anyone," he said. "In the right situations, for the right reasons."

"So, you really think I killed Paulie?"

He hesitated before speaking, which I didn't think was a very good sign. "I don't think you would have killed Paulie because he'd hurt you in the past. Or even if he was threatening you now for some reason. That's business. That's the life you chose." He cleared his throat, and there was a sense of resignation in his voice. I looked away from him, out the passenger-side window. "But I do think you would protect Ben, and the boys, and Lorelei."

"I would," I agreed. "You would too, if it were you," I added.

"Yes."

"Paulie wasn't threatening anybody I care about. And I'm all square with him and Vince," I said, telling him now what I wouldn't in the interrogation room. I don't know why. It was something to do with how stupid I'd felt when I realized that I was being treated just like anyone else that had dealt with Paulie and Vince.

I didn't want to be just like anybody else to Jack.

"Okay," he said.

"Okay? Just like that? You believe me?"

"Yes."

"Huh."

He let out a long-suffering sigh. "Johanna," he said softly. Hearing the name he—and he alone, except for my mother when I'd really pushed the boundaries—called me, made me take my eyes from the road and look at his rugged, lived-in face. "When we were together, did you ever lie to me?"

"No," I said without hesitation. I'd made a point of it. Even against my better judgment. If I had, we might still be together.

But Jack, much like myself, had a strong, albeit skewed, moral code. And I knew he would much more easily accept my gambling and the extremes it drove me to than he could my lying to him.

My moral code consisted of only two elements—never bet on a game that JoJo had fixed, and never knowingly involve a player in a fixed game.

I'd recently broken both those edicts and was trying to fight my way back to being able to look myself in the mirror each morning. I'd only bet on a game once, and those winnings went to a much-deserved pair of diamond earrings for Lorelei.

But involving a player...my mind went back only a dozen hours or so ago. To my meeting with Raymond Joseph.

I had involved him. I'd intended for it to be a one-time deal, but Raymond had gotten a taste and now was calling me. Still, I had gotten the kid into this seedy world, I wasn't about to involve him any further by naming him as my alibi.

"I didn't think you'd lied to me," Jack said now, pulling me away from my self-loathing thoughts.

"I didn't," I said.

"So, you tell me that you're not into Vince right now, that Paulie wouldn't be a threat to you or yours..."

"Yes?"

"Why can't you tell me where you were last night?"

I looked over at him, waited until he turned his head from the road to meet my gaze.

"*Because* I won't lie to you, Jack."

We'd reached my house. I was relieved to see that Gus and Ben had arrived safely and that our Lexus SUV was in the driveway. So was my beloved Porsche and Lorelei's BMW. There was a small, beat-up Nissan, which I didn't recognize, parked at the curb. Jack parked behind it.

"Does that belong to one of your people?" I asked Jack, pointing at the Nissan, suddenly furious at the thought that Jack had sent some of his guys around to question Ben, Gus and Lorelei about my whereabouts while he had me at the station.

It would have scared Ben witless, and Lorelei would have probably started making up alibis for me on the spot.

Jack shook his head. "Nope, not one of our guys. You don't know who it belongs to?"

"Nobody I know drives a piece of shit like that," I said.

He snorted, looked around the interior of his own piece of shit, "Almost nobody," he clarified.

"This belongs to the cops," I said, realizing I didn't even know what Jack drove.

As if answering my unasked question, he said, "Mine's about the same."

I reached for the door handle. "Are we done? Am I free to go, officer?"

He lifted one brow at me—a look I'd tried to copy, to no avail. "We're far from done, Johanna."

I didn't think he was talking about Paulie's murder.

Okay, I *hoped* he wasn't.

"Nothing's changed," I reminded him. Stupid. If the man decided to just forget the reasons he felt we couldn't be together, who was I to remind him.

"Maybe I…" He didn't finish, and I kept my mouth shut this time.

He looked toward my house. Drew his hand roughly down his face and let out a long, slow, breath.

And said nothing.

I finally reached over, smoothed down a patch of his hair that stuck up in the back. The man had a permanent case of bed head…and the audacity to make it look sexy. "You look tired, Jack," I said softly.

He nodded, then looked over at me. He bent his head into my hand, as if a dog wanting to be petted. And I desperately wanted to pet him.

But I didn't. After all, as I'd just said, nothing had changed.

I couldn't even tell him where I'd been last night.

I took my hand slowly away, placed my other one on the door handle. "I'd better go inside. Ben's probably freaking out about me going with you. I'm sure Jimmy put it together for them all that you were looking at me for Paulie's murder."

"A situation you could easily remedy by just telling me where you were last night."

"What if I told you that I was with a man all night, but I didn't want you to know that?"

I don't know if it was relief or grief that passed over his face, but he quickly set it to cop mode. "Is that the truth?"

Technically it was, I'd been with Raymond Joseph, but we both knew that's not what I'd meant. "No," I said. He started to say something, but I interrupted with, "I've gotta go, Jack."

"How's Ben doing anyway? Since Danny and Saul?"

Now it was my turn for a long, deep breath. "Okay, I guess. He misses them. I miss them."

Jack was looking out the front windshield, slowly nodding.

"He misses you, too, Jack," I said.

He kept on nodding, not missing a beat. "I miss him, too."

His profile was so familiar to me, the shape of his nose, the soft brown eyes. A wave of guilt washed over me.

I was keeping a secret from both him and Ben.

"Jack, I—" I said at the same time as he said, "Do you mind if I go in with you? Spend a little time with him? At least let him know that you're not in any trouble."

"Am I not in trouble?"

He snorted. "Probably no more than usual."

I pushed the secret down farther. This wasn't the time. And until I knew for sure if what I thought was true, it wouldn't be. "Sure," I said. "Come on in."

"You're sure? That wouldn't be weird? Me being at your place to see Ben?"

I snorted. "Probably no more than usual."

We both got out of his car and made our way slowly up the driveway and to the front door. It felt both familiar and strange to be walking into my home with Jack. I almost reached for his hand, but stopped myself. At one point I thought he raised his arm to wrap around my shoulder, but at the last second he scratched the back of his head and lowered his arm.

We went through the front door. I looked to my left, past the foyer to the living room. "Anyone home?" I called out, seeing it empty.

"In here," Lorelei called from the dining room off to our

right.

Lorelei's a dancer, having danced in some of the biggest shows on the Strip. But when forty hit, the opportunities waned, and she threw herself into running our small household. Which she did with razor-sharp precision. She was able to roll with the punches that come with having a professional poker player as the main breadwinner.

Jack and I walked into the dining room together. Gus, Ben and Lorelei sat at the large table with a young man I'd never seen before. They each had a coffee cup in front of them. I noticed a carafe of coffee on the sideboard along the wall, along with what looked like a tray of pastries.

Lorelei's a statuesque redhead, pure showgirl material. I do okay on a good day, looks-wise, but I always feel like a troll standing next to her. She had on her usual casual wear, track suit over a leotard, like she'd just returned from a dance class, though I don't think she'd taken in one in nearly six months. My fault. My ups and downs with gambling had kept her hopping with trying to spend lots of cash at times, and coming up with it at others.

A notebook and pencil sat on the table in front of her. That wasn't unusual; Lor always had some kind of list or another going.

She didn't meet my eye, though, and that was unusual.

"Everything okay?" Ben asked Jack and me.

Jack nodded.

"Everything's fine," I said.

Ben looked closer at us, probably trying to discern what exactly "fine" meant—the fact that I wasn't being booked for Paulie's murder, or that Jack and I were back together. Knowing how Ben felt about Jack, he'd probably be okay posting my bail if it meant Jack would be hanging around the house again.

"Everything okay here?" I asked, nodding my head toward the stranger.

He was in his late twenties, with longish hair that had no discernable style, glasses, and a small spot of toilet paper on his chin where he'd cut himself shaving. He had on a blazer that looked brand new, a too-tight tie, and a white shirt that looked as if the collar was choking him. So somebody not used to business attire, despite the folder with papers in it lying in front of him. He shuffled some of them now, looking nervous as hell.

As a professional poker player, I tried to read him. But then, I tried to read everyone.

He looked like any of the hundreds of druggies and homeless guys I saw every day. But like somebody had cleaned him up, put him in some new clothes and hoped for the best.

But what would a guy in a suit be doing in my dining room? IRS? Nah, they wouldn't send somebody that green to duke it out with a professional gambler. Besides, my accountant made sure that I was squeaky clean on my taxes.

They couldn't have found out about JoJo? Nope. Again, this puppy is not who they'd send if that case ever broke.

They'd send somebody like Jack.

Lorelei raised her head, flipped her flaming mane back—a move that caught both the kid's and Gus' attention—squared her shoulders, and looked over at me.

Oh, shit. "No, Lor," I said. "Not again. Not today. I'm too tired."

She ignored me and said, "Jo, you are surrounded by people who love you." I looked at the kid I didn't know. "Not him," Lorelei said with exasperation, following my gaze. She glanced at Jack standing beside me. Opened her mouth, then—thank God—shut it. "And as people who love you, we're worried about you."

I looked at Gus, who just shrugged and took a sip of coffee. Then I turned to Ben, and the look in his eyes quelled any smart-ass comment I was ready to throw at Lorelei. He *did* look worried about me.

For him, I'd listen to this farce. I motioned for Lorelei to get on with it.

She sat up straighter, now in the spotlight, the showgirl in her coming out, and said what I knew was coming.

"This is an intervention."

Four

❖❖

"YOU CAN LEAVE," I said to Jack.

He chuckled, walked to the sideboard and started to pour himself a cup of coffee. "Not on your life." He motioned to the coffee cups, I shook my head no, and he made his way to one of the empty chairs. He was about to sit down when he asked Lorelei, "Is this one okay? Should I sit somewhere else? Is there a seat especially for Johanna, or does she have to stand there and take it."

I shot him a screw-you look, which he only raised a brow at. He took off his jacket, hung it on the back of the chair and sat down. He rolled up his shirtsleeves, as if settling in for a game of cards.

"No, no, that's fine, Jack, right there," Lorelei said, quickly recalculating the ceremony now that there was a guest star. "Oh, this is great." She pointed to the young man's stack of papers in front of him as if he should write this pertinent information down. "Jack and Jo used to be…" I waited for her to define what I couldn't. I noticed Jack seemed to do the same. "Well, anyway, whatever it was, it ended because of Jo's gambling."

The young man seemed to think that very important indeed and wrote it down.

Jack and I both opened our mouths, ostensibly to correct Lorelei, but then our eyes met, and we both kept quiet. Jack buried his head and took a very long drink from his cup.

"This is Monty, by the way," Lorelei said pointing to the young man. Monty shook hands with Jack, who sat on his left. He started to get up and shake mine, but I waved him down.

I sat at the head of the table, where Lor seemed to want me.

"This is his first intervention," Lorelei added with a warning in her voice.

"Don't worry, Monty," I said. "It's not my first one, I'll talk you through it."

Monty sagged with relief, then seemed to remember that I was not the one who should be leading this thing. Flustered, he shuffled some more papers, pulled some note cards out and quickly looked through them. He placed them on the table in front of them.

Note cards. Too cute. Jack looked at the cards and then at me with a small smirk on his face.

"Be nice," I mouthed to him. He raised a brow at me, our eyes locked, and God, it felt like the time apart had fallen away and that any minute he'd be leading me down the hallway and to my bedroom.

Monty cleared his throat. "Ms. Dawson...um..." He seemed to have lost his place already.

Ah, well, at least he got my name right.

"Why don't you tell me how my addiction has hurt those around me," I said to Monty, avoiding Jack's gaze.

"Oh...oh..." That seemed to set Monty off, and he quickly reached for his folder. He finally found the paper he was looking for, set it in front of him and began. "Actually, the newest studies are placing compulsive gambling in the Impulse Control Disorder family."

I looked at Ben and Lorelei. "Who needs you guys, I belong to a different family."

Gus chuckled, Ben shook his head, and Lorelei ignored me. "Go on, Monty," she encouraged.

"Yes, Monty, go on. Tell me about this family. Who are my new siblings?"

Monty looked from me to Lorelei, who nodded for him to go ahead.

"Well," he said, his voice cracking. "Excuse me, I'm a little nervous."

"That's okay," I said, feeling sorry for the guy. Poor Monty, his first intervention, and I knew damn well that it wasn't going to end with him checking me into rehab. I hope he didn't have a quota or anything. "You want something other than coffee? We've got everything. Water? Soda?" I looked pointedly at Jack. "Bourbon?"

"It's a little early for that, isn't it?" Monty said, though it looked like he could use a stiff belt.

"Is it?" I replied to Monty, my eyes still on Jack. If I had to endure him here during this humiliation, I wasn't above hitting below his belt.

Monty cleared his throat again, took another sip of his coffee. "This is fine. Really. Thank you."

"Why don't you just tell us about this new study," Jack said coolly.

Monty fished through his file cards until he found the one he was looking for. Apparently, my bringing up addiction threw him off his schedule.

"Compulsive gambling is now thought by some to belong to the Impulse Control Disorder family."

"You already said that," Gus said.

Monty registered Gus' comment, but tried to stay his course. "Many psychological problems are characterized by a loss of control or a lack of control in specific situations. Usually, this lack of control is part of a pattern of behavior that also involves other maladaptive thoughts and actions, such as substance abuse problems or sexual disorder."

I looked at Jack. "Any problems there?"

A slow, shit-eating grin crept across his mouth. "Substance abuse? Nope, that's more my thing. The other? No disorder there."

Gus snorted. A small smile tugged at the edges of Ben's mouth. Lorelei sighed, I wasn't sure from frustration or thinking about Jack and me in the sack. I know the thought made me sigh on a regular basis.

Monty was looking at Jack, measuring his substance abuse claim. I thought I saw his eyes grow wide, possibly with the thought of a two-fer. He brought his thoughts back to me and continued to read. "But, there are several psychological disorders that are defined primarily by loss of control. They are..." He paused, waiting for a drum roll?

"Intermittent Explosive Disorder," he said, looking at all those around the table.

"And that is?" Ben asked.

Monty looked down at his papers. "Episodes of aggressive outbursts resulting in either destruction of property or physical assaults on others. Typically, this problem results in legal problems as well, because the individual is often charged with assault, or a domestic violence charge."

"Well," I said. "I was just questioned in a murder case..."

Monty got a gleam in his eyes. Ben gasped and I reached for his hand. "It's all fine, Ben," I said and squeezed his hand. I noticed Jack didn't say a word, just watched me.

"That's not it, Monty," Lorelei said, dismissing with a wave of her hand the last two hours of me being in an interrogation room with Jack and Frank Botz. "There are no aggressive outbursts with Jo. Go on."

Monty seemed disheartened that he wasn't going to get not only a trip to rehab but possibly a murder arrest on his first shot. "Domestic violence," Monty continued.

I looked at Lorelei. "Nope, but I'm seriously considering it."

"Next," she said to Monty.

"Kleptomania," Monty said, almost hopefully.

"Ya got me," I said. I held my hands in the air, arrest style. "Officer," I said to Jack, "take me in." I looked over to Lorelei. "Those earrings of yours?" Her hands sprung to the sizable diamond posts. "Total five-finger discounted them. Of course, you'll have to give them back, they're evidence now."

Of course I hadn't stolen them, but they were ill-gotten gains of a kind, though nobody but me knew that.

She took her hands away, gave me a sneer and was about to have Monty move along, but he hadn't seen our exchange and must have taken me seriously because he began to rattle off statistics about kleptos.

"A common misconception is that kleptomania is present in career thieves. This is generally not the case. Kleptomania is a relatively rare problem, and occurs with a much higher incidence in women than in men." Monty, getting into it now, put a dramatic emphasis on the word "women". "It is also out of character, or as psychologists describe it, ego dystonic. This means that the person does not want to steal and feels guilty about the behavior. In fact, other than the focus on an illegal act, this disorder has many features in common with Obsessive Compulsive Disorder. The essential difference is that, in addition to functioning as an anxiety release, the compulsive behavior in kleptomania also results in a temporary gratification."

Everyone around the table had pretty much zoned out on this one, figuring, rightly so, I wasn't a klepto. But me…well, I found that last part a little too close for comfort. The temporary gratification I felt when placing a sports bet was such a high, but later came the guilt.

When Monty saw he was losing his crowd, he went for the show-stopper. "Pyromania," he said with dramatic flair.

I had hopes for Monty in this biz.

"Next," Jack said, looking at his watch and totally stealing

Monty's thunder.

"Trichotillomania," Monty said, with a bit of attitude in his voice. I could tell he'd really wanted to explore pyromania.

"Tricho what?" Ben said.

"Habitually pulling out your own hair, to the point of seeing noticeable hair loss, and experiencing pleasure or tension relief from the behavior."

I looked at Lorelei again. "What if I achieve pleasure by pulling someone else's hair out?" I got another dirty look from her.

"Or what if you achieve pleasure from having your hair pulled by someone else?" Jack said, his voice soft and low.

A flash of a hotel room in Pittsburgh rushed through my mind.

"Next," Gus said. Poor Gus. The ladies' man had been out of circulation for too long.

"And finally," Monty said.

"Thank God," everyone but Lorelei said.

"Pathological Gambling."

"So I'm pathological now?"

"Shhh," Lorelei murmured, her attention all on Monty.

She meant well, I knew that. I kept quiet and waited for Monty to continue.

"This impulse control problem consists of persistent maladaptive gambling that creates serious life problems for the individual. This is different from recreational gambling and is diagnosed by the impact it has on your life and by the lack of control rather than the amount of money gambled or lost."

I waited for somebody to yell next, or to make a joke, but there was only silence. Monty kept reading. "Individuals with this problem engage in recurrent maladaptive gambling that usually disrupts their personal life, and frequently interferes with their work as well. Some individuals develop severe financial problems, resulting in personal bankruptcy, and others engage in criminal activity to cover their financial losses, such as embezzlement. This does not include uncontrolled gambling that occurs as part of a manic episode."

He looked up. All eyes were on me. I refused to put my head down, to show emotion of any kind. I waved for Monty to go on.

"There are some social differences in the pathological gambling patterns of men and women. Men usually begin a pathological gambling pattern during their teen years, while women are more likely to develop the problem when they are older."

"How much older?" Lorelei asked.

"It doesn't say," Monty said and started to flip through his cards.

"Just get on with it," I said, and Monty's head bobbed up. He looked around the table, saw that the joking was gone and ducked his head back to his papers.

"Pathological gamblers frequently need to increase their risk to stay involved. They have often tried to stop without success, and tend to gamble as an escape from problems. In particular, they may gamble to relieve depression. They may commit illegal acts to hide their losses, and frequently chase their losses by making bigger bets to get even. They may endanger their job or their family relationships because of this problem, and they will probably lie about the extent of their gambling."

My head turned quickly to Jack. "I never lied to you," I said, repeating what I'd told him in the car.

"I know," he said quietly.

Monty wrapped up, "Participation in Gamblers Anonymous is often helpful, but the individual should also seek psychotherapy, especially for the underlying depression."

You could have heard a pin drop.

I looked at Ben, saw concern on his face. I turned to Lor, expecting to see triumph, but was met by a look that was so poignant that I quickly turned to Gus, hoping—praying—for a little levity. He only placed his hand on mine and gave a little shrug.

And then I looked at Jack. It wasn't pity. No, I would never get that from Jack. That's why he was the one that got away.

It was a look of defeat, and of complete understanding. And that hurt most of all.

Monty pulled something else out from his folder. "I have a list of several psychotherapists in the area that specialize in—"

I abruptly stood up with more force than I'd planned, causing my chair to crash dramatically to the floor behind me.

"We're done here."

Five

❖

I PICKED UP MY CHAIR, embarrassed by my petulance. I left the room, avoiding eye contact with…well, everyone. I walked slowly down the long hall to my bedroom at the back of the house.

Poor Monty. I felt bad for him, but if this were truly going to be his livelihood, he would see worse. In Vegas, he would see a lot worse.

I pulled off my jacket, taking my odds sheets out and throwing them on the dresser. If I rushed, I could probably make it to a casino in time to make book on the later games, but I was too drained to contemplate it.

And to not contemplate placing a bet…well, I was pretty damned beat.

I toed off my shoes and was about to pull my shirt over my head when there was a knock on my door. "I'm fine, Ben," I called. "I just need some sleep."

I heard the door open and turned to reassure Ben, but it was Jack at the door.

"Got a sec?" he asked as he entered the room, closing the door behind him.

"Sure," I answered, though it appeared I didn't have much of a choice.

He looked around the room. It hadn't changed much since

he'd last been in here. Right down to the odds sheets scattered all over any smooth surface.

But the last time he'd been in here sure wasn't this awkward between us.

"You okay?" he asked.

"Fine."

"That was...that was..." He pointed to the door, but he meant the scene that had just played out in the dining room.

"Lorelei trying to help in her poor, misguided way," I finished his sentence for him.

"Was it? Misguided?"

I sighed, sat down on the edge of my bed. "I'm not going to have this conversation with you, Jack."

"But I—" He was cut off by his phone ringing. He pulled it out of his jacket pocket, looked at the caller ID. "Sorry, I have to take this."

I waved for him to go ahead. All I wanted to do was peel off my clothes and climb under my covers. It wasn't like Jack hadn't seen me in panties before. Less. But I stayed clothed. Stayed perched on the edge of the bed and waited for Jack to leave the room for privacy to take his call.

"Hey Frank," he said, making no movement to leave. "What's up? Yeah. Okay. That makes sense." There were pauses between each of his responses, and I wondered if this was about Paulie's murder.

It could have been about any one of their cases. Hell, it could have been about what to eat for lunch.

"Give it to me again," Jack said. Pause. "Okay, I got it." Pause. "Right, in about an hour." He closed his phone, put it back in his pocket.

"You still have the same number in case I need to talk to you...about Paulie?" he asked me.

It looked like I was going to be spared his rehashing of the intervention. Thank you, Frank Botz.

I pulled my iPhone out of the left-side pocket of my cargo pants. I nodded and placed the phone on my bedside table. "Yep, same number."

He watched my movements, his eyes staying focused on the phone for a moment before coming back to rest on me. "Did you speak with Paulie via phone last night?" he asked. All concern over my disastrous intervention was gone from his face.

"If you want me to answer that, you'll have to take me back in," I said. I wasn't trying to be a bitch, but I *had* spoken with Paulie last night, before and after meeting with Raymond Joseph. It hadn't been on my iPhone, but I still didn't want anything to tie me to CIU and Raymond.

Or to tie him to me, and therefore Paulie, and ultimately Vince Santini. The kid did not deserve to get dragged into any of this.

"A simple yes or no. You won't give me that?" Jack tried.

"Not unless you charge me with something and take me in. And then only after I speak with my attorney."

"Do you even have an attorney?"

I shrugged. "Jimmy knows a guy."

Jack snorted. "I just bet he does."

He circled around the room, stalking me. He'd done it before in this room. But then it had been foreplay.

"So, you won't answer the question."

"No."

"Is that because you won't lie to me?"

"Maybe that. Or maybe I don't want to end up right in the middle of a murder I had nothing to do with."

"Or maybe you could give us a close approximation on Paulie's murder based on the time you spoke to him."

"Look at his phone records for that."

"We did," he said as he pulled out his phone and dialed a number.

His face never left mine as a phone started to ring. Neither of us looked at my iPhone on the bedside table. That's not where the ring came from. He raised one brow. "You going to answer that?" He motioned to the right-side pocket of my cargo pants.

I let the phone keep ringing, not moving an inch, until Jack shut his phone and put it back into his jacket. The ringing in my pants pocket ceased.

"It's time for you to leave, Jack."

"**FIVE THOUSAND ON UCLA,**" I said, digging my roll of cash out of my jacket pocket.

The cashier at The Bellagio didn't bat an eye.

After Jack had left, I'd thrown my shoes and jacket back on and headed to the casino, deciding to place that bet after all.

Okay, *needing* to place a bet. Happy, Monty?

I took my bet slip, found a chair and settled into the deep leather, waiting for the feeling to wash over me, to take everything else away.

The Hummer. Jimmy called it a cock squeeze. It was the feeling that I got when I placed a bet, that exhilaration, the fear, the complete focus on the game and nothing else.

Nothing else. Usually.

The Hummer took longer to blot out the world as I thought of Paulie being killed. And Jack. And how to keep Raymond out of this, whatever "this" turned out to be.

UCLA and Stanford were tipping off, and yet the smooth ease of knowing I had money on the game did not come over me. I felt the weight of my cell phone in my pants pocket. Not my iPhone, the other one. JoJo's phone.

UCLA dunked in an easy bucket, but instead of being glued to the game, I got up and walked across the book area to a small alcove used for phone calls. The room years ago would have been banked with pay phones, but now was just used for people with cell phones who needed a bit of solitude to hear. You also weren't supposed to have cell phones out in the Sports Book area—they didn't want you calling around for better lines—but they've eased up on that a little bit lately. Probably trying to compete with online betting.

I pulled JoJo's phone out and dialed Raymond's number. He answered on the third ring. "What?" he said curtly.

"Can you talk?"

There was a moment of silence, then a muffle, then the sound of a door closing. "Yeah."

"This phone, the one I called you on. The one you gave me the number for..."

"Yeah?" he answered.

"Is it your main phone? Do lots of people have the number for it?"

"No. I got a burner phone when we started...when we... decided to stay in touch. You're the only one with the number."

Smart kid. But then that's why I'd chosen him. "Lose it. Now," I said. "Dump it in the trash somewhere public, but not on campus. Then get a new one."

"Shit. What's going on? Christ, JoJo, if they find out—"

"Nobody's found anything out. This doesn't have anything to do with you. But I want to make sure it stays that way."

"Are you tossing your phone?"

The damage had already been done with Jack, but I didn't like the idea of this number—one associated with me, Vince, Paulie and Raymond—being out there.

"Yes. But I'll wait until you get a new one and call me with the number. Use a payphone to make that call."

"You know what? Fuck this. Toss your phone, I ain't gonna call you anymore. I'm out. Done."

"Okay."

"Okay? You're just going to let me go?"

"You don't owe me anything, Raymond. Me or the man

who funded this little venture. Nobody's going to bother you if you say you're out." I prayed I spoke for Vince when I said this. "It's not about letting you go. You were always free to make the choices you did."

He snorted on the other end of the line. No, he wouldn't want to believe that.

"But, Raymond, I won't toss my phone until Wednesday. So if you want to call me back with a new number, you have a couple of days. After that, you'll have no way of getting in touch with me."

Raymond didn't know my real name, only JoJo. He didn't know where I lived, though I supposed he guessed it would be somewhere I could easily place a large bet. But really that could be anywhere these days with backroom bookie joints and online betting. He didn't know I barely knew how to Google my own name let alone place bets online. And Lorelei had strict instructions not to give me credit cards or open any online accounts for me. Instructions given to her by me when she first moved in.

"You might as well toss your phone now, I won't be calling with no new number," he said.

"If that's the case, take care of yourself. Have a good rest of the season."

I don't think he even heard the last part because he hung up on me.

I left the alcove and went back to the book room, slumping deep into the chair I'd vacated to make my call. I probably should toss the phone right now, but did it really matter? Jack had gotten this number by tracing Paulie's calls, trying to see who he'd spoken to the last night of his life. There'd be no reason to trace the calls from this number unless I was a serious suspect, and I just didn't believe that Jack would think that.

UCLA was up by three points early in the first half. That was good, but I needed them to win by fifteen to collect. I ordered a coffee from Brandi, one of the cocktail waitresses who knew just how I took it, pulled out a five for her tip, and waited for the Hummer to hit me.

Brandi brought the coffee, we thanked each other, and I took a deep gulp, hoping the stuff would wake me up. Stanford hit a three-point shot to tie it up, and the need for caffeine evaporated as the Hummer washed over me. The anxiety, the hope, the dread, the...aliveness. This was all I needed, all I wanted.

"Who'd you take," a deep, silky voice said over my shoulder.

I turned around to see Vince Santini sitting behind me. He was in an expensive and tasteful suit as usual. His black hair was combed back, his olive-toned face freshly shaven. Handsome. Elegant.

"UCLA," I said. He checked the board where each game was posted to see the point spread, then looked at the game where Stanford just went ahead.

"There's a lot of game left to be played," he said as he left his chair, moved to my row of chairs and sat down beside me.

Vince typically had a book with him, usually a biography of some famous world leader, but today he was empty handed. In fact, I was pretty sure it was the first time I'd ever seen him empty handed.

Had he come to see me specifically?

"I heard they pulled you in, too," he said. Yep, guess so.

"Yes."

"I'm sorry about that."

I shrugged. "It's not your fault."

"Yes, but I hate to see any of my clients bothered by this mess. This should be handled in-house."

I didn't want to ask about how Vince intended to handle Paulie's killer. I only existed in the fringe of their world. And happily so.

"They called you in, too?" I asked.

He nodded. "Last night. Not long after they found the body. I'm assuming I'm who they came to first."

That made sense. I wanted to ask if it was Jack or Frank Botz, but I didn't. It could have been any number of policemen at that point. Maybe the case hadn't come to Frank and Jack until this morning.

"It was that detective of yours," he answered my unasked question. "And his partner. The one with the bad ties."

I kind of liked Frank's ties, but could see how they would bug classically dressed Vince.

"He's not mine," I said. "Not anymore." Vince didn't say anything to that.

"Did they tell you anything?" I asked, knowing that Jack wouldn't let Vince know anything that he didn't want to.

"No. Nothing of any help. But then, I suppose I'm a suspect."

"Yeah, me too."

He gave a snort—a small, elegant snort, if that's possible. "Right. I gave them my alibi. I assume they'll check it out. I'd like to stay involved, see what suspects—what real suspects—they come up with, but I can't imagine them keeping me in the loop."

No, neither could I. No way would Jack lead Vince to Paulie's killer. He'd just have another homicide on his hands.

You didn't mess with Vince's people. And honestly, I was okay with that.

He turned to look at me. "So, no pillow talk with Detective Schiller about who might have done this?"

I gave him a small smile. "Nope. No chance of that."

He nodded, turned back to the front. We sat in silence for a while, and I thought about how long Paulie and Vince had been together. I knew they predated me by quite a bit, so probably nearly twenty years. "I'm sorry for your loss," I said quietly.

Vince looked at me. It wasn't the Jack Schiller eyebrow

raise, but the skepticism was just as obvious.

Yeah, Paulie had beaten the shit out of me years ago, and I'd always held it against him. But that was business, and I'd never held it against Vince. Odd, but there it was. I put my hand on Vince's arm and gave a small squeeze. "I'm sorry that you're hurting, Vince," I said with all honesty.

His look turned from skeptical to accepting. He let out a deep sigh. He put his hand over mine and kept it there. He looked tired, and Vince never looked tired, even with the hours he must keep to loan money to Vegas' most degenerate gamblers.

He took his hand off mine and pointed toward the screen where UCLA had not only caught up, but gone a few points ahead. "They're looking good."

I brought my hand away from his arm. "It's still early," I said.

He turned to me again. "I wanted to make sure you were okay." He lowered his voice to a near whisper. "And that our friend in the Midwest is set."

"I saw him last night, and he's been paid in full." Vince nodded. "But," I continued, "I don't know if I'd say he's set. He says he's out."

"He's told you that before."

"I know."

"Do you believe him?"

I thought of Raymond's vehemence last night in Dubuque. Then about the phone conversation I'd just had with him. And then I looked around me, saw the people hooked on every play made on the screens. The rows of people betting on horse races taking place half a continent away.

"No," I said. "He'll call again."

Vince nodded. "I'll be in touch," he said, then got up and walked away.

I nestled deeper into the chair, watched UCLA dominate and waited for another Hummer that never came.

Six

❖

"GOD, THIS IS INCREDIBLE, LOR," I said as I helped myself to seconds of the lasagna.

"My dinners usually are when they're eaten fresh," she said with just a hint of zing in her voice.

She was probably still a little pissed that I'd walked out on Monty, but she'd put a plate on the table when she'd seen me come in so I wasn't pushing it.

Besides, she was right. I very seldom got to eat her dinner fresh from the oven. Usually I was raiding the fridge at four in the morning or nuking leftovers at three in the afternoon after I'd woken up.

"Anna's right, Lorelei, this is really wonderful," Gus said, giving Lor a wink.

She took his compliment much better, actually giggling at the old goat.

Ben just picked at his plate, finally setting his fork down and letting out a large sigh.

"What's wrong, Ben?" I asked between forkfuls. It really was the best lasagna I'd ever had.

"Oh, nothing," Ben said, slumping his shoulders.

I should have been concerned, but actually I was pleased. This was Ben's long-suffering, beg-me-to-tell-you-what's-wrong sigh and shoulder slump. He'd been much too depressed lately to play at being upset.

"What is it?" I prodded, knowing that was what he wanted.

"I just thought, what with Jack tracking you down and all, and then seeing you home..."

"Yes?"

He shrugged again. "Seems like an awful lot of food for only four people. That's all I'm saying."

"You want me to call Jimmy?" I asked innocently, getting a hmmmph from Ben. "You know," I said after a moment, "Jack would come by and visit if you wanted him to, just let him know."

"Do you want him to come by?" Ben asked. Lorelei and Gus both looked up from their plates and waited for my answer.

"Not if he's going to question me for murder."

"Bah," Ben said and waved me off.

After dinner, and after I helped Lorelei clean up, the boys started setting up the dining room table for a card game. If I was home in the evenings—which wasn't often—we almost always played cards. Most nights it was just Ben and me and we'd play canasta, unless we could talk Lorelei into playing and then it was blackjack with Ben and me taking turns being the dealer. But with Gus staying with us, it opened up a whole array of card games that could be played.

"You two need to play two-handed something," Lorelei told Ben and Gus. "I need Jo to go over schedule and budget stuff with me."

Ben looked at me. I shrugged. Lor didn't ask much of me, but every once in a while she and I sat down and touched base on household issues, things that were upcoming in the world of professional poker, and expenses.

"Does it need to be tonight?" I asked Lor.

"Yes."

"Are we going to be long?" I asked. Ben got a hopeful look in his eye.

"Yes."

Ben's shoulders slumped. Gus started dealing cards to Ben and himself, and I followed Lorelei into the office she and I shared.

We had one of those writer's desks, the kind that two people sit at facing each other. But, I seldom sat at my side. I really just used my side as a dumping ground for losing bet slips, expense receipts and odds sheets.

Lor took good care of me. In two of the desk drawers were the media guides of almost every Division I football and basketball program in the country. Before each season began, I studied each one. I pulled them out every now and then to check averages and stats of particular players.

Of course, you could know all the facts, stats and averages in the world (and between Ben, Gus, Jimmy and myself we probably did) and some eighteen-year-old kid could get hot at the three-point line one night and you're down five thousand.

But not today. Today I was up. I took my wad of cash from my pocket. I put five thousand of it in a cigar box on my desk and handed the rest to Lorelei as I pulled my leather chair around to her side of the desk.

She didn't count the money, barely even looked at it, and placed it in her top drawer. I knew that it wouldn't stay there long. I'm not sure where Lorelei keeps the excess money. That was much discussed when she came to live with Ben and me. There was never to be ready cash in the house, or at least not where I could find it.

When I needed some for an upcoming tournament, I let Lorelei know in advance. My other...ventures...I financed from my winnings.

Most of the time. Until I needed cash to place a bet I knew would win. And then I'd play in one of Vince's back-room games to get the cash because I could play on credit.

But a few times, okay more than a few, my outstanding

balance with Vince—and Paulie's strong-arm threats—had me calling for JoJo's help.

Lorelei opened up her weekly planner, pulled some tablets out of her desk drawer, and a leather-bound ledger out of another.

"Okay. Let's see," she said to herself, going down a checklist on her tablet. She checked a few items off, and I wondered if I really even needed to be here. Lorelei ran the house pretty much single-handedly. I think it was just consideration that had her call these meetings, ostensibly to get my input.

She looked at the calendar planner, then dug into another drawer and pulled out a poker magazine. She had a page dog-eared and she flipped the magazine open to it. "The Marathon is coming up. Should I set the buy-in money aside?"

The Marathon was one of the biggest poker tournaments in the world and was played once a year in Vegas. It was six days of grueling hours with low blinds and antes, allowing people to stay in longer with crappy cards and thus long, long, long hours of play to get down to the final ten players by the end of the sixth day.

It was not on timed sessions like most tournaments. It was the Iron Man of poker.

"Oh, God," I groaned. "Is it really? That soon?"

With the turmoil of losing Danny and Saul, Gus coming to live with us, and dealing with Raymond Joseph, I'd totally forgotten about the upcoming tournament. One I'd played in every year since coming to Vegas. One I'd won six years ago.

We were living in what that prize money had bought.

"Do you want to skip it this year?" Lor asked.

"No," I said quickly.

There was money to be made playing poker every day in Vegas. Every casino had a daily tournament and of course continuous cash games. But the really big paydays were the tournaments on the tours. Those were played all over the world, and most pros traveled to them. Because I didn't want to leave

Ben, I stayed in Vegas.

So, when a big time tournament was played in Vegas— about five times a year—I made sure I was there. I could pay for our family expenses for five years in one week if I did well.

"Okay," Lorelei said, then looked at the ad in the magazine for The Marathon. "The buy-in is twenty-five thousand," she said, and wrote that down on her tablet. "I'll have that ready for you by then."

"Hopefully, I'll play my way in," I said. Big tournaments usually lasted two weeks. The first week, there were a series of satellite games where you played a much smaller buy-in and the winners won their buy-in to the main tournament. I've played my way into lots of tournaments.

I've bought my way into a few, too. "But you probably should have it just in case," I added, but didn't need to. If it was on Lor's tablet, it was as good as done.

"I better start clocking some serious hours in cash games," I said, thinking of how runners train for their marathons. This wasn't that different. The pain, the leg cramps, sore backs, a feeling of futility until you passed the finish line.

"Seems like you've been playing a lot lately," Lorelei said innocently as she flipped a page on her planner.

I didn't correct her and let her know that much of the time I'd been gone lately was dealing with, first, the man who wanted to kill The Corporation, and then, Raymond Joseph.

Thinking of him reminded me of something I meant to ask Lorelei, who was much more technical than I was. Which wasn't hard.

"Hey Lor, do you know much about tracking cell phones?"

"Just what I've seen on *48 Hours Mystery*. Why?"

"If you knew somebody's cell phone number, there's no way of knowing where they actually were when they made a call, right?"

"Oh yes, they can tell from the towers."

"What towers?"

"The towers that transmit the cell signal. They can tell exactly where you are within a small mile radius based on that tower. If you were driving, say up the coast of California, your signal could jump from tower to tower as you drove."

"Wow. Really?"

She nodded, her red mane bouncing softly with the movement. "That's how they always get them on *48 Hours*. The cell towers."

"Hunh." The weight of my prepaid cell phone seemed to burn my leg in my pants pocket. If it went that far, the police could find out that I was in Iowa when I called Paulie last night from that phone.

It could be my alibi.

Or it could involve Raymond.

Lorelei went over a few other things that she'd had on her list. What did I think about a new couch? Dillard's was having a sale, would I like new bedding? Did I mind if she redid Gus' room?

"Gus' room? You mean the guest room?"

She shrugged. "He hasn't made any move to leave." Her voice was vague, and the usually readable Lorelei suddenly created a great poker face.

"Do you want me to ask him to leave?" The idea didn't sit well with me, but taking care of two old men with very little help from me was not what she'd signed on for.

"Oh, no," she said much to my relief. "I love having Gus here." I looked at her. The poker face had dropped, and there was a flush crawling up her swan-like neck. "He's so good for Ben," she quickly added, but I wasn't buying it.

I decided not to touch that Pandora's box, but I thought about the fact that even in his seventies, and with a bullet hole in his leg, the charm of Gus had not been tarnished.

Hell, the bullet hole probably helped.

"Is that it?" I asked, and she seemed happy to let the matter drop and let me go.

"Yes."

"Do what you want with Gus' room. Go to town."

She nodded and wrote something down in her book.

"We have enough for that and my buy-in for the Marathon?"

"Yes," she said, then added, "But you're not going to need it, right?"

"Right." I rose, wheeled my chair around to my side of the desk. I noticed the urn with Saul's ashes. It was all so recent and raw, I hadn't wanted to bother Ben with them, so I'd stashed them away in here.

"Lor, what do you know about DNA testing?" I asked.

She looked up from her tablets and planners. "Not much. Again, just what I've seen on *48 Hours*."

"How often is that show on?" She shrugged. "What I want to know..." How to ask her when I wasn't even sure myself. "I want to know..." She leaned closer, her planning forgotten. "What do you need to do DNA testing, and can just Joe Blow get testing done, or do you have to go through the police?"

"I'm not sure," she said. Just as I was about to tell her to forget the whole thing, she started writing furiously on a new tablet. "But I'll find out and get back to you."

"Okay. Thanks." I started walking out the door, but turned back. "While you're at it, find out if you can get DNA from someone's ashes.

She looked at me, then looked at the urn with Saul's ashes then—and this is why I trust Lorelei with all my worldly possessions—she just nodded, wrote something else down and said, "I'm on it."

"THAT DOES IT FOR ME," I said two days later as I rose from the poker table at The Venetian. I stretched my arms over my head, tried to get some kinks out of my back and waited as the dealer turned my impressive stack of chips into a smaller stack of larger denominations that would be easier to take to the cashier.

And of course, my mind turned to what games were playing that I could bet it all on.

I looked at my watch, then asked my fellow players, "It's Wednesday, right?" To which they all nodded. "And this is four in the *afternoon*, right?" Again, more nods.

I took my stack, flipped the dealer two black chips with a thank you, and made my way to the cashier's cage. I'd played poker for seventeen straight hours, taking small breaks when I needed to pee, eat or ingest massive amounts of caffeine.

Training for The Marathon.

I cashed my chips in and headed for the Sports Book room. Once there, I grabbed an odds sheet and took a seat at the back of the room in one of the carrel-like desks that the horse race bettors liked to sit at.

Fishing my iPhone out of my pocket, I scanned the list of college basketball games on the docket for this evening. The early games on Eastern time had already started. I checked my phone for messages from home. The poker rooms are much quieter than the main casino floors, but sometimes it was still hard for me to hear my phone ring. Which it seldom does. Lorelei has it set to vibrate too, but I still checked. Nothing.

Lorelei knew I was going to clock some long hours playing, so she was taking Ben and Gus to breakfast if I wasn't home, unless Gus was back behind the wheel again.

I put the iPhone back in my pocket and pulled out my JoJo phone. Wednesday at 4 o'clock. Six in Iowa. No missed calls. So, maybe Raymond was out for good.

Good for him. If only it'd been that easy for me.

As if I'd rubbed the proverbial bottle and woken the genie, the phone in my hand—the JoJo phone—rang. I didn't recognize the number, but I knew the area code.

"Yes," I said.

"The spread still seven for Saturday?" was all he said.

"It's not on the board yet, but I don't expect it will change more than a half point either way." The advantage of living with retired odds setters.

"I'm in."

"Okay," I said, trying to hide the disappointment from my voice. I could make some serious money on the information I just got—I wouldn't, but I could. At the very least I'd make Vince very happy, and that could only help me in the long run. But I had really hoped that I wouldn't have heard from Raymond again.

I wanted him to be better than that.

Better than me.

"I want thirty this time. Half up front. The other half bet for me."

"I'll pass that on," I answered.

"You can't okay that?"

"No. It's not my money."

There was silence, then a curse. "When will I know?"

I thought about how long it would take to talk to Vince without having Paulie set things up. I didn't know if cutting out the middleman would make things easier or harder.

"Before Saturday," I said.

"Bullshit. I need to know sooner than that."

"I'll get back to you as soon as I can. Probably tomorrow."

Another curse. "You got this number?"

I looked at the caller ID, making sure the number still appeared. "Yep."

"Nobody else has it," he said.

"Keep it that way. I'll call you back on a new phone. Lose this number."

I waited for acknowledgement of that, or at the very least a good-bye, but he just disconnected.

I wrote down his new number on a losing betting slip somebody had left in the carrel and shoved it in my pocket. Then I deleted all my history of made and received calls from my phone. I didn't have any numbers stored in it, so I didn't need to delete those.

The money I'd just won was itching in my pocket to be bet, but I didn't care for any of the games on the board. Knowing that wouldn't stop me from plunking the whole wad down, I got up and left the Sports Book. I made my way through the casino and to the walkway to the Grand Canal Shops. I stopped, as I did every time I played at the Venetian, at the fountain area and sat patiently waiting for the living garden show to start.

Well, not patiently. My mind raced with the games that were on the board, point spreads, over/unders, favorites. Come on. Come on. I looked at my watch, noting the fifteen-minute show was due to start in five minutes.

I could do this, I could sit quietly and not think about betting. Go over the poker hands I played. Any mistakes? Anything I should have done differently?

But instead of poker hands, I envisioned a point guard for Arizona hitting a three-pointer at the buzzer to beat the point spread. In my jacket pocket, my hand clenched around the pile of money I'd won. I started to rise, to head back to the Sports Book when lovely classical music began to play.

The show was starting. Three women, dressed as statues, their hair in wigs, makeup to make them look like granite, rode down the escalator spaced exactly four steps between each other.

There was a crowd gathered around the fountain area, tourists with cameras, parents pointing out to children the statue women. I didn't take pictures. Their movement, or lack of, soothed me, calmed me.

The women exited the escalator and, slowly under their widely draped togas, made their way to the fountain. They got on their pedestals, bent down with uncommon grace and—I knew because of my many visits—discreetly hooked up a water hose to the minute hose that ran down their opera-length gloves.

Then they got into position and the music changed. The statues began to move. The first time I walked by, I thought that was the show, moving statues. I'd seen that many times. Caesars had a huge show with moving, speaking statues in their Forum Shops area. And then I'd seen the eyes of the front woman and I stopped, realizing they were real women.

I sat now for the entire show, watching the slow, steady movement, the water spray that came from their gloved fingers, the careful choreography, amazed as always that they didn't get each other wet being in such close proximity.

My breathing became steadier. My fist unwound from my money, and I pulled my hand out of my pocket. When the statues were nearly done, I walked to the up escalators and rode to the second level to see the two women who were dressed as trees. On stilts, with poles extending from their arms mimicking branches.

I watched as the women did incredible moves on the stilts, their bodies fluid and languid. When they finally made their way back to a door, I wondered, as I always did, if these women sit in a room somewhere in full costume and makeup, playing cards, chatting on the phone, doing God knows what until their next fifteen-minute show in an hour and a half.

The idea of their lives fascinated me. And watching them soothed me.

So much so, that when I left, I didn't veer back toward the Sports Book, but instead went straight to the parking deck and got into my car.

On my drive home, past the Strip, I took my JoJo phone out of my pocket. I reached into the glove box and pulled out the charger for the phone that I'd put there yesterday when I left home. About a mile off the Strip, at one of the stoplights, I motioned over one of the panhandlers that stood on the median begging for money. I say panhandler and not homeless person because in Vegas you never really knew.

Jimmy knew a bunch of guys that lived in nice apartments, had nice stuff, and would put on their armor of rags each morning and head off to the corners to beg for their living.

I held the phone in my hand, thinking. If Lorelei was right about cell phone towers—and I'm sure she was—this phone could be my alibi. I'd made a call from Dubuque to Paulie only an hour before he was killed. There was no way I could have done it.

On the other hand, the phone could lead them to Raymond Joseph.

I'm sure there are all kinds of technology that could figure that out without having the actual phone, but I didn't want to make it easy on anybody.

I swiped my shirttail over the phone, all its buttons and the charger, hopefully wiping any prints off of it.

Like I was on *48 Hours Mystery* or something.

When the bum got to my car, I rolled down my window and handed him the phone and charger. "It's got about a thousand minutes left on it," I said.

Like he was given cell phones every day—and who the hell knows, maybe he was—the man looked at it, nodded and said, "Got it. Thanks," and walked away from my car.

I could have thrown the phone in the trash, but I kind of liked the idea of Jack and Frank Botz tracing calls that might be made from that phone in the future. If they went that far. And I didn't think they would.

But I had to protect Raymond.

Seven

❖❖

ON MY WAY HOME, I stopped at a CVS and got a new
pre-paid phone. Once I got home, I handed most of my cash
to Lorelei after taking out what I'd need for more poker playing
and for a possible impromptu trip to Iowa.

She took the money and told me dinner would be ready in
an hour. She'd found some fresh mahimahi and wanted to try
out a new recipe.

Closing the office door behind me, I unpacked the new
phone and started charging it and pulling out the instructions
on activation. Usually Lor did this kind of stuff for me, but
I'd have to muddle through alone this time. I took all packag-
ing and put it in my bottom desk drawer. I'd take it out myself
some other time, not wanting to throw it in the trash.

I rummaged through the numbers on slips of paper in my
desk drawer until I found one for Vince. I hadn't called him in
a long time, always going through Paulie when we needed to
speak. I wasn't even sure this number was still good.

After dinner—definitely a keeper new recipe—I declined
Ben and Gus' offer of cards, saying I needed to take care of a
few things in my office. They didn't say anything, but I saw the
look they exchanged. "It shouldn't take long," I said a little defensively. "Keep a seat warm for me."

"Of course, Hannah, darling," Ben said a little sadly.

"Really, I just have a couple of calls to make, and then I'll take all your money."

Gus snorted, but Ben just gave me a small smile.

Back in my office, I activated the new pre-paid phone, secretly proud of myself for mastering something any thirteen-year-old could do. I called the last known number for Vince.

It went to voicemail. The voice was Vince's but he didn't give any name in his message.

I wondered if I needed to be as equally cryptic in the message I left. "Hello," I said. "I'm not sure if this number is still active. But if it is, and you get this message, there's something I'd like to talk to you about. You can call me back at this number. It's new."

Now what? Go out and play cards with the boys and take this phone with me in case Vince called back? And how to explain the phone when it rang?

I didn't even have time to go through other scenarios before the new phone rang.

"Hello?" I said.

"Are you available now?" Vince said.

"I can be. I'm at home."

"How about The Bellagio Book room in an hour?"

"How about the gelato stand there instead?"

I could almost hear his smile through the line as he thought about why I wouldn't want to go to the Sports Book room.

"See you then," he said then hung up.

I put my phone in my pocket, made sure my iPhone was still in my other cargo pocket, and headed out of the office. I stopped at the door, turned and saw the stack of cash on my desk. Mocking me. Taunting me with the amount it could turn into if only I wasn't such a baby and would place a bet already.

I tried to conjure up the serenity of the statue ladies, pictured their grace and fluidity. But the money won and I went back and grabbed it, shoving it in my leather jacket pocket.

It didn't mean I *had* to place a bet. Or even that I would. It was just good to have in case...

Disgusted with myself, I didn't finish the thought.

"You boys are in luck," I said as I reached the dining room. I scooped up my car keys from the side table. "You're going to be able to keep your money for one more night."

Gus chuckled at my joke, but Ben's concern shown in his face. "Is everything alright, Hannah, dear?"

"Fine. Everthing's fine. I just need to run out for a bit. Does anybody need anything while I'm out? Gus, can I pick up anything at your place for you?"

I'd stopped with Gus on our way home, to pick up some clothes for him, when he'd first been discharged from the hospital. I knew Lor had made a couple of more stops since. I honestly didn't know if Gus had officially moved in or what. Not that I'd mind that. It would be great for Ben to have Gus around.

Maybe he'd stop moping about Jack not coming around anymore.

"No," Gus answered me, "I've got what I need." I happened to notice that Lorelei had walked back into the dining room, and Gus had been looking at her when he spoke. She giggled.

Giggled!

"You're going out?" Lorelei asked me.

"Just for a little while. Do you need anything?"

"No. But you must be exhausted after playing for so many hours."

"I am. I'm going to crash for a day when I get back."

"If you're not up, do you want me to wake you for breakfast?" Ben asked. There was just a tiny bit of hurt in his voice.

My body needed the sleep, but harmony with Ben was better for my soul. "Yes, wake me. But I'll probably be back before you guys hit the hay."

Ben nodded, mollified, and he and Gus started shuffling cards without me.

Because I had to go take care of JoJo's business. That bitch.

At the gelato stand I eyed the frozen treats, still stuffed from Lorelei's dinner but willing to find some room. "The Amaretto's my favorite," Vince said from behind me.

I looked over my shoulder. He looked as handsome as usual, totally put together, even with only an hour's notice. I, on the other hand, looked like I'd played seventeen straight hours of poker. Probably smelled like it, too.

"Sounds good," I said.

"Two Amarettos," Vince told the clerk, then proceeded to pay for mine over my objection. He waved me away. "Don't worry, it's not going on your tab."

"I don't have a tab with you," I reminded him, though I knew Vince would know to the penny what anybody owed him.

"So far. But we haven't finished our dessert yet."

"I didn't call for that. Our friend from the Midwest called me."

"Ah," he said as he led the way to a table far away from anyone else.

"Yeah," I said.

"You're disappointed in him," Vince said.

"I guess," I said, then took a spoonful of my treat.

"But you more than anybody should understand his... need...to call."

"His need is financing his little sister's drug rehab."

"He's made enough to cover that by now."

"Who knows? Maybe she needs to be in longer. Maybe they needed to get her in a better one, a more expensive one." There was almost a desperation in my voice. Like if there was a reason Raymond was hooked, maybe there would be a pinpointable reason for me, too.

"You're making excuses for him, now?" He took a bite of his gelato and looked at me with penetrating eyes.

I pushed my dish away; it suddenly seemed way too rich. "No. You're right. He made the call because he wanted to."

Vince just nodded and took another bite.

"*Do* you understand?" I asked him.

He shook his head. "Not really. I deal with gamblers, obviously, and I get that there's a...need." He looked at me closely. "But no, I don't really get it."

"Lucky you," I said quietly.

"Yes, I've always thought so."

I smiled. "He says he wants thirty this time."

"That's a jump," Vince said.

I shrugged. "The more he does it, the higher risk of exposure."

"Are you making his case for him?"

"He knows that. He's a sharp kid, Vince."

Vince took another bite, looked around the nearly deserted room. "Would he take twenty-five, do you think?"

"Yes," I answered.

"Fine."

"Half up front."

"Fine. When will you be flying out?"

I shrugged. "I'll call him tonight. Probably Friday."

"Friday's Paulie's funeral."

"Oh," I said. Was I expected to go? Was that done? Attending the funeral of your loan shark's muscle? The man who beat me to a pulp ten years ago?

Where was Miss Manners when I needed her?

"You weren't going to go?" Vince asked.

"I guess I really hadn't thought about it." And I hadn't. Beyond the first few hours, after being questioned by Jack, I hadn't given Paulie's death much thought. I knew Vince ran a clean operation, but who the hell knew what else Paulie was into? Who else he dealt with? Or, like I originally thought, maybe he'd just broken one too many kneecaps and somebody came after him.

"I think you should go," Vince said, but didn't explain why. "In fact, I was hoping you'd go with me."

"Like a date?" I blurted out before I could stop myself.

A small smile quirked over his olive-toned face. "I don't think a funereal is a great first date, Anna."

"No, probably not," I said not testing his assumption that there may be a first date for us.

The truth was I'd always thought Vince was an attractive man. I'd put him in his mid-forties, and I admired the way he'd worked himself up, hadn't sold out. Although he was a loan shark, he ran his business with a certain degree of integrity. Though he always treated me professionally, I kind of got that he liked me, too.

But this was the first time he'd ever even mentioned the words date and me in the same sentence.

"But I do want your take on things, I'd like your opinion at the funeral."

"My opinion of what?"

"Things. People. You're a professional poker player, Anna, you can read people."

"Yeah, I can read someone to know if they're holding pocket aces, not a smoking gun."

He chuckled. It was a nice melodic sound. His laugh was much easier to come by than Jack's.

Shit. I did not want to think of Jack right now.

"Whatever you can observe, I'd appreciate your thoughts."

"Okay," I said.

"Paulie always really liked you, you know," he said.

"I know." And I did, but unlike Vince, Paulie had creeped me out. "Right when he was breaking my foot, I could see the admiration in his eyes."

Vince looked around again, then leaned across the small table toward me. "You know the order to do that came from me, and yet you hold Paulie responsible. You never seemed to hold it against me."

He was right, and I had no basis for that reasoning. I shrugged. "You can't even begin to imagine the things that don't make sense in my life, Vince."

He put his hand over mine, and it was smooth and cool. "No, but I wouldn't mind getting to know them. Getting to know you better, Anna."

It was a gut reaction to pull my hand back, but I didn't. Hell, I was a free agent. Jack had thrown me over. I admit, my ego was still a little bruised and could use a little stroking. And while I was still gambling, I didn't stand a chance of getting Jack back. Vince knew what I was, knew about JoJo—*was the reason I created JoJo*—and still wanted to be with me.

"I'd like that," I said honestly.

He took his hand back, nodded slowly. "But first Dubuque, and then the funeral."

"Right," I said.

"And then finding out who did this to Paulie," he added.

"Right," I said again although I honestly didn't care about that other than idle curiosity and what it would mean to both Jack and Vince to find Paulie's killer.

Though they would surely deal with the culprit in different manners. Jack with handcuffs, Vince with cement shoes. I didn't much care about that, either. In his world, Vince had every right to avenge the murder of one of his own.

The circle of the under life.

Jack's livelihood as a homicide detective would never be in jeopardy.

"So I guess I'll head to Iowa tomorrow." I was already thinking about flight schedules and leading Lor and Ben to believe that I was out playing poker without outright lying to them if I could.

"I can have the cash to you whenever you like."

"He's probably going to want his other half bet on the game. He has before."

"Would you like me to bet that for him, or would you rather?"

Not wanting to tempt myself to bet on the game myself, I answered, "If it wouldn't be too much trouble…"

"No trouble at all. I'm obviously placing a bet of my own."

Right. Of course. Why would you pay a kid to throw a game then not bet on it? Only I'm that stupid. "Thanks."

"What works for you for the first end?"

"Let's see," I thought out loud, "I'll take Ben and Gus to breakfast first thing…"

"Can you hang around here for about a half-hour, and we can take care of this right now?" he interrupted.

"Sure."

He nodded. "I'll be back," he said, then got up and left.

I didn't know anything about Vince's private life. Did he live nearby? Did he have a stash somewhere? Or was he just walking to the cash cage here at the Bellagio and writing a check for twelve thousand? He probably had that kind of account here. Here and several other places on the Strip.

I used the time by calling Raymond and telling him it was a go. As I expected, he settled for twenty-five after an initial balk. And as I'd told Vince, he wanted the back end bet on the game. I told him I'd call him when I arrived in Dubuque tomorrow evening and set up a meet.

Vince came back with five minutes to spare, handed me an envelope, which I put in my inside jacket pocket.

"I don't think I've ever seen you with a purse," he said.

"And this is only the second time I've seen you without a book."

"Things are a bit...up in the air...for me right now."

Besides being Vince's strong arm, Paulie, with Carla, also ran Vince's after-hours, backroom poker games for high-rollers. I didn't know what had happened to those games in the last few days since Paulie had been killed. "Yes, I imagine they are."

"You looking for a job?" he teased. At least, I think he was teasing.

"Running games, or enforcing?"

He snorted, which seemed so out of character.

"Should I be complimented or insulted by that?"

He threw his hands up. "Take it how you want to."

I got up to leave, and so did Vince. "I'll call you tomorrow with the details for Paulie's funeral," he said.

"Okay." I started to walk away but then turned back to him. "Call me on my other phone about the funeral."

"What's that number?" He took out his own phone and programmed my number in when I told him. "Which number do you want me to use to…" he looked over his shoulder.

"The one I called you on tonight for any of the JoJo stuff."

"JoJo stuff? Who's JoJo?"

I suppose he was thinking I had an accomplice, or maybe JoJo was my cute pet name for Raymond Joseph. "That's the name I use when I…"

"To the players, you mean?"

I shrugged. "To them, to myself." His brow furrowed. "It's easier for me that way," I tried to explain. "I've come to think of her—of her actions—as a different person. I can remove myself from it that way."

He looked closely at me. I bit down the urge to hang my head. He brushed a finger lightly across my cheek. "One of those things about your life that I can't imagine?" His voice was soft, understanding, and for just one moment I wanted to believe that I could be normal, that a man—any man—would find that side of me, the JoJo side, acceptable.

"Yeah," I said.

He nodded, started to leave but then stopped. "Believe me, I can imagine that. It even makes a certain kind of sense. Give me a chance to imagine your worst." He turned then and walked away.

Eight

❖

RAYMOND GAVE ME DIRECTIONS *to a different bar this time, but it was still out of the way and nearly empty. Another dive, barely populated save for a couple of grizzled old men on stools and the bartender. I didn't bother buying any CIU clothing this time, but I did dress as nondescript as possible in jeans, sweatshirt, tennis shoes and a warm winter jacket I'd found in the back of my closet from when I'd visit my family in Wisconsin.*

I got there first and ordered a pitcher of beer and two glasses. I paid for it, thanked the bartender and took the pitcher and glasses to a booth near the back.

Raymond came in half the pitcher later. He made a beeline for me after a small nod to the bartender who looked closely at Raymond and then me. Here's hoping he wasn't a Hogs fan.

I didn't rag on Raymond for his choice of meeting place, just poured him a glass of beer and placed it in front of him, like we met for beers all the time. He took a long drink from the glass, set it down. He pulled off his parka, settling it next to him in the booth. Then he finally looked at me.

"Fuck," he said.

"Yeah, I know." And I did. I knew how he felt, what drove him, the disgust he was feeling right now, even though he was probably mentally allocating the money he'd win. Earn. He earned his money, I won mine.

"Was it the voice or the feeling," I asked him, wanting to know which demon he was trying to drown in his now empty glass of beer.

"What?" he said, refilling his glass.

"The voice or the feeling. Which was it that made you call me?"

"It was my sister. Helping my sister, that's it, that's all it's about."

"No. That's how it started, but that's not where you're at now." I knew that even though I'd thrown his sister up to Vince myself as a reason that Raymond might call me. *"You've earned enough. You can stop."*

"But I want to get her to a better place if she needs to. To make sure there's enough in case she relapses or something. To be able to get her and my momma out of that neighborhood. And maybe even enough so that my momma won't have to work two jobs. So that she can watch over my sister when she gets out."

I leaned back against the back of the booth. *"Right. That's the voice talking."*

"What the hell is the voice?" His tone never raised, but I could hear the anger, the frustration.

"It's what answers you when you say to yourself, 'I'm through. No more.'"

He leaned forward, his arms on the table. *"Shit. You don't know what you're talking about."*

"It usually starts with 'Yeah, but.'"

That got him. He slowly placed his glass on the table, his head lowered, hung as if in defeat. I barely heard him when he said, *"Go on."*

"You tell yourself you're done. That was the last time. There's no need to risk anything else."

He didn't say a word, but his head nodded. I admired the precision of his braids, the exactness of the scalp that shown between the rows.

"And then the voice says, 'Yeah, but.'" I took a sip of beer. Raymond didn't move. *"And the voice knows its shit. It knows what you need to hear. What's going to make it easy, what's going to make*

it all alright. Hell, it makes you feel like a fool if you don't do it."

"But it makes sense," he said, his head still hung low, and his hands going under the table. I took the opportunity to slip the envelope I'd carried across several state lines under the table and tapped it in the general vicinity of his knee and hand. He took it from me without looking up.

"Of course it makes sense. The voice always makes sense. I'm not even saying the voice is wrong."

He sighed loudly. I saw the movement where he put the envelope in the back pocket of his jeans. "The voice. Christ, I hear the voice."

I made a wave of dismissal. "Everybody does. Every day. It's what gets us through. It's just sometimes…sometimes it gets us through something we wouldn't ordinarily do."

That analysis didn't seem to make him feel better. I took another drink of my beer. "How about the feeling. Do you get the feeling?"

"That's different than the voice?"

"Oh yeah."

"I don't think so," he said, but he didn't seem to hold out much hope.

I leaned forward, trying to get him to look up at me, but his head still looked down at his legs. "Do you remember your first kiss, Raymond? I mean your first real kiss?" He still didn't look up, but I saw a small smile tug at the corners of his mouth. His head nodded slightly, but I caught it.

"Part of you is terrified. You're thinking you don't know what you're doing. What if she laughs? What if I do it wrong?" I waited, then went on. "But the other part of you…ah, that other part of you…elation, joy, you're thinking this is the best thing that's ever going to happen to you. A feeling of total shock and awe. You know…you know… you'll never feel this good again in your life."

He was nodding, his face in a real smile now, but his head still looked down.

"That's the feeling I get when I place a bet, Raymond. I call it a Hummer." He opened his mouth, but I cut him off. "Not that kind."

He shut his mouth. "Do you know the feeling I'm talking about?" He nodded. "Do you feel that when you're about to...work...a game?"

He thought for a minute. Longer maybe, but I didn't speak. "No," he said. "I get that feeling right before a game—a regular game. But not any of the games I...worked," he said, staying with my euphemism.

I let out a breath I hadn't realized I was holding. "That's good. That's good. The voice you can learn to recognize, to deal with, to talk back to. But if you had the voice and the feeling, you'd be..."

"Screwed."

"Pretty much, yeah."

"Then why do I feel so fucked now?"

"Conscience."

"Shit."

"Yeah."

After a moment he said, "You call the feeling a Hummer, you got something you call the voice?"

I shrugged. "I've heard lots of people call it different things— the devil on their shoulder, their demon, their inner child. I had a gambler friend once who even named his Stan." I chuckled, remembering Lonnie and wondering what had happened to him. Best not to guess.

Raymond looked up at me for the first time since we'd started talking. "What do you call your voice?" he asked.

I pulled my jacket on, and slid out of the booth. As I walked past him, I leaned down to whisper in his ear.

"JoJo."

"WOW, YOU LOOK GREAT," Lor said to me Friday afternoon as I came into the living room. "Where are you off to so dressed up?"

I had on my black suit, the one I wore when I made a final

table. My hair was pulled back in a tight bun. The look had earned me the title "Black Widow" on the poker circuit after that first final table. Well, the look and the fact that I'd annihilated the men at that table.

"A funeral," I said quietly hoping only Lorelei would hear me, but Ben and Gus both looked up from the newspapers that they'd been reading.

"Whose?" Ben asked with suspicion in his voice.

"Paulie's."

Gus didn't try to hide his look of surprise. Lorelei looked from me to Gus and Ben. She didn't know about my particular history with Paulie, and I preferred to keep it that way.

"Why?" Ben asked.

I cleared my throat. "I'm going as a favor to a friend."

That seemed to satisfy Lorelei and Gus, but Ben kept on. "What friend?"

I sighed. Vince was picking me up here, so it wasn't like I could hide it. I'd even remembered to call the guard at the gate to have him let Vince through. Besides, it wasn't any of Ben's business. "Vince Santini."

I ignored his bluster and turned to Lorelei. "Where do I keep my purses?" I used them so infrequently—and usually left them lying on the side table in the foyer when I was done with them—I had no idea where they were kept. God, what a mess my life would be without Lorelei.

Ha. What a mess it was anyway.

She pointed to the guest closet door. "In there. On the shelf."

I took out a small, black leather one and went back to my bedroom to grab my necessities, pulling most of them out of my cargo pants pockets. I took the fake ID that I flew to Iowa under and put it in the bottom of the cigar box on my desk that kept all my receipts.

Lipstick. Brush, in case the bun bit it. Real ID. Cash.

iPhone. I started to leave, then turned back and grabbed a tin of breath mints and tossed them into the purse as well.

When I got back into the living room, Lorelei was just opening the door to Vince. He always looked sharp, but he seemed to exude extra debonair today. "Hello, Anna," he said.

"Hi, Vince. Vince Santini, Lorelei Samuels."

The two shook hands, and Lorelei, who had definitely seen her share of good-looking men, stood transfixed at Vince. I pointed him into the archway leading to the living room. "You know Ben and Gus, right?"

"Yes, of course. Gentlemen," Vince said as he went to first Gus then Ben and shook their hands while he urged them not to get up, which they didn't.

"Wow," Lor whispered in my ear. I only nodded.

"Ready?" Vince said to me.

"Yes," I said as I went to the closet and got a shawl for a wrap. It was mid-February and though it was Vegas, it was still chilly.

Not Iowa cold, but not suntanning weather, either. Vince took the soft wrap from me and held it open. I turned my back to him and let him drape the sides over my shoulders.

With the old folk looking on from the living room, it kind of felt like we were headed to the prom, not to the funeral of a man I didn't particularly care for, to see if I could sniff out something about whoever killed him.

How had my life gotten to this point?

I almost told Ben not to wait up, but decided not to push it. He knew what Vince was, and I knew he wasn't thrilled with me leaving with him. The irony was, Vince was completely up front about what he was. I was the one with all the secrets from Ben.

And I had a big one.

Vince opened the door for me when we reached his black Infiniti. When he'd gotten in on his side, started the car and buckled his seat belt, he looked over at me and said, "It's probably not appropriate to say given the circumstances, but you look very beautiful today."

I looked down at myself. Totally put together. Totally Vince. Totally not me.

"This really is more your speed, isn't it? More than my usual attire anyway."

He pulled away from the curve, and we headed out of my subdivision. "You look good to me in whatever you wear," he said smoothly.

"But maybe a little bit more your taste like this."

He smiled, his perfectly white, straight teeth gleaming. He had the tact not to answer that one.

"Truth is, Vince, I'd find it exhausting dressing like this all the time. Like you do."

He shrugged. "I like nice things. For a long time in my life I had nothing. Now that I can afford it…" He didn't finish. He didn't need to. It was probably his version of the Hummer… having what he never could.

I'd led a perfectly normal, upper-middle-class life. I never really wanted for much, especially not the basics. I certainly didn't begrudge Vince his appreciation of finer things. I just wondered how he thought I might fit into that world. If, in fact he even did. I could be reading way too much into a casual comment about a possible first date.

We rode in silence to the funeral home, but it was a comfortable silence. I was relieved to see that it was a different place than we'd used for Saul. Danny's funeral had been at his Catholic Church.

"Seems like I've been doing this a lot lately," I said as we parked.

"Yes, it does," Vince answered. He'd come to both Danny and Saul's funerals. He'd told me it was to pay respect to the forerunners of Vegas. Vince was a history buff in his reading, and as such, appreciated those who came before.

It was something I admired about Vince. Most guys trying to make their mark in this town acted like they discovered Vegas. Not Vince.

We entered the funeral home, and Vince was greeted right away by the funeral director. "Mr. Santini," he said as he shook Vince's hand. "There are just a few more minor details I need to discuss with you."

"Of course." He turned to me. "Will you excuse me?"

"Sure. I'll just go pay my...respects." The last part was a little hard to get out and Vince lifted a corner of his mouth.

"I won't be long," he said and headed off into an office with the funeral director.

I realized that Vince was probably paying for all of Paulie's funeral expenses. The way Paulie used to hit on me, I assumed he wasn't married—though I don't know that that would have stopped Paulie.

Looking around the room confirmed that thought. There was nobody that looked like a mourning family, and other than Carla, Vince's bookkeeper and the person who ran the poker games with Paulie, who sat in the front row, I was the only woman.

I looked around the room. God, it was like an open casting call for *The Sopranos*. Goombas everywhere you looked. I avoided eye contact and headed to the front of the room, to the open casket. To pay my respects.

As if I'd ever respected Paulie.

But I did respect Vince, so I reluctantly stepped up to the casket.

Even in repose Paulie looked a little slimy. They had tried to make him look respectable. He wore an understated suit and tie. It looked like something Vince would wear. In fact, I didn't recall ever seeing Paulie in a suit that nice, and I wondered if Vince had gone out and bought him one for the afterlife.

They'd taken most of the product out of his hair. It didn't

shine as much as it normally did.

Paulie didn't really fit Vince's current image, the man he'd built himself into, but from what I understood, the three of them had come up together and Vince kept Paulie and Carla on even when he'd outgrown them.

Loyalty I understood. And revenge.

No wonder Vince wanted to find Paulie's killer himself. I could understand that, I'd wanted it desperately myself just a few weeks ago when somebody was targeting The Corporation.

Be careful what you wish for.

I bowed my head to say a prayer for Paulie's soul, but all that came out was, "Please, God, don't let me end up like him."

I turned around and looked at the milling group of shifty-looking men and mentally thought, "Or him. Or him. Or him."

Carla waved me over to her, and I sat down beside her in a straight, but soft, upholstered chair. The first two rows were made up of these chairs, and then folding chairs took up the rest of the room. I figured the nice chairs were for family and closest friends and wondered if maybe I should sit back a few rows. But then I realized that Vince would be sitting in this row, so I stayed where I was.

"It's nice that you came," she said to me.

"I'm sorry for your loss," I said softly to her.

It was quiet, but I swear she snorted. "The only loss is that it didn't happen sooner," she nearly seethed through her teeth.

"Wow," I whispered.

She shrugged. "He got what was coming to him. He couldn't have expected his life to turn out any differently."

"Geez, Carla, I thought you guys were friends."

"Hardly."

"But you seemed to get along well enough at the games you ran." But as I said it, an image of Carla sitting at a table, reading a magazine, ordering food and taking care of drinks came into my mind. After the initial start of the game where they "arranged" loans of money and handed out chips, Paulie and Carla went their very separate ways during a game. Even in a relatively small hotel suite.

She sat up a little straighter, pulled at her blazer. "That's 'cause I'm a professional."

"Well, I guess you don't have to pretend anymore."

"Oh, I'll keep it together for the funeral. There'll probably be plenty of people who spit on his casket, so I won't have to."

I chuckled then stopped myself as a man with a definite limp who had come up to the casket looked over his shoulder at me. I hung my head and tried to pretend I was muffling a sob.

"Besides, I would never do anything to embarrass Vince," Carla added.

I nodded at that. I guess I'd have to keep my saliva to myself, too.

"He should have been here by now," Carla said, looking behind her scanning the room.

"He is. The funeral director needed to speak to him."

"Oh. I thought I'd handled all the details."

I shrugged. "Probably something that just came up."

Carla looked closely at me. "Did you and Vince come together?"

I nodded, still looking straight ahead, pretending deep thoughts about the dearly departed.

"Hmm," was all she said. After a moment, it was killing me, so I turned to her.

"Hmm?"

"Interesting, that's all," she clarified. Clear as mud, really.

"In what way?" I was looking closely at her now, trying to read her.

But Carla had been around good poker players for a very long time and didn't give anything up. "I think it's nice, that's all."

"It's not like it's a date," I said, with not quite as much

certainty in my voice as I'd hoped.

"No?"

"No."

"Hmm," she said again. Gaining nothing from each other's faces, we both turned forward again.

A line had formed now of men passing by the casket and Paulie's body. They each stopped, some for just a second, some for a minute or two. Some heads bowed in prayer, some words were said quietly, but with a sneer on the mourner's face. I swore one man pinched Paulie's arm and I was reminded of hearing about some Eastern European dictator whose mourners pushed pins in him to make sure he was dead.

I suppose there were a great many people who didn't want Paulie coming back from the dead. Although they'd be fools to think that just because Paulie was gone their debt to Vince was washed out.

It might take Vince a bit to find some new muscle, but he never forgot a dime anybody owed him. It was all right there in Carla's blue ledgers. I knew, I'd signed a line in that ledger myself too many times to remember.

The line had dwindled and Vince still hadn't come in. The last man lumbered through. He was a large man, wearing a very ill-fitting and out-of-date suit. He seemed very upset and I thought in some sad way that it was nice that at least one person was honestly mourning Paulie.

He had his back to the room, but at the angle I sat, I could see him a little bit from the side. He leaned over Paulie's body, visibly upset, a small moan coming from him. He ran his hands along Paulie's arms, bending deeper over Paulie, and I wondered if he was going to kiss the corpse.

It looked like that's how it was headed and I was about to turn my head, not wanting to witness that sight, but just then my poker player's sixth sense of people's behavior kicked in. Instead of watching the man bend down to kiss Paulie as

I'm sure everyone in the room was, my eyes went instead to the man's right hand, which was on Paulie's left wrist. The mourner's positioning was such that his hand was blocked by his body, except for the small angle that I had.

And damned if he didn't lift Paulie's watch and diamond pinkie ring (yeah, Paulie was a pinkie ring guy—'nuff said) just as he gave Paulie's waxen cheek a loud kiss. It was a thing of beauty, the smooth sleight of hand that left Paulie's corpse jewelry free. The man gave Paulie one last semi-hug—as much as you can hug a stiff corpse. He was probably making sure Paulie wasn't to be buried with his wallet. He turned and walked down the aisle, nobody but me noticing his full fist easing into his suit jacket and releasing the ill-gotten gains.

Ill being the key word, as I tried to swallow down the gag of disgust rising up from inside me. "Jesus," I whispered to myself, but Carla heard me.

"I know, I can't believe it either," Carla said. At first I thought she'd seen what I had, but then I realized she meant the amazing fact that someone was actually visibly upset about Paulie being dead.

The disgust turned to loathing. Of that fake mourner. Of Paulie. Of all these men, many with limps that mirrored the one I'd sweated through six weeks of physical therapy to lose.

Of myself for even being here. Of living a life that would call for me to be here.

"I've got to get out of here," I said to Carla and left my chair before she could even respond. I walked quickly down the aisle. When I was almost to freedom, Vince and the funeral director entered the room and came down the aisle. Vince stopped when he met me, but the funeral director kept walking to the front of the room.

"Where are you going?" Vince asked. "We're about to start."

"I can't," I said.

"Why?" Vince asked. And it was a valid question. I couldn't

possibly be too upset to sit through a funeral of a man I detested.

"I just...I just..." I stammered, trying to find a way to explain to Vince my loathing of all these people. But I couldn't. He was one of them.

So was I, and that's why I couldn't stay.

Vince's deep brown eyes bore into me, looking for something. A kindred spirit, I suppose.

And because I did respect Vince—and yes liked him as much as I did—I said, "I was in the front row, but then figured if you really wanted me to try and pick up anything, that I'd be better off watching from the back."

He nodded, while he judged how close I was to the door and how I had nearly passed the back of the room for the exit. "That's a good idea," he said, "I'll see you after. It's not going to be a long service, for obvious reasons."

Because Paulie had been murdered? Because Vince would be hard pressed to find someone to speak well of Paulie? I didn't ask, I just nodded and stepped to the side, still inside the room, but near the back wall. There were two upholstered side chairs with an end table between them along the wall a few feet away from the last empty row of folding chairs and I sunk into one.

Vince watched me until I'd settled in, then turned and walked to the front of the room, sitting down next to Carla in the seat I'd just vacated.

Determined to just get through the next half hour, and then away from these people, I tried to drown everything out. I should have been watching people for Vince, but knew it would be a waste of time. At this moment everybody looked like a killer to me.

"Another funeral. Another back row." Jack Schiller's soft whisper drifted over me as he sat in the chair next to me. I turned to him and saw his gaze sweep over my body, slowing as he visually slid over my crossed legs and down to my suede pumps.

Nine
❖

"But same incredibly hot black suit."

"**WHAT ARE YOU DOING HERE?**" I whispered to him, but of course I knew. It was the same thing that had brought him to Danny and Saul's funerals, a homicide investigation.

"I was just about to ask you the same thing," he answered. "I wouldn't have thought you'd be the first one in line to mourn Paulie Gonads."

"Seeing as I killed him and all."

He raised one brow at me. Damn, I wish I could pull that look off, it'd be so useful at the poker table.

"I'm here for a friend," I said and felt him slightly stiffen. His eyes swung from me to the front of the room, to the back of Vince's head. "How's the investigation going, anyway?" I asked.

"You know I can't tell you anything," he said, still facing forward.

"Because I'm a suspect or because I…" I didn't finish the sentence. I didn't know how.

"Finish your sentence," he said.

"You finish it for me." There was a near petulance to my voice that made me inwardly cringe.

"Because you're a suspect or because you'll tell Vince Santini anything I tell you. That sound about right?"

I shrugged. "Paulie meant a lot to Vince. It's not unnatural

that he'd want to be kept apprised of your investigation. I wanted
to know what was going on when Danny was killed."

"That was different."

"How?"

"Danny was a good man that didn't deserve what happened
to him."

"Playing judge and jury for Paulie?"

He was wearing his usual work outfit, leather jacket, blue
chambray shirt, tie and chinos. He looked fine, totally suitable
for a funeral, and a heck of a lot more dressed up than a couple of
lowlifes here. But he'd worn a suit to Danny and Saul's funerals.
I don't know why that little wardrobe tidbit made me feel good,
but it did.

"Vince tell you anything? He have any ideas who did this to
Paulie?" Jack asked me.

"Nope," I answered, not willing to tell him that Vince was
just as eager to find out who killed Paulie as Jack was. More so.

"Would you tell me if he did?"

"I don't know," I answered truthfully. "Not if he asked me
not to."

"What if he does in the future? And doesn't ask you to not
say anything."

"I won't spy on Vince for you," I told Jack.

"You'd protect a man who wouldn't hesitate to have you
killed if you owed him money?"

"Vince wouldn't...well, at least he would hesitate."

Jack softly snorted at that and sat back in his chair. He stuck
out his legs, crossed them at the ankles and his arms crossed his
chest.

We sat in silence while the funeral director droned on. He
spoke of generalities about life and sudden death, probably not
daring to delve into Paulie the man.

I scanned the men in the rows ahead of us since that's what
I'd come here for after all. I noticed Jack was doing the same.

"Jesus, what a bunch of deadbeats," he said.

I agreed with him, but got defensive in a twisted kind of way. "Watch it. I play cards with these guys all the time." Which wasn't quite true. The real big guns in Vince's high-stakes, back room games weren't here. To them, Paulie was only a voice on the phone telling them when and where for a game.

Their pockets were so deep that they never had to play on marker, never owed Vince, never would have taken that car ride with Paulie.

"You are so not in these guys' league," Jack said to me. He was right. I wasn't.

"Yet," he said adding the word I couldn't say out loud.

He turned back to me, waited until I faced him—until I *could* face him.

"Okay, Johanna, I'm Bob Marley now."

"What?"

"Bob Marley."

"The Reggae singer?" Jack could be esoteric at times, and I always took pride in sticking right with him, but this was a jump I couldn't follow.

"What? Oh. No, not Bob Marley. The Marley guy that comes to Scrooge. You know, in *A Christmas Carol.*"

"Oh. Jacob Marley."

"Right. The guy who tells Scrooge he's about to be visited by ghosts."

My hands tensed. I sat up straighter. I nodded at Jack to continue.

He stood up to leave, but instead leaned over me. He put his fingertip lightly on my horseshoe pendant. Silly to wear a lucky horseshoe to a funeral, but I always wore it. His lips were close to my ear, his breath soft against the wisps of hair that had loosened from my bun. He smelled like leather and Jack...but not bourbon, my twisted mind registered.

He whispered in my ear then left. I spent the rest of the

service replaying his words: "Look closely around you, Johanna. You are being visited by the ghost of gambling future."

OF COURSE I KNEW what my life could end up like. It surely would have had I not met Ben ten years ago. And it still could, I knew that, I've seen it happen to more stable people than I over the years. But this…seeing all these degenerate gamblers in one place—Jack was right. If I wasn't careful, I could one day be reduced to stealing a dead man's watch to place my next bet.

The service was over, everybody was filing out, but I sat glued to my chair, too exhausted with dark thoughts to move.

I watched the men leave. Vince and Carla were still at the front of the room speaking with the funeral director.

I counted twenty-seven men walk past me. Of that, there were ten with discernible limps—Paulie's signature. There were at least seven noses that had been badly broken and repaired even more badly. Too many cheap suits to count.

I sunk back in the chair as the last man walked out the doorway behind me.

Call it an epiphany. Call it my Scrooge moment. But it became crystal clear to me in a way it never had before.

I had to stop gambling.

"THINK THAT DETECTIVE would tell you anything about Paulie's case?" Vince asked me on the way home.

Déjà vu all over again.

"No," I said. "He asked me the same thing about you."

Vince smiled at that. I admired his profile as he kept his eyes on the road. He was more classically handsome than Jack, whose face was much more rugged and lived in than Vince's.

Which was odd, because they both had seen a lot of bad stuff in their lives. Done a lot of bad stuff, too, probably.

It showed on Jack's face, but not on Vince's.

I wasn't surprised that Vince knew Jack had been at the funeral. "You know, you two should team up. You both want the same thing," I said to Vince.

"Not exactly."

No, not exactly.

"So, anybody stand out as someone who would have shot Paulie point blank?" Vince asked me.

I snorted. "Who didn't?" Right away I wished I could take the words back. "Sorry," I said quietly.

Vince shrugged. Well, Vince didn't exactly shrug, it was a much more elegant movement.

"No. I didn't see anything that stood out. Or anybody."

He nodded. "Neither did I."

I didn't tell him about that guy stealing Paulie's watch and pinkie ring. I didn't know how Vince would react to that. And I figured if a guy was desperate enough to steal a dead man's jewelry, he probably didn't need Vince Santini showing up on his doorstep.

When we finally reached my house, I reached for the door handle, but Vince put a hand across to stop me then got out of his side and came around to open the door for me. He put out his hand to take mine and I let him.

He kept his hand wrapped loosely around mine as he walked me up the pavement and driveway. It felt smooth and cool, and I liked the feel of it over mine. There was an awkward moment at the front door where I wondered if I should ask Vince in. He didn't seem disappointed when I didn't, but he did wait for me to speak first.

"Sorry I wasn't much help," I said.

"Thanks for coming with me."

"No problem."

"I'll call you tomorrow," he said.

For a real date, I wondered. Until he said, "After the game."

"Right." Right. CIU played tomorrow.

"Did you place a bet on it?"

"No," I told him.

"Would you like me to lend you money to bet it?"

I shook my head. "No. Thank you. I'm actually pretty flush right now. I've had a good run at cash games."

"That's good."

"That's not why I don't bet the game. I mean, I still won't bet it even though I've got some extra change."

"Why is that?"

I shrugged and looked back toward the street, not wanting to meet his eyes. "I don't bet on games JoJo is involved with."

He was silent for a moment. At least he didn't laugh at me like Paulie had when I'd told him my rule. "JoJo was just the middleman on this one. It's not like you—she—slipped a roofie in his drink and he's playing like hell and doesn't know why."

This time, I thought, and silently thanked Vince for not saying it.

"Still…" I hedged.

"Okay. I get it. Sort of."

I looked at him, and he really did. Sort of.

"Tomorrow," he said.

"Okay," I said. I waited to see…I don't know what I waited to see. I honestly couldn't tell you what I wanted to happen right then.

But nothing happened. Vince just left, got in his car and drove away. And I went inside my home to see what Lor and the boys were up to.

"AND AT THE HALF," the game announcer droned from the

television, "Central Iowa is up by ten. I guess you could say much like we expected."

Not me. I'd expected it to be closer than ten. I needed six. Well, I didn't, as I hadn't bet the game, but Raymond did to get his back end and stay on Vince's good side. A side I highly recommended.

I got up from my leather chair and was slightly surprised to remember that I was in my own home watching the game and not a book room at a casino.

When Ben's hip started really getting bad, and I was on a particularly hot streak, I charged Lorelei with making the seldom-used family room into a home theater. No, the instructions had been more implicit than that. I had taken her to the book rooms at the Bellagio and the Venetian and told her to set up something similar so we could watch several games at once.

She'd taken my instructions—and a considerable amount of my money—and delivered. In spades.

Eight flat-screen plasma televisions hung on the wall, circling a huge projection screen. The masterpiece took up an entire wall. Eight luxurious leather seats, some recliners, some wide enough to hold two people, were set for maximum screen access. Along another wall was a concession stand of sorts. A sideboard filled with snacks, a coffee maker, a mini-fridge.

Not to confuse it with the living room, it had become known in our house not as the family room, but the book room, and I don't mean a library.

But Lor's masterpiece was better than a book room. No smoke, no crowds. Our own fabulous cocktail waitress in Lor. That we didn't have to tip.

But no odds board flashing its delicious lights. No counter across the front of the room manned with lovely people just waiting to take your money.

Which is why I didn't spend much time here.

But from seeing all the little sheets of paper with odds and point spreads scattered here and there and in the wastebasket, I knew that Ben did. His tablets, and thus paper remnants, were different than Lor's. She used tablets the size of a steno pad whereas Ben's were much smaller, the size that would—and did—fit inside a shirt front pocket.

I didn't look too closely at what it said about me that I'd surrounded myself with tablet freaks.

Retired for years, Ben still set the odds for every game every day, on little sheets of paper from his numerous little tablets, even though they never ended up on a casino board. They could have, they were more deadly accurate than the incredibly accurate ones set by the current odds maker.

Suddenly, I felt like shit that I didn't watch all the games here with Ben. There was no reason not to. I could place my bets in a book room then come home and watch with him. He'd love it.

But Ben was astute. He would notice the way the Hummer took me over. I could sit passively and watch a game that I had ten thousand dollars on go down the drain—I had, many times in fact—and not even the anonymous guy sitting next to me would have been able to tell.

But Ben would have.

I could hide about as much from Ben as I could from Jack.

Which suddenly made more sense to me.

"You need anything?" I asked Ben now as I rose from my seat.

He checked the level of his coffee cup and shook his head. "No, Hannah, darling, I'm fine." He smiled at me, his sparkly brown eyes almost disappearing within the multitude of crow's feet in his weathered face.

A face that now seemed even more familiar to me.

I nodded at him, and started to leave the room. "You're coming back?" he asked, with just a tiny bit of neediness in his voice.

"Yep. Just hitting the john and my office. I'll be back by the second half."

He seemed to relax as I left the room and walked down the hall and across the house to the office Lorelei and I shared, hoping to find it empty. It was, and I shut the door behind me, settled in at my desk and booted up my laptop.

It was state-of-the-art, as was everything in the house, but I didn't use it much. Much to my Wisconsin family's chagrin, I wasn't a reliable e-mailer. They pretty much had stopped trying, calling me when needed, or sending news to me via Lorelei's e-mail address.

It wasn't that I couldn't figure out the computer. But the more familiar I was with all the online things, the more likely it was that I'd find myself sucked into online poker or sports betting. That was why Lor was keeper of my credit cards, so I couldn't open an online account. But there were ways around that if I really wanted to, and I supposed that if I were online a lot, I'd find that way.

I'd known a lot of good poker players that had lost their fortunes by playing addictively online. When you had to go out for a game—get dressed, drive to a casino, plop down cold, hard cash, sit at a table, need to get up eventually—it was a lot easier to walk away. When you could play in your pajamas at any hour of the day and the money was just an icon on a screen…well, it wasn't an experiment I felt I was strong enough to play with.

But I could find out stuff I needed to online. Stuff JoJo needed.

But as I called up Google, I knew that this search was solely for me. In fact, it could—and I hoped would—mean JoJo's demise.

I typed in "12-Step Programs".

I knew Lorelei had tons of this sort of information at the ready for me. Hell, I think I saw Monty's information still sitting on her desk a foot away from me.

But I was still feeling a bit raw from this, like a colt trying to stand up on wobbly legs, and I didn't want Lor—or anyone else in my immediate circle—watching me stumbling my way into walking.

A fleeting thought went through my mind that Jack would get it. He would understand. I pushed the thought aside.

Jack wasn't an option.

But maybe he could be, a voice deep in my head said, *if this works, if you could stop.* It was a voice I didn't recognize, certainly not JoJo's twang.

No, this wasn't for Jack. Nor Ben nor Lorelei. This had to be for me, or it would never work. And still it would be tricky. I couldn't stop playing poker; it was my livelihood. And I'd become accustomed to fine things, much like Vince had. Mine were just not worn on my body.

But poker, played either in a tournament form or cash games in a casino—where you had to have the cash up front—had never been the problem. Where the problems had arisen—and JoJo had been born—had all come from sports betting. I'd play in one of Vince's games on credit because I had no cash and wanted—needed—to place a bet on a game.

If I could stop placing bets, there'd be no need to play on credit, no need for JoJo to ever come out again.

Poker was fun, and I was good at it, but I could walk away from a game at anytime. Unless I was playing for a stake to bet on a game.

I knew these types of programs were all about support, not doing it on your own, but I wasn't ready for that. I was barely ready to admit that I wanted to try this.

I clicked on one of the Google results. The "12 steps" came on the screen, and I scanned through them.

I could totally do this on my own.

Give myself up to a higher power? I did that every time I placed a bet.

Admit that I was powerless against my addiction? Ahhh… that might be a sticky one. I didn't much like the idea that I was powerless. Wasn't that the whole idea of my creation of JoJo? Taking back some type of control?

Deciding to skip that step for now, I read down further on the list. Make amends? I could do that. I hadn't really hurt anybody but myself, anyway, right?

A flood of faces raced in front of me. The many players that JoJo had set in her sights. Ben looking at me with concern every time I went away for more than a day. Lorelei spending her time trying to figure out ways to help me.

But the two faces that seemed to stay front and center were those of Jack Schiller and Raymond Joseph.

Make amends to Jack? He'd broken my heart.

And Raymond Joseph? Wasn't he doing just fine? And really, if it hadn't been for me, his poor sister would probably still be strung out on the streets of Chicago's South Side, not getting the help she needed in rehab.

Okay, that was definitely JoJo's voice coming through.

There was a soft knock on the door. "Jo, are you in there?" Lorelei asked.

I clicked the browser window closed. "Yeah, come on in." I grabbed for some sheets of paper on my desk as Lorelei came in. "Just getting some odds sheets," I said, like I had to justify my presence in my own office, on my own laptop.

She shut the door behind her and sat down on her side of our partners desk that we shared. "Good, I wanted to get you alone."

Oh, no. If she started in on pleading Monty's case, should I just go ahead and tell her that I was going to turn over a new leaf? Would the odds sheets I'd just grabbed defeat that purpose?

But I needn't have worried, Lorelei had other things on her mind. "I found out a bunch of stuff on DNA testing," she said.

Immersed in my new-found morality, I'd forgotten I'd asked

Lorelei for her research help. "What'd you find out?"

"There's a bunch of labs—all over the world—that will do whatever testing you need done. It's expensive, and even more expensive if you need it fast…" She looked at me questioningly.

The information I sought was nearly forty years old, but now there did seem to be a sense of urgency to it. "I'm willing to pay for that," I said.

Lorelei nodded, then took out a file folder from one of her desk drawers. "There's even a lab here in Vegas that does it."

"What kind of…sample…do they need?" I asked.

"What exactly are you looking for? Evidence type gathering? Genetic tracking?" She seemed to be going down a list of options.

"I want to know if somebody could be somebody else's father." My eye caught on the urn with Saul's ashes. "Or, if somebody is definitely not their father."

Lor nodded, and went back to her papers. "Ideally a swab taken from the inside of that person's mouth works best."

"What if I can't get access to that sort of thing?"

"Then a strand of hair would work. Or something that still had saliva on it. There's a list of things here that we could gather."

"We?"

She looked almost hurt. "Yes. We."

I smiled and nodded for her to continue. She looked pointedly at Saul's urn. "As for cremains…"

"What?"

"Cremains. That's what they call ashes from a cremation."

"God, it sounds like some dried fruit you'd put on a salad."

"Ewwww."

"Go on," I waved to her, trying to not think about the mental picture forming.

"The DNA testing industry is a bit divided on cremains. The feeling is that if the cremation was done correctly, there's no way any testing could be done on just ashes. All the DNA would have been burned out."

Ah, well, that put a different spin on my little project, but it wasn't completely dead...no pun intended.

"But, apparently, the information that comes from non-mortuary related places is that most cremations are not done the same way and that many times tiny bone fragments remain. Those *are* testable and still contain DNA."

I looked at the urn. "And how do you know if there are bone fragments?" I looked to Lor with disgust.

"You...uhm...put the ashes through a strainer and see what's left."

"Jesus," I whispered, eyeing the urn warily.

"Jo," Lorelei said quietly, and I looked up at her. "You know I'd do anything for you..."

I held up a hand. "I won't ask you to do that, Lor, don't worry."

"No, that's not what I meant. I meant that I'll help you in any way you need me to."

I was just about to get down on my knees and kiss her feet. I so didn't want to strain Saul's ashes by myself.

"But..." she said, halting my movement of gratitude. "If I'm going to paw through Saul's ashes, and gather saliva from some stranger, I'm going to need a good reason."

"Not a stranger," I said.

"No? Who then?"

"Jack."

"Jack?"

"Yes, and no, you can not gather saliva from him in the preferred method."

"Why Jack?"

"Well, actually, Jack and Ben. And Saul, of course."

"Jo, what the hell is going on?"

I sat up straight, cleared my throat, and voiced the secret I'd held since Saul had died in my arms.

"I think Jack may be Ben's son."

Ten
❖❖

I WAITED IN MY RENTAL CAR *in the deserted parking lot Raymond had directed me to during our brief phone conversation. I was glad he wasn't pushing his luck and choosing another bar, but it was cold as hell in Iowa in February. I kept the car running and the heater blasting.*

A bright, sunny, Sunday afternoon. Beautiful day, really, if you didn't mind the frigid temperatures.

I'd met Vince to pick up Raymond's winnings late Saturday night. He'd asked me if I was in JoJo mode. When I'd said yes, he handed me an envelope with the cash and said he'd call me on Monday, when Anna was available.

No judgment. No shaking his head at my alter ego. He just wanted to talk with Anna, not JoJo.

I'd almost kissed him.

Instead, I'd said I looked forward to his call then tried to get a flight to Dubuque under my fake flying name, Marie VanSipe, only to find that I'd missed the last flight out that night. So, I got a flight for Sunday morning and went home.

I came home after everyone was in bed, and I was gone before anybody was up, so Lor and Ben would have thought I was still playing cards. And given that I was planning on playing some long hours this week, it wouldn't raise any flags.

I wouldn't outright lie to them if they asked, but they probably wouldn't. With the time change, I'd be home in time for Sunday dinner.

I started thinking about all those great meals of Lorelei's that I'd be available for now that I wasn't betting games. My vision of her homemade mac and cheese was cut short by a burst of cold air as Raymond Joseph plunked down in the passenger seat.

Great secret agent I was. The kid—hell, his whole car—totally snuck up on me.

I looked across him to see a beat-up, late model piece of shit parked next to me. Happily, I noted that Raymond hadn't raised suspicions by using any of his ill-gotten gains on new wheels.

Not surprised, though. Raymond was smarter than that.

"JoJo," Raymond said, distaste evident in his voice.

"Raymond," I said and handed him the envelope Vince had given me. "Nice work yesterday."

He snorted. "Shit, I let it get too close. We almost lost."

"But you didn't"

He shot me a if-looks-could-kill glance. "But we almost did."

I ignored his look. "It'll help you during tournament time. People will underestimate you."

"Yeah, but if I do this shit then, I—"

"Raymond," I cut him off. "You won't be asked to do this in the tournament."

I wasn't sure what emotion was keener in his eyes, the relief, or then the panic. "What do ya mean?"

"You're at the top of the conference, yes, but everybody says the Big Ten is overrated this year."

"So?"

"You'll be underdogs."

He looked at me questioningly. Of course he didn't get it. Only a degenerate gambler like myself would.

"You'll be no good in the tournament. CIU will be the underdogs after the first round."

"So?"

"So? You can't fix a game if you're the underdog. What are you going to do, have people put thousands of dollars on your promise that you'll try really, really hard to win? It's a situation you have no control over, Raymond."

"Shit, like I have control over any of this." The disgust on his face was obvious.

I almost patted his arm but knew he'd rebuke me.

"There are two weeks left of regular season, then the conference tournament, and then this is all over. You have a shelf life, Raymond."

"You gonna leave me alone next year?"

"Yes. Pros don't hold any interest to my...associate. Pro players make so much money it's not enough incentive to them for the risk that's involved."

"That's why you go after the refs in the pros." Raymond had apparently done his point-shaving homework.

"I don't go after anyone," I stated.

He shot me another look. "You came after me."

He was right. I nodded. "You're the only one."

"The only one that knew." It wasn't a question. His eyes bored into me.

"Yes."

"Fuck," he said and looked away from me, out the window.

"Yeah," I agreed.

"They say I'm too little for the pros," he said softly. "That I'm a great college ball player, but that's as far as I'm gonna get."

"I'd heard that, too."

"Another reason you picked me?"

"Yeah. But you know what? I've never seen a player play with as much heart as you, Raymond. I know it's a cliché, but it's true. Prove them wrong."

Raymond Joseph had better people in his life to give him a pep talk than the woman who'd lured him to the dark side, but I said it anyway.

"Get to the Final Four and show them what you've got."

"Christ, shut up," he said.

"Sorry."

He started to chuckle. "You know how you were telling me about the voice you hear?"

"Yes?"

"I call my voice L'il Roy."

"Is that a rapper or something?"

He looked at me. "Man, you sure are white, aren't you?"

I shrugged.

"No, L'il Roy's no rapper. He's somebody I grew up with in Chicago."

"Oh, that's nice."

He let out a half snort, half laugh. "There ain't nothin' nice 'bout L'il Roy." His voice seemed to grow more...city...as he went on. Maybe just thinking about the South Side of Chicago did that to him. I know a week back in Madison for the holidays and I'm talking like a character from Fargo.

"He was a year older than me, but got held back so we were in the same grade growing up. He had an older brother named LeRoy, so he became known as Little Roy. His real name was James."

I stayed silent. This was the most Raymond had ever said to me, so of course I didn't interrupt him.

"James and I played together as kids. Played hoops every night. Until 'bout the ninth grade. I kept playing hoops at night, but James fell in with LeRoy. And LeRoy was no good."

I turned the heater down a little. It was warm enough, and Raymond's voice was getting softer as his memory deepened.

"Anyway. Basketball saved me. Gave me a place to go in the evenings, after school, something to shoot for. That, and my momma wouldn't let me fall in with that crowd."

"She sounds like a great mom. Looking out for you the way she did. Trying to help your sister, now."

His shoulders tensed. "Yeah. She is. And she always said no

good would come to L'il Roy."

"And was she right?"

"Depends who you ask. He'd say he was doing just fine."

"Oh," I said, surprised.

"You thought I'd say he was dead."

"Well, yeah."

"Nah. He's too mean to die. Did some time, though. But now he runs three blocks."

"Is that good?"

"For him, yeah. For everyone else that lives there, no. And not for his brother, LeRoy."

"Why?"

"He ran those blocks…before L'il Roy killed him."

"God."

"He's the voice I hear. Just like when we were ten-year-olds and he'd try to get me to come with him at night and I'd stay to play ball. In that same voice of his. 'Come on, Raaaaymond'," he said, his voice sing-songy. "I hate that fucking voice."

Raymond's self-loathing was like a third passenger in the car.

God, what had I done to this kid? He only had the voice now, but the feeling was coming, I knew it. And once the voice met the feeling it was all over.

It wasn't really making amends, and he certainly wouldn't see it that way, but it was something I could do for Raymond.

I could quiet his voice. Silence L'il Roy.

He turned to open the car door, and I slipped my JoJo phone into his jacket pocket. His only connection to me. I waited for him to notice, but he kept on with his exit. Too hasty to make a getaway to notice, plus his bulky parka helped.

"This was the last time," he said over his shoulder just before he slammed the door. Repeating what he said to me every time. But this time he was right, even if he didn't know it yet.

"Yes, Raymond," I said to my empty car. "It was."

♠ ♥ ♦ ♣

MONDAY MORNING WITH the boys, I pulled out a magazine—and not even a *Sports Illustrated* or *ESPN*, but a *Cosmo*—to read after breakfast while the boys discussed the day's games.

And even though I appeared to be deeply engrossed learning a hundred and one ways to please my man (assuming I ever got the chance to try any of them out on anyone), I couldn't help but overhear when Jimmy took a call on his cell phone then told Gus and Ben that his guy had just heard that the center for an ACC powerhouse was about to be picked up for questioning for allegedly beating up his girlfriend, and would most likely be out for tonight's game.

News that hadn't broken anywhere yet.

Jimmy knew those types of guys from his odds setting days and still maintained contact. Especially with tips like this.

You have about an hour to place that bet before the news breaks and the point spread changes, JoJo said in my head.

She might as well have spoken out loud, for Jimmy and Gus both looked at their watches then signaled our waitress for the check.

"You getting in on this?" Jimmy asked me as he pulled some bills out of his wallet.

I shook my head. "Thanks, but I think I'll sit this one out."

I didn't explain. I still wasn't able to say the words, "I'm going to stop betting." They could have thought I didn't have any money on me. And though they'd be happy to lend me some if I asked, they wouldn't offer.

That's not how things were done within The Corporation.

Ben, of course, wouldn't make the bet. Ben never bet on games, never gambled at all beyond the friendly—well, okay, totally cutthroat—poker games at our dining room table.

Saul once alluded to Ben's "past" with gambling. Ben never spoke of it, so I didn't pry.

"I'll bring Gus by your place later if you guys wanna get going," Jimmy said.

I looked at Gus. "Is that okay with you?"

Gus looked at Jimmy. "Can we make a couple of stops?"

Jimmy shrugged his mammoth shoulders. "Yeah, sure, why not."

Gus looked back to me. "I'll see you later? Cards tonight?"

God, yes, that would keep me from thinking about the game I didn't bet. "Sounds good. Jimmy, can you stay? We'll do dinner then cards? I'll tell Lor."

"Yeah," Jimmy said, and I knew he was already dreaming about Lorelei's cooking.

"Okay," I said, glad that Gus was going with Jimmy, and that Ben and I would be able to leave and not wait around for Gus to place his bet. I didn't know how long I could be tempted with a tip like Jimmy got and not bet.

Gus and Jimmy left the table after we settled up. I stood and waited for Ben to ease his way away from the table and slowly glide his walker out of the casino.

I looked the other way as we walked past the book room.

LORELEI NEARLY TACKLED me when we came in the house. "There you are. Finally."

Poor thing. I'd dropped the bombshell about Jack possibly being Ben's son two days ago, and since then had either been gone or Ben had been around us.

Which he was now. I tried to be discreet but widened my eyes and nodded my head toward Ben who stood in front of me.

But Lor was sharper than that and had her alibi at the ready. "I got this bill in the mail for something that I didn't order. Can you come into the office and take a look?"

"Sure, let me get Ben settled."

Ben was about to wave me away when Lor piped in. "I'll get him settled. Go take a look. I left the receipt right in the middle of your desk. I'll be there in a second."

She'd already started walking with Ben into the living room, helping him with his jacket as they went.

One did not wave off Lorelei.

I went down the hall to our office, prepared to take a seat and wait for Lorelei so that I could answer her sure to be many questions.

At least answer the ones I could. I probably had just as many questions myself.

But as I entered the office, I stopped dead in my tracks in the doorway. In the middle of my desk sat not a questionable receipt, but a white tablecloth spread out to cover every inch of desktop and upon that a box, several plastic sandwich bags, the urn with Saul's ashes, and a colander.

I WON'T GO INTO THE NASTY DETAILS, but try to imagine dumping three or four full ashtrays into a colander and hoping it sifts through. The grittier stuff went through pretty easily, but there were lots of large flakes that just kind of sat there in Lor's stainless steel strainer.

"You are so buying me a new colander," Lor said as she gently shook the thing back and forth while I held the box underneath.

"Fine," I answered.

"And not some Walmart one. I want one from Crate and Barrel. Or Sur La Table."

"Fine." I didn't know any of the places she was talking about, but knew without a doubt that Lor would find the best colander on the market.

One of the larger flakes floated up and came to rest on Lor's thumb, holding fast to the colander handle. She closed her eyes, swallowed down whatever she was feeling, and flicked the ash back into the pile. "And a manicure."

"Throw in a pedicure. I really appreciate this, Lor."

"Then explain to me why we're doing this."

We switched places, she holding the box and me taking the colander, its handle already covered with a light film of...Saul.

"When Saul died, he said that Ben and Rachael had a child together that Rachael gave away and Ben never knew about."

"Rachael was Saul's wife?" The same disbelief I'd felt when Saul had told me about Ben and Rachael having an affair was evident on Lorelei's face.

"Yeah."

"Holy crap."

"Yeah."

"And he told you Jack was this child?"

I shook my head. "No. He died before he could tell me that."

"Then why do you think it?"

"A couple of things Saul said about Jack moving to Vegas... kind of like he'd been keeping tabs on Jack."

"That's it? That's kind of thin."

I shrugged. "The very first time I met Jack, there was something so familiar about him." I didn't bother to tell her it was in front of a municipal building that housed all sorts of twelve-step program meetings. Jack was there to attend an AA meeting. I was there to go to Gambler's Anonymous. Neither of us had ended up going into the building.

Kind of said a lot about what was to happen between us.

"And then when I looked at that picture of Rachael, Saul and Ben. The one in the dining room?" Lorelei nodded. "I mean, I'd seen that picture every day for ten years, but after meeting Jack, it was just so astonishing, the resemblance to Rachael. Except the eyes. Jack has Ben's eyes."

Lorelei was looking away, off into space, I suppose trying to picture Jack and Ben's eyes. She lost her hold on the box and it slipped a bit to the side, some of Saul's ashes floating onto the white tablecloth.

"And a new tablecloth," she added to her inventory.

"You got it."

"If you're so sure Ben is Jack's father, why are we getting samples from Saul?"

"Because Saul and Rachael were married at the time. Saul felt he wasn't able to father children, but I don't think he knew that for sure." I shrugged, causing the colander to kick up more dust. "I guess it's just for process of elimination. This could all be a wild goose chase and the parents that raised Jack in California are the ones who gave birth to him."

"But you don't think so?"

"No. I don't think so."

In the end we were able to find a couple of bone slivers… sheesh…and we bagged them up. As we were cleaning up the mess, I mentioned to Lorelei that Jimmy would be coming over for dinner and cards afterward.

"Why not call Jack and invite him over, too?"

I looked at her like she was crazy.

"Why not? Ben misses him. Jack liked playing cards with us before."

"That's when it was foreplay."

She snorted. "Don't give yourself so much credit. He loved playing cards with us."

"I know," I admitted.

"We'd be killing two birds with one stone. Ben gets to spend some time with Jack, and we get a hair sample or saliva or something from Jack."

"I can't call Jack and ask him to come over," I whined.

"I can," she said. She took a pencil off of the desk and, so as not to touch the phone with her dusty hands, pushed first speaker then arched a brow at me until I told her Jack's number.

"Johanna?" he answered.

"Uh, no. Sorry, Jack, it's Lorelei." She shrugged at me.

"Is everything alright? Is Johanna hurt?"

I admit it, I got a thrill over how concerned his voice sounded.

"She's fine," Lorelei said quickly, and I could hear Jack's loud exhale through the speaker.

"Ben?"

"He's fine. Look, Jack, totally social call, here."

"Oh." That seemed to stop him.

"We're having the boys over tonight for dinner and cards. And they've all been missing you at the table, so I thought you might want to join us."

"Is Johanna in town?"

"Yes, where else would she be?"

It was a small snort, but I heard it. He was probably lifting that one damn brow, too. "And she knows you're inviting me?"

"Yes."

Silence. Then, "Am I on speaker phone?"

"Yes, but only because my hands are...dirty."

More silence. "Johanna?" he said so softly I barely heard him. It was the exact same tone of voice he'd whisper to me in bed.

I cleared my throat. "Yes?"

"You okay with me coming over?"

No. God, no. Verbally sparring with him at the station or a funeral was one thing. But in my home? Where he'd spent so much time? Playing cards and trash talking with the boys, our eyes meeting across the table? No.

"Yeah. Sure. It's fine," I said with as much nonchalance as I could muster.

"What time?"

"Dinner's at six," Lorelei said.

"Can I bring anything?"

She gave me an "isn't he the sweetest thing" look, but answered, "No, I've got it all covered, thanks."

"Never had a doubt about that," he said, knowing just how to stroke Lorelei. "See you then." When he hung up, Lorelei punched the disconnect button with the pencil then dropped it into the garbage bag she had at the ready.

We put the sealed Ziploc bags to the side and poured Saul's ashes back into the urn trying to kick up as little dust as possible. The box then went into the trash bag. I wiped the sides of the now covered urn with the tablecloth and set it back in its spot on the shelf. Lorelei and I both used the ends of the tablecloth to wipe as much from our hands as possible then put the once nice tablecloth—now rag—into the trash bag and sealed it up.

"Thank God the cleaning lady comes tomorrow," Lorelei said.

"You got that right."

"I'm going to take a very long shower," she said.

"Me, too."

We left the office, me carrying the garbage bag to the garage and the trash cans. When we parted at the hallway Lorelei would take to her bedroom and bathroom, I said, "Lor, throw in a massage and facial when you get your mani/pedi."

"Thanks, Jo," she said.

"If you haven't already," I said hoisting the trash bag as evidence of my gratitude, "you're certainly going to earn it tonight."

Eleven

❖

"**THIS IS GREAT, LORELEI**," Jimmy said through a full mouth.

"Thanks, Jimmy," Lorelei answered. "I know my ziti's one of your favorites, but I really felt like Mexican tonight."

"*Muy bueno*," Gus said, raising his fork in salute, which Lorelei answered with a sly smile. The old charmer chuckled in return.

"Whatever," Jimmy said, digging in for more enchiladas. "It's damn good."

"Absolutely," Jack said as he wiped his mouth with his napkin. "I forget, Ben, is Mexican kosher?"

"I'm more afraid of the gas tonight than the afterlife right now," Ben said.

Everyone laughed, including Ben. I hadn't heard him laugh like that in a while. And he'd eaten a big helping, which was good. He and Jack shared a look of shared humor, and I felt my gut clench.

Lorelei and I sat on one side of the table, Jack and Gus in the seats across from us. Ben sat on the end between Jack and me, and Jimmy on the other end, between Gus and Lorelei.

"So, Jack," I said, "has your son been to visit you yet?"

"No. Not for a few more weeks. During his spring break."

"Are you getting excited?"

He studied me closely, looking, I suppose, for my ulterior motive of my subject choice. I knew about his son, but hadn't really pressed him on details when we'd been together. "Yes," he answered.

"You have a son?" Ben asked, then looked at me as if I'd kept that fact from him on purpose.

"Yeah, I do. His name is Casey, he's six."

"And you're apart from him?" Ben asked, his voice soft.

Jack nodded. "He lives in Portland with my ex-wife and her new husband. I was there last month for a weekend. But this will be the first time I have him here. It's been a hard year without him since I moved here."

Ben nodded his approval. "A son is a blessing. You must treasure him." I felt Lorelei nudge my calf under the table. Yeah, I got it.

"I do," Jack said so softly I wasn't sure I heard him.

Ben turned his attention to Jimmy. "Let that be a lesson to you, too, Jimmy."

Jimmy took his face away from his plate long enough to glare at Ben.

"Jimmy has a son that he hasn't seen in what? Forty years?"

"Something like that," Jimmy answered with a shrug. But I'd bet this house—if I was still betting, which I wasn't—that Jimmy knew to the day how long it'd been since he'd seen his own son.

"It's never too late," Ben cajoled.

The look Jimmy shot Ben made us all crack up. Watching Ben and Jack side-by-side, I noticed how similar their smiles and laughs were. How could I not have noticed that before?

Or was I now looking for anything to substantiate my theory? Making square pegs fit in round holes?

Apparently not, because Lor again kicked me under the table. I shot her a sideways glance, but she was looking at Ben and Jack.

"And you, Jack, are you close with your own father?" Ben asked.

I moved my legs to the side to protect them.

"No, not really. He and my mom split when I was seven. I didn't see him too much after that. Birthday cards. A few days at the holidays. Not every day." His voice grew softer at the end, probably realizing how similar his situation was to his son's.

Ben did what I wanted to do and put his hand on Jack's arm. "We learn from the past. We have to."

Jack nodded. Ben took his hand away. People resumed eating. I moved my legs back to their normal spot.

"Besides," Jack added after a minute. "He's not my real father, anyway. I'm not sure who is. I was adopted."

Ouch. There was definitely going to be a bruise on my shin.

"THIS ONE'S JACK'S," I said, bringing the water glass I'd cleared from Jack's place to Lorelei in the kitchen. She had a Ziploc baggie open and waiting, and I dropped the glass—which I held on to by the base—into it.

We heard footsteps coming down the hallway tile, and Lorelei put the baggie in a drawer. We turned as Gus entered carrying more dishes.

"You didn't have to do that," Lor said, rushing to him to take the dishes out of his hands.

"No problem. A beauty like you shouldn't have to do the grunt work, especially after slaving so hard on the excellent meal."

Lorelei smiled brightly and brought the dishes to the sink. She started running the water. Gus leaned against one of the counters watching her. Watching her amazing ass, actually. Feeling like a third wheel, I started to leave, but Gus turned to me and said, "That was nice of you, inviting Jack over. It couldn't have been easy for you. But it was good for Ben."

"It wasn't me, it was Lorelei," I admitted.

"Still," he said, shrugging.

"It *was* good for Ben," Lorelei said, looking over her shoulder at us. "He hasn't eaten that much in a long time."

"I've been meaning to talk to you about that," Gus said with definite hesitance in his voice.

"Ben's eating habits?"

"Ben's other habits."

"I'm not following." I looked to Lor, but she shook her head. She'd turned around from the sink and now dried her hands with a towel.

"Lately Ben's needed some help with showering," Gus said.

"What?" Lor and I both said. "How do you know?" I asked.

"Why didn't he tell us?" Lor chimed in.

Gus raised his hands in a helpless gesture. "He was embarrassed."

"Embarrassed? With us?"

"We'd do anything for him."

"Of course you would," Gus said, trying to calm us both down. I'd lifted away from the counter, and Lor had a death grip on her towel. "But there are certain things a man does not want a young woman doing for him, even if he does think of her as a daughter. Especially if he thinks of her as a daughter."

"Well…well…" I looked at Lor for help.

"We'll hire him a nurse. A male nurse," she said.

"Right. Yes."

Gus nodded. "It might get to that point. It hasn't yet. So far I've been able to help out with the things he's needed."

An idea struck me. "Oh, Gus, have you been staying around here longer than you would have liked just to help with Ben?"

Gus smiled indulgently at me, then turned to Lorelei and gave a slow grin, one I had to admit was still sexy even at his age. He turned and started to leave the kitchen. "Yeah, that's exactly

why I've been staying, Anna, to help Ben," he ended with a low
and throaty chuckle.

WHILE THE BOYS SET UP the table for cards, Lorelei
shooed me into the office. She had the bagged drinking glass
as well as another, smaller, seemingly empty baggie. "This is a
strand of hair that I got from Jack's jacket when I hung it up."

"Did he see you?"

She looked insulted. "Of course not."

She opened a drawer on her desk and pulled out an NPR
tote bag. From inside she pulled out the bag of Saul's bone
slivers. She'd written Saul's name on the outside of the bag, just
as she was now writing Jack's on the glass and hair baggies.

"What about Ben?" I asked.

She pulled out two more baggies. One contained a
toothbrush. The other several strands of hair. "There are probably
used tissues in his bathroom trash. Do you think we'll need it?"

"No, this ought to do it. They'll let me know at the lab if
not, right?"

"Probably. Do you want me to take it all there?"

I sighed. Yes, I did. Badly. "No, I'll do it. This is my hunch."

"Oh my God, I almost peed my pants when Jack said he
was adopted," she said, which started my shin aching.

She started putting all the things into the tote bag. I
wondered how many samples were brought to a DNA lab in an
NPR tote bag. Probably not many.

"Jo?" she said absently as she set about her task.

"Hmm?"

"What do you think of Gus?"

"I love Gus."

"But?" she asked as she put the now complete tote bag on
my chair and pushed it in under the desk so it would be out of

sight.

"He's charming as hell, we both know that. But if you're looking for a sugar daddy, keep looking, Lor. Gus' wives wiped him out. And what he didn't lose in his divorces, he's spent on clothes."

"I'm not looking for a sugar daddy, Jo. *You're* my sugar daddy."

I laughed. "You work damn hard for your keep, Lor."

"Most kept women do," she said as we left the office.

THE BOYS HAD THE DINING ROOM table set for cards, poker chips out, Ben shuffling a deck of cards. Just as I was about to sit down, my phone, which I'd set on the entryway table, rang. I stepped through the open archway into the foyer and grabbed it.

I was facing everyone who would call me.

Except for Raymond Joseph and he didn't have this number. He didn't have *any* number. Not anymore.

I didn't recognize the number, but it was Vegas' area code. "Hello?"

"Anna, it's Vince."

I instinctively turned my back to the group at the table. "Hi."

My mind started whirring of thoughts of why Vince would call right now. I knew I'd have to let him know that Raymond was out of business, but I was hoping to put that off for a few days.

"Are you at home?" Vince asked.

"Yes."

"How would you feel about going for a ride?"

I hesitated. "A ride?" Most people would be scared shitless at the prospect of taking a ride with Vince Santini. Most people probably wouldn't come back.

"Yes. Maybe out to Red Rock or somewhere? It seems like we're always meeting in casinos, and I thought maybe we could do something different."

"Oh. Oh." My brain wasn't quite getting it. "You mean as a date?" I must have said it a little too loudly, because the chatter behind me stopped. I turned around to see all four men staring at me. Just then Lorelei entered the room and put a carafe of coffee on the sideboard. When she saw the poker chips, she said, "Oh, poker. I think I'll sit this one out, fellas."

The boys tried to cajole her into staying as Vince was saying in my ear, "Yes. As a date. Unless you'd like to do something else? I know it's short notice, you probably have plans."

Lorelei said she had stuff to do anyway and left the dining room as I told Vince, "Actually I was just about to sit down with the boys for a poker game."

Jimmy must have heard me because he said, "Whoever that is, tell him we need a sixth."

Ben looked at Jimmy like he was crazy then looked at Jack for his reaction, which, I hate to say it, is what I did, too.

"Oh. Well. Another time then," Vince said as I met Jack's eyes. He always told me I had a tell, much to my disbelief. I imagined if that were true, the trigger was going off in a big way right now.

He raised that damn one eyebrow at me, which prompted me to say into the phone, my eyes on Jack, "Would you like to join us?"

There was a pause on the phone, and I wasn't really sure what answer I was hoping to hear. "Okay," Vince answered. "I can be there in about fifteen minutes."

"Great. I'll let the guard know. See you then," I said and hung up.

Jack counted out another stack of chips, placed them at an empty chair, presumably for Vince. I called the gatehouse to give the okay for Vince to enter. The guard asked if I'd like to permanently add Vince's name to my approved list of visitors and I paused for a second before saying yes. I wasn't sure if Jack could hear the guard's voice, but by the way his shoulders tightened at my answer, I'm guessing he could.

Jack, as a cop, had never needed to get on my approved list. Not officially, anyway.

As I took my chair, Jack grabbed the deck of cards and started shuffling. He placed the shuffled deck down in front of me to cut. I rapped them with my knuckles, signaling my okay, and he took the cards back, placing them in front of him to wait for our sixth player.

I reached for my horseshoe pendant and tapped it three times for luck. I had a feeling I'd need it to survive this night.

"Game on," he said.

THREE HOURS LATER, he was singing a different tune when Vince had most of his chips. Jack's eyes kept straying to the bottle of bourbon on the liquor cabinet.

Can't say as I blame him. The rush of playing cards in such a weird atmosphere had me desperately wanting to place a bet. Too late now, all of today's games would have already been played.

Thank goodness.

"Are you sure you don't want a drink?" I asked Jack. He'd declined earlier, choosing to stick with coffee. As had Ben. Jimmy, Vince and I were having beers and Gus his usual Manhattan.

It seemed odd to watch Vince being relaxed, drinking a beer, his usual suit replaced with a dress shirt and slacks. He was still the best-dressed person at the table, but still several levels down for Vince.

Of course, Vince's casual—by his standards—attire wasn't even close to the oddest thing about the evening.

"No, thanks," Jack said to my offer of a drink, instead rising to refill his coffee mug from the carafe that Lorelei had refilled several times, along with bringing out sopapillas at one point to cap off our Mexican feast.

She'd greeted Vince, gave me a questioning glance and wished us all luck.

Apparently, Vince hadn't needed it.

Hand after hand Vince had raised, and Jack, with seemingly nothing, had called only to have his ass handed to him.

I knew Jack was a better player than that. Was he setting Vince up? If so, he'd better change his strategy soon because he only had enough chips for a couple more hands.

Or, was he so uncomfortable with the fact that Vince and I were dating—I think it was safe to say that we kind of were— that he just wanted to lose his chips quickly and get the hell out of here?

But no, he'd never gone all in head to head against Vince, which he could have easily done and been out the door hours ago.

"So Vince," Jack said, his back to the table, getting his coffee, "any information about Paulie come your way?"

Vince didn't look up from the chips he was dragging from the center of the table to his pile then methodically stacking them. "No. You?"

"Nothing I'm at liberty to talk about."

Jimmy snorted at that. He'd never been much of a fan of the police, though he seemed to have a grudging respect for Jack. Vince didn't say a word.

"Can you tell us anything? Do you have any leads?" Ben asked what Vince probably wanted to but wouldn't.

"We're looking into a few things. But no, no strong leads."

Jimmy snorted again. Because he didn't believe Jack or because he had so little faith in the solving of Paulie's murder, I wasn't sure. I didn't ask for clarification.

Jack sat back down. "Shuffle up and deal."

THERE WERE SIX OF US at the table, but it might as well have been just Jack and Vince the way they played for the next two hours. They stayed out of pots that the boys or I played heavily in, but never missed a chance to play against each other.

Re-raising, going over the top, any kind of aggressive play, and they dealt it to the other. It got so as soon as one of them made a bet the rest of us would fold our cards, knowing that we'd only be in the way of their private match.

At one point, Jimmy said what I'd been thinking, although a bit more bluntly. "Why don't the two of youse just whip 'em out, we'll measure 'em, see who wins, and then we can *all* play some cards."

"Shut up, Jimmy," Ben said, although the rest of us, save for Vince and Jack, were chuckling.

"Unless Anna already knows who the winner is?"

"Shut up, Jimmy," we all said. No one was chuckling now.

The next hand, they went at it again. Raise. Re-raise. Call. Raise again. It got to the point that although they weren't all in, whoever lost would only be in for a hand or two more. The pot was huge, and when the river card was played, even I couldn't tell who was going to win. Usually, with betting like this, I'd have a good idea what cards players were holding, but these two weren't playing like smart, professional players.

Jimmy was right, they were leading with their balls, not their heads.

There was no obvious help from the community cards, nothing high to make a strong pair, nothing connecting for a straight, mixes of suits so there wasn't a possible flush in one of their hands. They probably both had pairs in their hands, or one of them was bluffing.

"I think you're bluffing," Vince said, mirroring my thoughts. Although, I guess if I had to choose, I would have picked Vince for the bluffer. And maybe he was.

"You might be right," Jack answered, "but you'll have to pay to find out."

Vince looked carefully at Jack's small remaining stack, and bet an amount just slightly below that total. He didn't want to put Jack all in. He didn't want to kill Jack in one blow. He wanted to maim him, let him bleed for a little while.

Jack counted out the bet, still keeping it in his chip area. It wasn't a call, or a bet, until the chips left the player's chip area. His own personal space, if you will.

He watched Vince for a long while, then pushed the chips into the pot. "Call."

When Vince flipped over a pair of queens, all eyes turned to Jack.

A small smile tugged at the corner of his mouth, and I waited to see him turn over kings or aces, but he only shrugged, then mucked his cards, pushing them, face down, into the discarded cards.

"You got me," he said to Vince.

I thought Jimmy or Gus might leap across the table to turn over Jack's cards. I admit, I wanted to, but that simply wasn't done at the poker table.

When a player mucks his cards, he does it because he doesn't want the other player to know what he had. So that we wouldn't know if he'd been bluffing, or if he'd had a good hand but gotten beaten by a better one.

Vince didn't look at the cards, instead keeping his eyes on Jack. "I guess I did."

As Vince had planned, Jack bled chips for a couple more hands before it was ultimately Ben that put him, almost apologetically, out of the game for good.

After Jack had said his good-byes to the boys, including a

hug for Ben and a curt nod to Vince, I walked him to the foyer where I got his leather jacket out of the guest closet.

"Step outside for a sec?" he said.

I nodded, and grabbed a shawl off a hanger. It was the same shawl I'd worn to Paulie's funeral. I wrapped it around me, called, "I'll be right back. Play a hand without me," into the dining room, and walked outside with Jack.

"Do you really not have any leads?"

"Why, so you can rush in to tell Vince anything I might say?" There was an edge to his voice. And just a tinge of petulance, I happily noticed. Jack didn't do petulance.

I shrugged. "He wants to know who killed his friend. You can't blame him for that."

We got to his car, but instead of crossing to the driver's side, he leaned up against the passenger door. "What are you doing, Johanna?"

I could have given half a dozen smart-ass comments, or even pretended I didn't know that he was talking about me and Vince. But this was Jack, and beyond his dumping me—hell, even then—we'd been pretty straight with each other.

"I'm not really sure."

"Do you know how hard this is for me?"

"*You* dumped *me*."

"Not because I didn't want to be together."

I had no answer for that.

He looked at me for a bit too long. Then he rubbed his hands across his face, almost as an attempt to wipe the whole conversation away, and pushed off from the car door. He made his way around to the driver's side, opened the door and looked at me from across the top of the car.

"Be careful," he said, then got in the car and drove away.

Twelve
❖❖

THE GAME WOUND DOWN shortly after Jack left. Vince and Jimmy were the only two players on the plus side.

I asked Vince if he wanted to hang out until I got Ben settled. Ben balked, but not as much as usual, and I realized he was up much later than he'd been lately. And even though he looked tired, I thought that wasn't such a bad thing.

"Sure. I need to call Carla anyway, see how the game's going."

"Carla's running your game?" He nodded. "Alone?" He nodded again.

Not that Carla wasn't capable. I just would have thought that she'd want to have some muscle like Paulie around in case... well, I wasn't really sure in case of what. It wasn't like thugs off the street were invited to Vince's games. There really was no need for enforcement.

Maybe there never had been.

I walked with Ben back to his room, tried to help him, but he shooed me away. Gus was probably right, and Ben would never allow me—or Lorelei—to help him with certain things. The thought broke my heart that I wouldn't be able to be everything Ben needed.

I started to leave his room when he said, "What are you doing, Hannah darling?"

"You sound just like Jack," I said before the possible meaning of that hit me.

"Maybe Jack is right."

"Jack left. Vince stayed."

He looked at me a little too long—much like his possible son—and muttered some Yiddish that I neither fully heard nor would have understood as he turned away.

As I passed the kitchen I heard Gus' low chuckle, and I put my head down and kept walking back to the dining room. Vince was holding his phone as I came back. I looked into the living room. "Do you want to sit down?"

He nodded, but hesitated in the archway to the room. "Actually, I need to look at some scores." He motioned with his phone.

"Let's go to the book room. You can get highlights and everything there," I said, my palms itching at the thought of watching scores and knowing I didn't have money on any of the games. I led the way to the book room.

"Wow," he said appreciatively as we entered.

"Nice, huh?"

"Yes. Very."

"It was Lorelei's creation."

"Why do you even leave the house?"

I laughed. "I know. There's really no need. Some of the best poker players are in my dining room every night. I don't even need to go out to get some good playing time in."

"And yet you do. Go out." And he knew why I went out. To place bets.

"Yes," I said quietly.

"But not so much lately?"

"No." I took a seat in one of the huge leather chairs, the kind that would seat two cozily. Vince looked at the spot next to me, but instead sat in his own large chair. I turned three of the televisions on, got ESPN, ESPN2 and ESPN News up, then curled my legs up under me, leaning against the arm on the chair next to Vince.

"Do you need paper or anything?" I asked.

"No, that's okay. Thanks."

He's probably used to not putting things down on paper. Good practice for his line of work. Carla kept the ledgers for him on the poker games money.

The night's scores scrolled across the bottom of each channel.

I turned to take in his handsome profile. His eyes scanned the tickers, jumping from screen to screen, but his body, or head for that matter, never moved.

After several minutes of him watching scores and me trying not to, he seemed satisfied and turned his body toward me, his elbow brushing mine on the arms of our two, touching, chairs.

"And how's that working out for you? Trying to stay out of casinos?"

I shrugged. "I haven't placed a bet in six days."

"And that's good?" His voice was soft, gentle.

I took a deep breath, let it out, and answered honestly. "I have no idea."

He gave a small nod. He shifted his arm so its length ran the length of mine. He held his hand open, palm up, and it felt natural to place mine lightly on top of his. He closed his loosely over mine.

He leaned closer to me, but I stopped him with, "Vince, we need to talk about Raymond Joseph."

"You want to talk business now?"

"Just this little bit. Just to get it off my chest."

He slid his hand away from mine and sat up a little straighter, the smooth, always in control Vince firmly back in place. "Okay, shoot."

"Well, I'm kind of hoping there'll be no shooting," I said with a small chuckle. Gentleman that he was, he tried to smile, but it was as lame as my joke.

"I've cut off communication with Raymond Joseph."

"*You've* cut off communication with *him*?"

I nodded. "The last time we met, he said it was the last time."

"Doesn't he say that every time?"

"Yes, but this time I made sure he meant it."

"How?"

"I slid my phone into his pocket. When he finds it, he'll realize he has no way to get in touch with me."

Vince's brown eyes stared straight ahead, his shrewd mind working. "So, he can't contact you?" When I nodded, he continued, "But you could still contact him?"

"Yes. But I won't."

"But someone else could."

Vince, Paulie and I were, to my knowledge, the only three people who knew about Raymond's involvement in point shaving. Paulie wasn't going to be calling Raymond.

"Vince, lose his number."

"I don't have his number."

I tried to pull off Jack's one brow raise, but it didn't work. Still, Vince got it. "He's a good kid, Vince."

He looked at me for a few seconds, then turned back toward the televisions. Probably mentally tallying up the money he could make off of Raymond versus the lost revenue from me if I took my business elsewhere. He'd be much better off staying with Raymond.

Especially now that I didn't need to play in his games so that I could get a quick stake to place a bet.

Six days and my life had already changed for the better.

He let out a long sigh. "All right," he said.

"All right?"

"I'll leave him alone."

"Really?"

He lifted his hands in resignation. "All wells dry up

eventually, Anna. It's a lesson I learned early."

"I imagine you learned a lot of lessons, Vince."

A small, faint smile crossed his face. "Not as many as I should have," he said with a hint of remorse in his voice.

It seemed like the perfect opening to ask about his upbringing, his past, what had brought him to where he was now. I think he sensed that's where I was going and as if to cut me off, he leaned over the arms of the chairs and kissed me lightly.

His mouth was soft and warm and was gone before I could register his taste.

And it was Vince Santini. Gambler. Loan shark. Man to be feared. Man I *had* feared.

"Does this feel weird to you?" I whispered, his mouth still close to mine.

"No. It feels very, very good."

He kissed me again. Coffee laced with cognac. That was his taste, even though there wasn't cognac anywhere on the premises and I didn't think Vince had had any of Lor's coffee.

He smelled of something expensive. And elusive.

His kiss didn't hold the desperation that Jack's did, but there was hunger, like Jack's.

And I realized I was hungry, too. Hungry to be kissed by a man who wanted nothing more than to be kissed back. Who knew the worst of me and still wanted to be with me.

A man who knew JoJo. And still wanted to kiss me.

I inched up the side of the chair, reaching for him, trying to ease over the barrier. He grabbed my upper arms, pulling me toward him. I tried to gain leverage, but my knees slid on the soft leather of the chair. Our lips parted and I started scrambling to get back in position.

Because when I was kissing Vince, I barely thought about all the games that were going to be played tomorrow and what the point spreads would likely be. Or the fact that Ben would probably be needing some male help soon.

Or the fact that Jack had been here tonight. And left.

Okay, I thought about all those things, but only fleetingly. Mostly I thought about how soft Vince's mouth was for such a hard man. And how firm and yet gentle his hold on my arms was.

"Anna," he whispered as I got close again. There was more urgency in our kiss this time. And a lovely use of tongues. I was moving, rising up to cross over the arms when I felt the vibration of Vince's cell phone go off.

He pulled away, but he kept one hand on me as he took his phone out of his pocket. "I'm sorry. I have to take this," he said when he looked at the caller ID. He sat up, away from me.

"Yes," he said into the phone, all softness now gone from his voice.

"Do you want me to leave?" I whispered.

He looked at me, indecision in his eyes, then gave a short, curt nod. "I'm sorry," he said.

"It's fine, it's fine," I said quietly as I rose from my chair. "I'll be in the dining room." He nodded that he heard me, but he waited until I left the room to speak to whoever was on the phone.

I'd intended to clean up the remains of our poker game, but Lorelei had beaten me to it. The poker chips were neatly stacked in their case and moved to the sideboard as were the cards. The used glasses and coffee mugs had been removed to the kitchen. The carafe of heated coffee remained as did clean mugs, thoughtfully left out for Vince and me.

I started to reach for a cup then stopped. If Vince was staying, I wouldn't be needing it, and if he was leaving, I'd want to get some sleep. I turned off the hot plate that held the carafe, left the cups where they lay.

Vince appeared soon after. "I'm sorry, I have to leave." He rounded the table, took his suit jacket from the back of the chair where he'd been sitting earlier and put it on.

I almost said something about my being used to the crazy hours with the last person I dated being a cop, but I wisely kept my mouth shut. "That's okay," I said.

He stepped close to me, put his arms around my waist. "No," he said softly. "It's definitely not okay, but it can't be helped."

He leaned in, I thought to kiss me, but instead he rested his forehead on mine. He just stood there for a minute, and I relaxed my body into his. After a moment, he let out a ragged sigh and pulled away. "Are you free Thursday night?" he asked.

"Yes."

"I'd like to cook for you."

"You cook?"

He nodded. "Would you come to my place?"

I guess I'd never thought about Vince's home. I kind of just imagined him showing up in casinos or at card games. "Where do you live?"

"The Palms Place."

"Nice."

He nodded. "So, Thursday?"

"That would be great."

He took a piece of paper and a pen from his inside jacket pocket. "Here's my unit number. And here's my home phone number. I still keep a landline if you can believe that."

I had a feeling I might be the only person with this information. Well, maybe Carla. Or Vince's mother. Did Vince even have a mother? All things I could find out on Thursday.

"It'll be nice to finally be alone. No casinos, no..." he waved his hand in the general vicinity of the rest of the house, "roommates. Just us."

Hmmm, so maybe we wouldn't spend Thursday talking about his mother. "I'm looking forward to it," I told him honestly.

"Me, too," he said and left.

I went back to the book room and turned off all the televisions, careful not to look at the scores or to listen to news about upcoming games.

I went to bed at the end of day six without placing any bets.

Huh, this wasn't so hard.

BY EARLY THURSDAY MORNING, I was singing a different tune. I'd been playing poker for the last nine hours trying to get ready for the grueling hours of the upcoming Marathon tournament. I'd purposely chosen The Orleans as my place to play because I could enter through the parking deck and not have to walk past the Sports Book room to get to the poker room.

In most casinos, the poker rooms were situated near the Sports Books, but they were on opposite wings at The Orleans. And I was trying to stave off the temptation as much as possible.

The longer I played poker, the less time I had to tempt myself with placing sports bets. And that had to be a good thing. But, God, I missed the Hummer. Sure, I felt a twinge every time the dealer turned over the flop, but it wasn't the same.

I looked at my watch. I'd need to leave shortly to take the boys to breakfast. Then I was going to crash all day until it was time to get ready to go to Vince's.

I gathered up my chips, tipped my dealer handsomely when I realized I'd won big. My mind had been so occupied with thoughts of all the games I was going to not place bets on that I'd been playing poker by muscle memory. And apparently it had gone well, as I was up about four thousand dollars. Which meant I'd been grinding, because you didn't get the big fish that thought nothing of dropping thousands in one night at The Orleans, so I'd had to work for it.

I got to the doorway of the parking deck and stopped. The

four thousand burned in my pocket. I had been so good for six days. Seven if you counted this morning. Almost a week. I surely deserved some kind of reward for going so long. Six days. Seven. Seven. Six.

The Seventy-Sixers. Of course. It's like the universe was screaming at me.

I made a U-turn and headed toward the Sports Book, the tingling of the Hummer starting to thrum through me. The voice of certainty that Philadelphia would be on the board and would win tonight drowning out any peeps of promises that might have tried to be heard.

As I rounded the corner, seeing the brilliant lights of the betting boards ahead of me, my phone rang. I ducked into the lobby of the oyster bar and pulled my phone out of my pocket. Like whoever was on the line was going to see me heading to the book room. And what if they could? I hadn't told anybody but Vince that I wasn't betting.

"Hi, Jimmy," I said after looking at the caller ID.

"You near a TV?"

"I'm at The Orleans. I just finished playing, I'm heading home."

"Head to the bar there by the poker room," he said.

"I'm closer to the book," I said and left the oyster bar and headed to the far end of the book room where the televisions lined the wall.

Jimmy could have been calling me to watch a news story, I suppose, and that of course wouldn't be on the TVs in the Sports Book. But I knew that wasn't the case. This call had something to do with the sports world. It was too early for game results.

A feeling of dread seeped through my body, chasing all remnants of the Hummer away.

"What's up?" I asked cautiously.

"Your boy," was all he said.

The dread stopped seeping and started rushing. I'd never

told Jimmy about JoJo and Raymond, but a few weeks back I did give him a tip to bet against CIU. Couple that with the fact that I'd been absent quite a bit over the past weeks, and Jimmy was no dummy.

"My boy?" I played dumb.

Jimmy snorted. "Just get to a screen."

"I'm there," I said as I reached the line of televisions. Most of the leather chairs were empty at this time of morning, but I remained standing.

On three of the screens I saw Raymond Joseph's face smiling out at me. It was the head shot of him in his Fighting Hogs jersey, his trademark braids neat and tidy. His grin huge.

There was no volume on any of the screens, but I didn't need it. I really didn't even need to see the scrawl at the bottom of the picture to confirm my fears, but I read it anyway.

Central Iowa University star accused in point-shaving scandal.

Thirteen

❖❖

"WHAT DO YOU KNOW?" I asked Jimmy as soon as I could get him alone after breakfast.

I'd driven home from The Orleans in a daze, flipping through all my radio stations trying to find out anything I could, but they'd already moved on to different stories. Ben and Gus were waiting for me when I got home, so I didn't get a chance to get on the Internet.

Jimmy wisely hadn't mentioned it during breakfast, but now I had him alone while Gus and Ben went into the book room at The Barbary so Gus could place bets on tonight's games.

He shrugged. "Not much yet. The kid went looking for someone to stake him if he delivered under the point spread."

"What?" I gasped.

Jimmy nodded. "I don't think this has anything to do with…anyone in Vegas."

"He went looking for a backer?"

"That's what I'm hearing," Jimmy said.

I shook my head in disbelief. "He's so much smarter than that."

Jimmy shrugged. "Maybe. Maybe not. Or maybe he was desperate."

Because he had no way of contacting JoJo. "Yeah, maybe."

"Whatever. I guess he went to the wrong guy."

"I guess so. You still know guys in Dubuque?"

He looked at me as if I'd insulted him. I probably had. "Right. Of course you do. And Chicago, too?" I asked, thinking of Raymond's mother and sister. He snorted his response. "Can you have them keep an ear out for me? Anything at all."

"Sure, Anna." He patted my shoulder with his huge paw, a very un-Jimmy like sentiment, which only drove home to me how fucked up this whole situation was.

The drive home was quiet. After we parked, I walked slowly with Ben into the house, Gus ahead of us and already inside. "Is everything all right, Hannah, darling?"

"Sure. Everything's fine. Just tired from playing."

He ran his shrewd brown eyes over me, even opened his mouth to say more, but he thought better of it and just kept pushing his walker across the paved walkway.

I intended to head straight to the office and my laptop to see if there was anything new about Raymond, but Lorelei met me at the door, the NPR tote bag in her hand. She waited until Ben had passed into the living room, then handed me the tote bag and some papers. "Here's the MapQuest directions to the place. It's in Henderson." She pointed to the papers I now held. "Also their form on the information we're looking for." I nodded. She then handed me an envelope. "A check. You need to sign it, but don't look too closely, their prices are astronomical for a rush job." I nodded again, tucked the envelope into my cargo pants pocket and turned around to exit.

"Thanks, Lor," I called over my shoulder as I passed through the doorway. I'd just put my foot outdoors when I stopped. "Wait," I called to her, and she came out to me. I pulled out my wad of cash and handed it to her. "Keep it handy. I'll probably play tomorrow," I said as I handed it to her.

Her brow furrowed at my unusual request. I always gave her my extra cash, but kept my playing bankroll myself. "If you're going to play tomorrow, don't you just want to keep it?"

I thought of my close call at The Orleans. "No."

I HAD NO TROUBLE FINDING the place; Lor's directions—as always—were dead on. There must be good money in DNA testing because the lobby of this place was lovely with lots of marble and huge, white leather chairs in the waiting area. The place was bright and spotless, but not sterile, instead conveying a very warm feeling. I suppose when dealing with skin and saliva samples all day, you'd like to have nice surroundings.

"Oh, yes, we spoke on the phone," the woman at the front desk said when I handed her my paperwork. She was maybe thirty, very tastefully dressed in a dark suit. Polished. A female Vince in some ways. "I'm Jennifer."

"Uh, no, you spoke with my...someone else," I said, deciding not to even try to explain what all Lorelei was to me to a stranger who probably couldn't care less.

"Okay, well, it looks like everything is in order," she said as she stamped my paperwork and had me sign a couple of forms. "I'm going to label your samples in your presence and have you sign each label."

I nodded and started to pull out the bags from the tote. I put the bags with Jack's glass and hair sample in one pile, Ben's toothbrush and the bag with his gray hair in another pile. And lastly, the baggie with Saul's ash-covered bone slivers.

"Are those from cremains?" the receptionist asked with absolutely no inflection in her voice. Business as usual for her, while I stood dumbfounded that I had DNA samples from three men I—at various times—thought so highly of.

"Yes."

She brought out a different label for that bag, an orange one. "Just a flag for our techs," she explained.

"Oh."

She gave me a sympathetic look. "First time?"

"Yes."

She nodded. "From what the woman I spoke with said, and your forms, we have samples from three different people, is that correct?"

"Yes," I said, indicating the three piles I'd separated my booty into.

"We'll call them Subject A, B and C," she said placing a white label with an A on it onto each of the bags in Jack's pile. She turned the label around and pointed to two blank lines. "If you'd like to put in something more personal for you, like the subject's name, or a date, or something like that, it would go in the first line. Then you sign the second line."

I wrote "Jack" on the first line and signed the second, then did the same for Ben and Saul's bags.

"And we're looking for possible familial connections between two of the subjects?" Jennifer asked.

"Yes, between Jack—Subject A—and either Subject B or C."

"But not both?" Jennifer clarified.

"No, not both."

She nodded. "That's all I need. Once we receive payment…"

"Oh, sorry," I said, reaching into my pants pocket for the envelope Lorelei had sent with me. I took out the check, borrowed Jennifer's pen to sign it, and handed it to her.

Jennifer gave me an understanding smile. "Thank you. I'll just get you a receipt."

"You can just put it back into the envelope," I said, taking Lor's advice not to know what this probable wild goose chase was costing me.

Jennifer handed me back the closed envelope. "We'll call as soon as the results are in. We can also e-mail and FedEx results, but I understand you live in the area?"

"Yes. Summerlin."

"Then you'd probably like to pick up the results in person when they're ready?"

"Yes," I answered.

Jennifer nodded. "Very good. We'll call you when they're ready. Is there anyone else at your residence that you'd like us to leave the message with in case you're not available?"

These people knew discretion, part of their stock and trade. "Yes. You can tell Lorelei that the results are ready."

"Okay."

"But please don't tell her what the results are. I'd like to know first." Selfish of me, seeing as Lor had helped get the samples and did all the leg work with this firm, but I needed to know what I was dealing with before I could share with Lorelei. At the very least, we'd find out the results together.

"Your name is the one on the order and the check, so that's how we'll handle it."

I thanked Jennifer, took my receipt and my empty tote bag and headed for home.

There wasn't anything new online when I checked in my office. I went into the book room and turned on all the sports news channels, my eyes constantly scanning the bottom tickers for anything new, but there wasn't anything that I hadn't seen earlier. I called Jimmy, but he said his sources didn't know anything more yet, either.

I tried to get a nap, not wanting to look like a zombie when I went to Vince's for dinner, but sleep evaded me. Every time I closed my eyes, I saw first Raymond's huge smile as he'd take the floor for his team, and then the haunted look in his eyes as he'd tell me yet again that he was done with JoJo.

I should probably be worried about Feds knocking on my door, that Raymond would lead them back to me, but I wasn't. Somehow I knew Raymond was going down alone.

I wasn't sure how yet, but I knew it was time to make my amends to Raymond Joseph.

Vince met me at the door of his high-rise condo wearing jeans and a button-down shirt. The jeans were designer—and creased!—and the buttoned shirt he wore untucked was made of some very expensive material, but still, Vince in anything besides a suit was a sight to remember.

And he did look good. The shirt was a dark plum color, which highlighted his olive skin. He wore the top two buttons undone, and his black chest hair peeked out just a bit at the top.

I hadn't really thought about what I envisioned Vince's condo would look like, but I was surprised by what I saw when he ushered me inside. I knew it would be tasteful, elegant and expensive, like Vince himself. But I hadn't expected it to be so warm and inviting, which it definitely was. Earth-toned walls, hardwood floors with a gorgeous area rug in the sunken living room. His furniture was comfortable looking and in dark, solid colors. Jewel-toned pillows accented the sofa.

He had some interesting art pieces on the walls, which I admired as he took my coat and brought me a glass of wine.

"I should probably know these artists, but I don't," I admitted, taking the glass of red from him.

He shrugged. "An investment. It might prove fruitful, it might not."

"But they're pretty to look at," I said, my ignorance showing.

"They're pretty to look at," he agreed. I turned to see him smiling down at me. "Now come with me while I get the sauce going." He took my free hand in his and led me to the kitchen.

He set me up at the granite bar that looked into the kitchen area and set about work. I offered to help, but he could probably sense the halfheartedness in my offer. "Do you cook?" he asked, the surprise in his voice.

I guess I should have been offended, but hey, he was right. "No, but I could cut the veggies or something."

He chuckled and shook his head. "Sit. Relax. More wine?"

It was good wine, and it was giving me the nicest glow. "Hmmm, I'd better not," I said, taking another small sip from my glass. "I pulled an all-nighter at the tables last night. I'd be asleep before dinner was served." And judging from the delicious smells coming from Vince's kitchen, this was not a meal I'd want to sleep through.

"We wouldn't want that."

"No," I agreed. I didn't want to fall asleep on what I believed would be a big night with Vince. But I also couldn't shake my guilt that I was going to have a lovely night when Raymond Joseph was probably going through hell.

A hell I had created.

Or JoJo. Hell, even I couldn't keep them straight anymore.

Instead of dwelling on something I couldn't do anything about—for now—I concentrated on Vince. I watched his tall, lean body as he moved comfortably in his kitchen. "Where did you learn to cook?" I asked.

"I learned out of necessity. But later, when I didn't have to, I found I missed it. So, I learned to do it well."

"How?"

"I took a class, bought some books."

The thought of loan shark Vince Santini taking a cooking class brought forth a laugh from me that made him turn from the stove. "Sorry, I just...I can't picture you in a cooking class."

"It's the best class offered in Vegas," he said almost defensively.

"I'm sure it was," I teased. He grinned and turned back to the stove, throwing some other spice into his sauce. "And you're always reading biographies of famous leaders or artists."

"So?"

"So, nothing. Just an observation, that's all."

He turned from the stove and leaned his hips against the counter facing me. "Ask me what you want, Anna. I'll tell you."

I took a gulp of wine then leaned forward, placing my arms on the bar. "Who are you, Vince Santini?"

His eyes never left mine as he reached beside himself and grasped his wine glass, raised it to his lips, and took a sip. He swirled the wine in his glass. "A kid who grew up on the streets. Who knew that he had the brains to make something of himself. But even when I did, I knew I'd always be seen as a hood, a punk, so..." He shrugged.

I waved to the kitchen. "Cooking lessons."

He nodded. "And books, and good clothes, and the best wines." He took another sip.

"And yet, you kept Paulie with you all the way through. And Carla, too. She grew up with you guys, right?"

He gave a small nod. "And?"

"Nothing. Carla has seemed to adjust to her new station. Or at least she tries, seems to *get* that there is a new station. But Paulie?" I shrugged, not wanting to be unkind. Especially to a dead man. "It's just he didn't quite fit the mold of the new Vince Santini."

"The new Vince is all on the outside. The old Vince is still there. The one who knows the value of a dollar. How to get it. And more importantly, keep it. And..."

"Yes?"

He put his glass down, stepped across to the bar and put his arms down on either side of mine, his hands grazing my elbows. "That Vince Santini, the old one, the new one, the *real* one, holds loyalty higher than anything."

"And Paulie was loyal to you," I finished his thoughts.

"Until the day he died," he said quietly.

I turned my hands to the outside, to slide them down his arms. I gave a gentle squeeze, which he returned with a sad smile. "You miss him," I stated the obvious.

"I miss him," he said, then turned back to the stove. He took a spoon from a drawer and dipped it into his sauce. He

took a taste before bringing the spoon over for me to try. It was a
tomato sauce, not quite marinara, and better than I'd ever tasted.
"Yum. Those classes paid off."

He smiled. "Let's eat."

He did let me help with the clean up, or at least clearing
the dining room table while he put away the food. "Leave it," he
waved when all the perishables were taken care of and the dishes
sat soaking in the sink.

He grabbed the second bottle of wine we'd opened during
dinner and both our glasses and led the way across the living area
to the glass doors leading to the balcony. There was a wrought-
iron café table and two chairs outside and in the center of the
table a candle, which Vince lit.

"It's too cool to stay out here for very long, but I thought
you might like some fresh air."

"Yes, to clear my head. Too much good food. Too much
good wine," I said.

He grabbed a fleece blanket from the back of one of the
chairs and wrapped it around my shoulders, keeping his hands
there and my back to his chest. "Not worried about falling asleep
anymore?" he said as he nuzzled into my neck.

"No, not falling asleep, but driving might be questionable."

He put his hand gently under my chin and turned my face
toward him. "Were you planning on driving home tonight?" His
voice was low, soft.

"No."

He nodded, released my chin. I turned back around. "The
view is amazing," I said, soaking it in. Vince's condo was on the
twenty-fifth floor. Vegas didn't have many high-rises, and most
of them were casino hotels, none of which I stayed in. I was
in them for Vince's games, but if I was there, it was because I
wanted to place a bet and had no stake, so the view was the last
thing on my mind.

"A lot of people wanted the east side, looking toward the

Strip, but I liked the northeast corner better. You can still see the best part of the Strip, but you also can see the mountains."

"These condos aren't cheap," I said.

I could feel his shrug behind me. "A good investment."

"Like the art. Yet, pretty to look at. You like to surround yourself with beautiful things," I stated, but it sounded more like a question. It *was* a question of sorts.

"Yes?"

"And I'm not fishing here..." I said, turning around to face him. His hands slid from my shoulders to my waist. He motioned with a small movement of his head for me to go on. "But I wonder why you're seeing me. Pursuing me."

"You don't think you're beautiful, Anna?" There was no tease in his voice.

I held his gaze, not flinching, not putting up any womanly facades. "I know I can be pretty if I put the effort in. Which I rarely do." He didn't nod, didn't even acknowledge my statement. "But this town is full of truly beautiful women. Women who would fit into the world of Vince Santini that you've created much more easily than me." He started to answer, but I rushed to finish my thought. "Women with a lot less baggage than I have."

"That's certainly true," he agreed.

"So, why me?" I asked.

He looked beyond me toward the Rio across the way, the lights from the casino flashing in his eyes. He took a deep breath, let it out. He moved his hands from my waist around to my back and pulled me closer to him.

He dipped his head and just before his lips met mine he whispered, "Maybe I think you're a good investment."

Fourteen

❖

I WRAPPED MY ARMS around Vince's neck, the blanket falling to the balcony floor. His hands slid up my back, one going to my nape, the other pushing against the spot between my shoulder blades, trying to draw me nearer.

Which was impossible. My body was squashed, delightfully so, against his.

And then Vince's phone went off.

We both murmured curses, mine a bit more colorful than his. "Let me see if I need to take it," he said, stepping away from me and pulling his phone from his pocket.

"Carla?" I asked as he looked at the caller ID.

He shook his head. "Carla has strict instructions not to bother me tonight. I don't know this number."

I liked the thought of what Carla's no interruptions implied. Vince's brow furrowed and he answered the call.

"Yes?" After a second of listening, his eyes flew to me, and for one panicked second I thought something had happened to Ben. But no, Lorelei would have called me on my phone.

Which was in my jacket pocket hanging in Vince's closet.

"Is it about Ben?" I whispered. Vince shook his head, and I started to relax.

Until I thought of Raymond Joseph.

We hadn't talked about it tonight—I hadn't wanted to think

about it—but surely Vince knew about Raymond being caught. Was he getting information from somebody?

Was there anyone out there who knew more info than one of Jimmy's "guys"?

"Now is not really convenient," he said in a no-nonsense voice, then listened. "I see. Yes. All right. I'll be there in twenty minutes." He disconneted, let out a long sigh and reached out, putting his hand on my arm. "That was Jack Schiller," he said, watching carefully for my reaction.

And damned if I didn't give him one. I'm a professional poker player, I make a living at not letting people know what I'm thinking. But, on total reflex, as if Jack were right here on the balcony with us, I took a step away from Vince.

His hand dropped away from my arm.

"And?" I asked. "What did he want?"

"He says there's been a break in Paulie's case. He wants me to come down to the station."

"Right now?" I asked, although I knew the answer.

Vince nodded. He looked out into the night then down into the parking lots below us at Palms Place and even across Arville Street to the Loose Caboose and its parking lot. "You think you're being watched?" I asked.

He shrugged. "The timing's a little suspect, that's all."

I didn't say anything to that—what could I? I started to turn from Vince and head into the condo, but he pulled me to him, swept me into a deep dip and kissed the life out of me. When he let me back up, he said, "Just in case, I thought we'd give him a show." His eyes twinkled with mischief, and I was immensely sorry that our night was ending.

"I have a feeling this is going to take a while, but you're welcome to stay until I get back."

I shook my head. "Thanks, but I think I'll head home."

"You're okay to drive?"

"Yes, I'm fine." I really hadn't had that much wine, and the cold air—as well as Jack's phone call—had killed whatever buzz I had.

"I'm going to change before I go," Vince said. "So I'll say good-bye here." He had his hand on the doorknob, but I put mine over his.

"Vince, you haven't mentioned it at all, and I didn't want to, but you do know about Raymond Joseph, right?"

He nodded, just a small movement of his head. He didn't say any more, just took my elbow and walked me into the hallway, softly closing the door behind us.

"From what I understand, it has nothing to do with your transactions. He went rogue when he couldn't get ahold of JoJo," he said quietly.

"That's how I understood it, too."

Again, I wondered if Vince's informants were any match for Jimmy's? Hell, maybe they were even the same guys.

"If you hear anymore, I'd appreciate it if you'd let me know."

"Do you think he'll rat you out?" Raymond didn't know about Vince. JoJo was his only contact. And I was the only one who could link JoJo to Vince. Of course I never would, and I believe Vince knew that.

"No," I said, instinctively knowing that Raymond wouldn't do that.

"Then what's the problem?"

"The problem is I destroyed this kid's life."

"He was never going to make it in the pros anyway, he's too small."

"I know, but he might have had a good year or two at the league minimum—or in Europe—that would have set up his mom and sister for awhile. And then he could have, I don't know, gone into coaching or something. That's all dead to him now."

"You didn't destroy his life, Anna. You're not going to come forward, so only he can tie himself to the games he's already shaved. And he's not going to do that. I watched those games, there's no way to prove he shaved points. He's a very smart kid."

"Yeah," I said. "That's why I chose him." Vince's clinical eye to the situation didn't make me feel any better, but I could tell Vince didn't want to continue that line of conversation.

He opened the door behind him, stepped back. "I'll call you soon?"

"Thank you for what was—mostly—a lovely evening."

He gave me a small smile. "Rain check on dessert?"

"Definitely." He placed a quick kiss on my lips, much less dramatic than the one on his balcony, and went back into his condo while I turned and walked down the hallway to the elevator.

THE NEXT MORNING AT BREAKFAST Jimmy again got me alone to update me on Raymond. "My sources say he's left school."

"They kicked him off the team?"

Jimmy shrugged. "Nobody knew for sure. He mighta left on his own, they mighta kicked him out. He ain't playing tomorrow, they know that for sure."

"Jesus," I murmured.

"I do know all they got is the guy that says this Joseph kid came to him. Still nothing about…"

"Yeah." I nodded, trying to think. "So what do your guys think is happening?"

"They think the Feds are trying to make a case. Probably looking at games he's played in. But it won't stick if they can't either turn Joseph or find a paper trail."

"They won't."

"Which? Turn him, or find the money?"

"Both. Neither."

"Well. That's good, then."

"Yeah," I said, but I certainly didn't feel any better. "Keep me posted," I said to Jimmy, but didn't really need to.

I'd told Jimmy they wouldn't find anything on Raymond—he was that good at what he'd done. But there had been that Penn State game. Where he not only had to shave points, he had to make sure the Hogs lost outright. He'd had to do something extra in that game, and he had. The kid he'd guarded had had the game of his life.

Would it be noticed?

After I dropped Ben and Gus off at home, I headed back to The Orleans to play poker. After eight hours at a cash game, I was down about three hundred and decided to call it a day. Well, night actually, I thought after looking at my watch. It was past dinnertime, but I'd bet there'd be some leftovers in the fridge. My back ached a little, but I figured eight hours would only be half a session in the upcoming Marathon.

I left the table and cashed out. I got to the end of the poker room and stopped. I would turn left to go to the parking deck, right would take me to the casino floor. And from there to the book.

Friday night. All of the Saturday college basketball games would be on the board. I wondered if the CIU game would even be on the board, or if they'd pull it due to the allegations against Raymond?

Maybe I should just check. I wouldn't bet on it or anything. Just look and see if it was on the board. And if it was, what was the spread. I turned right. Four steps later and I was already mentally calculating how much money I had left in my pocket from my poker bankroll, my hand even reaching for it.

Damn.

I took a ninety-degree turn to my right, trying to get myself under control. After three steps I stopped, my head down, breathing much harder than normal.

"Hi, welcome to Fuddruckers, what can I get you?"

I looked into the pimply face of a kid behind a food court counter. "What?" I asked as I took in my surroundings.

"What can I get you?" he asked again.

Yes. Food. That's what I'd come this way for. "I'll have a large chocolate shake," I said, knowing better than to order anything that would take more than a couple of minutes to prepare. In my current state, I didn't think I'd stick around for it.

I paid the kid and thankfully one of his coworkers had my shake made even before the kid could make change. I took the shake to a table, used a spoon to scoop out some of the whipped cream. Dangled the cherry over my mouth and let it drop. Took a long drag from my straw, giving myself brain freeze.

And slowly, so slowly, I gathered control. My hand eased away from the wad of cash in my pants pocket. My breathing returned to normal.

I might need to get a firmer handle on this, or I was going to end up splitting my pants. I stood up, tossed my empty cup away and headed for the parking deck.

Eight days without placing a bet.

I CRASHED RIGHT AFTER raiding the fridge. Raided. Destroyed. Totally cleaned out.

Yeah, I definitely had to get a better handle on this. Can't just trade betting for eating. What was that called? Sublimation? Something like that. At least if I was going to sublimate, it should be with something not so fattening.

Shopping? I hated shopping. And it could prove just as costly as betting.

Exercise? I knew compulsive runners. Even a couple of pro players I knew were health nuts, which is hard to do when you spend hours and hours sitting on your ass playing cards. My idea of exercise was the walk from the parking deck to the poker room.

Drinking? Thoughts of Jack and his demons rushed through me.

I'd take my chances with Lorelei's leftovers. I could always buy bigger pants.

I set my alarm so I'd be up in time to watch the college games that started at noon on the east coast—CIU being one of them.

When I woke, I'd gotten a—for me—full night of sleep, but was still a bit out of it. I threw on some flannel pajama bottoms and a ratty Wisconsin sweatshirt leftover from my college days, slipped my feet into some slippers and groggily made my way to the book room.

Ben was there, already dressed and seated in the second row of seats, his little tablet and pen on a side table next to his chair, along with a steaming cup of coffee and a plate with a fully-loaded, half-eaten bagel on it.

The Corporation used to do breakfast every morning, but during college basketball season, they tended to do breakfast on their own on Saturdays and Sundays. Lorelei usually did bagels—that she ordered especially for Ben from New York—on Saturdays and then a nice, larger brunch on Sundays. Most Sundays, the boys came over for brunch, so it was kind of like meeting for breakfast anyway.

But this morning, it was just Ben and me, Lorelei having already left her breakfast contribution—the bagels and a large pot of coffee—on top of the little concession stand.

"Lor around?" I asked as I helped myself to a mug of coffee. I'd come back for a bagel later, once the caffeine had kicked in.

"She went to a dance class."

"That's good." Lorelei liked to keep up with a few classes a week. I'm not sure when she fit them in, maybe when I took the boys to breakfast. In the early years with us, she'd pick up a subbing gig every now and then, but it had been a long time since her last one. I don't know if it was hope or just maintenance that kept her going to classes, but I was glad she did it.

Dancing for my sublimation? Nah, when I took a class with Lor once, years ago, I discovered I had no grace. And I'd hated every minute of it.

I sat sideways on the large chair in the front row, my legs in front of me, knees in the air, toes curled under the arm of the chair. The same one I'd sat on when Vince was in here with me. It seemed like a thousand years ago.

I hadn't heard from Vince since Thursday night. I didn't really want to think about what that meant. Had whatever Jack had learned about Paulie's murder led Vince to discover who the murderer was? Would Jack purposely on accident let something slip that would give Vince the answer and then try to trip Vince up? Was Vince even now driving out into the desert with a body in the trunk of his expensive car? With Jack following?

I really didn't believe that.

Mostly didn't believe it.

I took a deep swallow of the hot coffee, let it wash down my throat, let it burn.

"That's a shame," Ben said, pulling me out of my reverie.

"Hmmm?" I turned my head to see him behind me.

He pointed to the center, large screen. "That guard from Central Iowa. Such a shame."

I turned my head forward, so that I stared at the wall, not able to look—not yet—at the screen. Knowing what I'd see.

"What have they been saying?" I asked Ben, taking another drink of coffee, burrowing myself deeper into the plush leather. Trying to hide.

"Not much. They don't know much. Too much speculation. Not any facts. Putz," Ben said. "They're ruining that boy's life."

No, I'd already done that.

"So, they don't really know anything for sure?" I almost said *yet*, but cut myself off.

"No, they've made lots of noise, shown clips of the boy missing some shots. Three-pointers with the defender right on him. Bah." He brushed his hand in a dismissive gesture in the general direction of the TV screens.

Good, keep looking in that vein, I silently urged the media. They'd never find what they wanted there. Raymond had shaved his points on defense. Being a step slower than the kid he covered, being half a step further back than normal when his guy would take a shot.

The media would never find it. But the Feds might. They'd know better where to look.

"And this is all from one guy accusing the kid?" I asked Ben.

"So they say. Probably some schmuck who wanted his name in the papers. Or lost money on them himself and wanted revenge."

"They've released his name?"

"Yes. Somebody named Bubba Kinney."

"Bubba? Are you serious?"

"I assume it's a nickname."

I thought about the clientele in the bar I'd met at with Raymond. Yeah, any of those guys could definitely have been a Bubba. Maybe Raymond had even gone back there looking for a…sponsor.

From the corner of my eye I saw Ben pick up his pen and tablet. I heard the rustle of pages. "Who do you have today, Hannah, darling?"

"Nobody," I said and took a gulp of coffee.

The rustle of Ben's tablet silenced. Then it began again. Ben never said a word about my lack of action on today's games.

I silently blessed him for that.

At halftime, they recapped the Raymond Joseph story, now having a picture of Bubba Kinney. It looked like a mug shot. That wasn't too surprising. Raymond would be smart enough to go to someone with a less-than-stellar reputation. It was just his bad luck that this guy turned out to have a moral streak about college basketball.

You never can tell with criminals.

All morning and into the afternoon my eyes flitted from screen to screen, seeing the games being played, but not really processing them. It was so much different when you didn't have money on the outcome.

When there was no Hummer.

I had more coffee than usual, hoping the strong brew might give me the jump-start that I needed, but no. It only made me use the bathroom about every thirty minutes.

The games were drawing to a close by seven. Lorelei had brought some sandwiches in at some point, and I remember Ben and I eating them, but mostly I sat and pretended to watch the games I couldn't have cared less about.

And thought about Raymond Joseph.

As the last of the game clocks ran out, I heard the rustle of Ben's tablet. "How'd you do?" I asked.

Ben didn't bet on the games. Never bet on them. Ben bet with himself. He'd take each game and declare the point spread and the over/under, writing them in his tablet. Before they were posted at the casinos. Then he'd write down the casinos' predictions. He won if his point spread was closer to the actual than the professionals' picks.

"I won," he said, not surprisingly. Ben almost always won. He'd been setting point spreads—for pay and for fun—for over sixty years.

"That's good," I said. At least somebody was a winner today.

"Hannah, darling," he said softly. "What is it? Maybe I can help."

I turned to my side in the seat again, pulled my legs up, just like when I first came into the room hours ago. I wasn't truly facing Ben, which was good. I didn't want to see the disappointment.

There was irony in here somewhere. The whole reason JoJo came to life was because I was too ashamed for Ben—and the boys, and Lorelei—to know I was in debt to a loan shark. And now, because JoJo's life had caught up with her, he was likely to find it all out anyway.

"I…I did something I'm not very proud of," I said quietly.

Ben didn't say anything, but he must have hit the mute on the remote for the one screen that had the sound going, because the room fell silent.

"And because of it, somebody got hurt."

"We all do things we're not proud of sometimes," he said.

I nodded, still staring at the wall ahead of me, giving Ben my profile. Like the side angle of a mug shot.

I didn't need to burden him with the gory details. He'd know if I was even bringing it up it was bad. And of course he'd know it'd have something to do with my gambling. I dreaded this, had dreaded this moment, since JoJo came into being. But a small part of it was freeing.

Like one of those steps, I was giving myself up to a higher power. Only, in this case, my higher power was Ben.

"Hannah, darling." He placed his small, wrinkly hand on my shoulder, and I turned my head to look at his warm, concerned, brown eyes. "You want I should help you with this?"

No need for details. No judgment. Just willing to help me out of whatever mess I'd gotten myself into. That was my Ben. Why I loved him. Why I so desperately did not want to tell him everything. To introduce him to JoJo.

"No, Ben. There's nothing you could do to help." I placed my hand on top of his. "But thank you."

He squeezed my shoulder and removed his hand, sitting back in his chair. "Can you make it right?"

"I don't know," I truthfully answered. I waited a moment and added, "But I'm going to try."

Fifteen
❖❖

THERE WAS A VOICEMAIL from Vince on my phone when I checked it after watching games with Ben. I called him back.

"Sorry I haven't been in touch sooner," he said when he picked up.

"No problem. I'm sure you were busy."

"I was."

I chased away a vision of Vince with a bag of lye at his feet in front of a big hole, a shovel in hand. Would never happen. Vince would never ruin a good suit like that.

"Do you have plans for tomorrow?" Vince asked.

"We usually do brunch around eleven, but nothing after that."

"How long is brunch?"

"A couple of hours. It usually leads to a card game, but I can skip that."

"How about if I pick you up at two?"

"That would be great. What are we doing?"

"I thought I'd surprise you."

After a moment of hesitation, I said, "Okay. But how should I dress?"

"Just casual."

I let out a little chuckle. "My casual or your casual?"

His voice rumbled, a sort of pseudo laugh that made me happy I'd only have to wait a day to see him. "My casual. Your normal."

"Done. Would you like to join us for brunch?"

"No, thank you, I have something to take care of before I pick you up."

"Okay. Two then. Vince?"

"Yes."

"What happened at the police station Thursday night?"

There was a long pause, but I refused to let myself speculate. Vince was obviously available to take me out tomorrow, so that had to be a good thing.

Finally Vince sighed, then said, "I'll tell you about it tomorrow."

"**BEST OMELET I EVER HAD,**" Jimmy told Lorelei at brunch.

"Thanks," Lor answered, while everyone else nodded their agreement.

We were pretty much done, Jimmy still working on his second—or third—omelet. I started to clear the table, taking trips to the kitchen. After my second pass, Jimmy caught my eye and surreptitiously pointed his head toward the back of the house. I made a small nod and went to my office, sat down in the chair on my side. Jimmy came in a few minutes later and closed the door behind him, then sat at Lorelei's side, facing me.

"My guy in Chicago got some news on your kid."

I put my hands on my desk, bracing myself. I nodded for Jimmy to continue.

"It ain't good."

"He turned?" I was astounded. Never in a million years did I think Raymond would turn on JoJo to get some sort of deal.

Although that's exactly what he should have done. It was the smart move, and Raymond was a smart kid.

But I wouldn't have done it, and I hadn't thought he would.

"Nah, nothing like that," Jimmy said, and a small degree of tension left my body. But there was plenty still there, waiting.

"There's no news on the legal side of all of this."

"Then what?"

"Word is he's not at his mom's."

"So?"

"He went there first. Either she kicked him out, or he left."

I didn't let myself think about which of those scenarios would be worse.

"So where is he? Does your guy know?"

Jimmy nodded. "He's holed up with some thug there. This guy is bad news. Apparently, he's some sort of high shooter of hoods. Name is—"

"L'il Roy," I said in a whisper before Jimmy could.

Jimmy only nodded, not asking me how I knew. You didn't poach on other people's sources. Jimmy couldn't have known, but might have guessed, that my info came right from the horse's mouth.

A chill shot through me. Raymond's words of never wanting to end up like L'il Roy played in my head.

"I THOUGHT WE'D DRIVE THROUGH Red Rock Canyon," Vince said to me after he'd collected me and we were in his car. "Have you ever done that?"

"No."

"Me neither. Even as long as I've lived out here. I'd always wanted to, but never have."

"Me, too. What's that saying about never seeing the tourist stuff in your own town?"

He smiled at me, making his strong features turn a touch softer. "Great. Let's do it, then." He pulled his car away from the curb, and I had the overwhelming urge to look back at my home, as if I'd never see it again. Feeling foolish, I kept my head turned forward.

"What happened with Jack?" I asked.

He let out a small snort. "Wild goose chase."

"Really? Nothing? You said he sounded pretty urgent on the phone."

"That's how he made it sound. Turned out to be a fishing expedition. He was playing me to see if I had any information he could use."

"And you played him to see what he had." Vince didn't respond to that, didn't have to. I remembered the tension at the poker table when these two men went *mano a mano*.

The drive from my place to the beginning of the Canyon Trail was a quiet one, but it didn't exactly feel like a comfortable silence to me. Not uncomfortable, necessarily, just…charged, I guess.

I'd been thinking about Raymond and L'il Roy all night, and I hadn't come up with a plan, per se, but I did know I couldn't go barreling into Chicago's worst neighborhood and take on its leader alone.

I needed backup. I needed muscle. Somebody that even L'il Roy would, if not be afraid of, would at least have to listen to. Or at least not shoot at.

Police or mafia were basically my choices. Cops or robbers.

I'd start with the latter.

"Vince?"

"Hmmm?" He'd just finished looking at the map that they gave us when we paid our entrance fee. The driving route was thirteen miles that formed a loping circle through the canyon. There were several pull-in places to stop, get out, take pictures. Lots of hiking trails sprouted from these points. Though we didn't get the Wisconsin winters I grew up with, it was still quite cool this time of year. And today, it was particularly windy. I didn't think we'd see many hikers. In fact, I didn't see any other cars ahead or behind us on the one-way road.

"Do you know anyone who's connected in Chicago?"

"Anna—"

"It's just that this whole thing with Ra—"

"Anna," he said forcefully. I looked at him. "Let's wait for a few miles to have this discussion."

"Okay."

"Enjoy the view."

"Okay," I said and tried to, but all I could think of was the favor I was about to ask of Vince and if he'd help me out. And if he did, what would I owe him? Would he charge interest, or something altogether different?

What was I willing to pay?

After a few miles and a few lookout points passed, Vince pulled into one. He parked the car in the lot that had room for about thirty cars. The place even had a small restroom facility. We were the only people there.

A shiver ran through me.

"Cold?" Vince asked and turned the heater up.

"No."

"Are you warm enough to step outside for a bit?"

"Really?" We could feel the wind whipping across the car.

"This is the highest point of the canyon, I'd like to see the view."

"Okay." I said. I zipped up my leather jacket, turned up the collar and got out of the car.

I'd taken Ben and Saul to the Grand Canyon a few years ago and it was spectacular. But this place, though much, much smaller, had its own beauty. A ruggedness. Today, a lonliness. And very, very high when standing near the edge, where Vince had led me.

"This is great," I said, making a movement to return to the car.

Vince took my arm, pulled me to him, circling his arms around me, my back to the cliff's edge. He looked at me closely. "Are you nervous being out here with me?"

"No," I said quickly. A little too quickly. "But when I said you'd have to cut out the middleman, I didn't mean it literally." I tried to make it a joke, but my voice sounded forced. I probably shouldn't have reminded him that I was the only link between Raymond Joseph and himself.

"Anna, I don't do that." I gave him a pointed look. "Well, at least *I* don't do that. You needed JoJo as a buffer. I needed Paulie."

"Okay," I said, understanding that. Not necessarily condoning it, but hey, the people who crossed Vince knew what they were doing. Knew what hole they were digging the minute they borrowed money from him. Besides, I didn't think there'd be many that it would get that far with—not good business, no chance to get your money.

"Now, what did you want to talk to me about? About Raymond Joseph?"

"Can we go to the car?"

"I'd prefer to talk out here."

I'm so dense. Here I was planning on waltzing into Chicago's seedy underbelly, and I hadn't even figured out that Vince needed to be somewhere where there was no possibility of being overheard or wire tapped, to talk.

Hell, that's probably why we went out to his balcony that night at his place.

"Right. Sure," I said and took a deep breath. "Raymond has left school. He went to his mother's first, but now he's living with a...I don't really even know what he is...in Chicago."

"L'il Roy. Yes, I know."

"You know all this?"

Vince nodded. "Some. Most. It's in my interest to know."

Of course it was. If Raymond turned, the Feds could find me, even though I'd never let Raymond know who I was or where I lived. They could still find me. And if they found me, from there they could find Vince.

The Vice Department that had never been able to get Vince for his loan sharking business would gladly take this case. Racketeering, extortion, it really didn't matter much to them.

He knew it. I knew it. And I stood encircled in his arms on the edge of deserted cliff.

"I'd like to find out what's going on, and hopefully get him out of there," I said now to Vince, taking a step closer to him, forcing his arms to go tighter around me.

"So, you think he's going to turn."

"No."

"Then why do you need to get him out of there?"

"He's in a very dangerous situation. It was his worst fear to end up back on the streets with L'il Roy. I just want to help him."

"This is a man who could make things very difficult for you."

"He won't," I said, but with less conviction than I previously had.

"So, if I did know somebody connected in Chicago…what do you propose?"

"That we go to Chicago and with him as backup, get Raymond out of that situation."

"We?"

I shrugged. "Or just me if you think your guy would trust me without you."

"Go on. So we, or just you and an acquaintance of mine, burst into the drug dens of Chicago and rescue the kid. What then? How are you going to get rid of him? Or is that for my friend in Chicago to figure out? That kind of favor costs a lot of money, Anna."

I shook my head. "No. No. Not take care of him as in get rid of him. Really take care of him. Get him set up somewhere, if he's not welcome at his mother's. Get him off the street. Away from L'il Roy."

"Where, Anna?"

"I'm not sure yet. I want to talk to his mother first. But I could put him up somewhere for awhile, until this blows over and he can start over."

"You expect this to blow over? The Feds love a case like this."

"But they don't have much of a case. Just this Bubba Kinney's word that Raymond approached him about point shaving. They can't prove that he actually did anything. And from what I understand, this Kinney guy isn't exactly the salt of the earth."

"Anna, I can't go with you."

I knew that, but had hoped…well, it didn't matter what I'd hoped. "I know. It was stupid. I thought we could go in there quietly and find out what was going on, get him and his family out of there. You're right. I'll have to figure out a different way."

"I can't go, Anna. But you need to. Or should I say JoJo needs to."

"What do you mean?"

"We, I, could be exposed by this kid. You need to go and find out what's really going on. Jimmy's connections, my connections, they're not good enough. You need to talk to Raymond yourself. Help him if you want, I don't really care. But he needs to know he'll have a very angry *sponsor* to deal with if anything beyond this Bubba Kinney comes out."

"I don't know if I can do that, Vince. I'm not much for strong-arm tactics."

His arms left my waist, went to my shoulders. One strong push and I'd be over the edge. But I didn't duck. Didn't flinch. Didn't dive for the ground behind him. He looked at me for a long time, then looked beyond me. Looking for possible witnesses? He looked back to me, squeezed my shoulders. "Handle it how you want, Anna, but I need to stay out of this."

I nodded. "I know," I said softly.

He pulled me to him, put his arm around my shoulder and turned us back toward the car. "This might work itself out on its own."

"What do you mean?"

"You didn't think he'd survive long with this Li'l Roy."

"Right?" I said, not sure what he meant, but I had a guess.

I felt his shrug, but I didn't look at his face. Instead, I kept my eyes on my feet as we neared the parking lot. "If he doesn't survive, then problem solved."

THE DRIVE HOME WAS SILENT. Still charged, but now with a different explosive. Did Vince have something planned for Raymond? And if so, should I stop it, or just sit back and let my problem disappear, as if over the side of a cliff?

We pulled up to the curb in front of my house. Vince didn't ask for me to go with him anywhere else, and I didn't ask him in.

I thanked him for showing me Red Rock, he nodded, and I turned to get out of his car. He put a hand on my arm to stop me. "I'll call you tomorrow," he said.

"Okay."

He kept his hand on my arm. "So, you'll go?" He paused, probably trying to figure out how to phrase what he wanted to ask in a way that could never be incriminating in case his car was bugged. "You think you'll be out of town?"

"Yes?"

"And you're going alone?"

I took a deep breath, looked at his handsome face. "I'm not sure yet."

I didn't know for sure if he suspected whom I'd turn to next.

Well, yes, from the look in his eyes I guess he did. I was actually thankful for his paranoia of being bugged so he didn't ask me.

He let go of my arm and I left the car. Walking up the drive, I realized I'd just given Vince more incentive for wanting me off the cliff.

Sixteen

❖❖

"JACK, I NEED to talk to you."

There was a pause and I almost hung up. But then he said, "Do you want me to come to you?"

"No," I said quickly. "Can we meet somewhere?"

"My place?"

"No, not there either. Someplace..."

"Neutral?" There was a tiny hint of humor in his voice.

"Public," I clarified.

"Johanna, are you okay?" The humor had turned to concern.

"Yes. I'm..." I stopped. Was I okay? I didn't really know.

"Hey?"

"Yeah, I'm okay. This isn't about me. Not really. But I need some help."

"I'm done for the day and I'm not far from the Strip. Can you meet me over there?"

"Sure."

"A book room somewhere?"

"No," I said firmly.

"Okaaay." He waited for an explanation that I didn't give.

"Just. Not." I let out a sigh. "How about somewhere in the Forum?"

"Okay. Where exactly?" The Forum was the mall of high-end shops connected to Caesars Palace. From where I parked, I wouldn't have to walk through the casino to get there.

"Outside The Cheesecake Factory?" It was the furthest point from the casino entrance, plus I could bring home some cheesecake for Ben. He said it was the closest he'd found to the New York style cheesecake he'd grown up with.

"Sounds good. I can be there in a half hour."

"See you then. Thanks," I said as I hung up.

It was Monday night. I'd spent most of the day working up the guts to make that call and checking back with Jimmy on any news out of Chicago. Nothing.

A knock came on the closed office door, and Lorelei poked her head in. "You have a minute?" she said, looking at the phone still clutched tight in my hand.

I put the phone on my desk and waved her in. "Sure. I need to talk to you, too. Better close the door." But I didn't even need to say it. She'd already begun to shut it behind her.

She sat on her side of the double desk, facing me. "The DNA place called today. The results will be ready for you to pick up tomorrow."

Crap. I'd totally forgotten about Jack's parentage. "Really? So soon."

"You paid extra for the speed."

"Yeah." My hesitation must have been obvious in my voice.

"Jo, you don't have to pick them up if you don't want to know. They can just stay there forever. Or we can tell them to destroy it."

"No," I said.

She let out a breath of relief. "Oh, thank God. I don't think I could have stood it not knowing."

I laughed. "But you would have let me have them destroy it?"

She looked sheepish. "Well, I probably would have tried to talk you out of it, first." She straightened in her seat. "But ultimately, it's your choice."

I put my elbows on the desk and buried my face in my hands. "God, it doesn't feel like my choice anymore. It feels like everything is out of my hands."

"Jo?"

I sighed, scrubbed my hands over my face, trying to rub sanity into my head. It didn't work. "Lor, I'm going to need a credit card. Maybe two depending on what their limits are."

Her body tensed, and she straightened even more, if that was possible. She looked down at the desk, as if trying to gather her thoughts, or remember a previously rehearsed speech. She most likely was, as she'd probably been waiting years for this. For me to come to her with the request I'd made her promise to deny me.

"No," she said calmly.

I held my hand up as if to stop her, but she'd already said her piece in one, succinct, harsh word. "But this is different."

"That's what you said you'd say, and to tell you no."

I smiled. She was right. "You're right, I did. And thank you for remembering that. But this really is different."

"You said you'd say that, too."

I sighed. "Okay, here's the abbreviated edition. I have to go to Chicago for a couple of days. I need a card."

A look of relief came over her face. "Why didn't you say it was for travel? Of course you can have one. Just like when you go home to Wisconsin and then you give it back to me when you get home. I'll have it for you…is tomorrow morning okay? Do you need me to look up flights for you?"

"I probably will, yes. And tomorrow morning is fine. But I might be making more charges on them than just traveling, so you're going to have to tell me the limits on them, and like I said, I might need more than one." She started to speak, and I tried to stave off any argument. "I'm not buying stuff to hock for gambling, I promise."

A look of concern mixed with pity and, yes, horror, came

across her face. For the first time in a long time—maybe ever—I was glad for the conception of JoJo so that I hadn't had to see that look in Lorelei's eyes before now. Now was bad enough.

"This has nothing to do with gambling?" she tried to nail me down.

"Not directly. But..." Well, shit, I guess I might as well practice for Jack on Lorelei. "My gambling indirectly got a friend into trouble. He's in Chicago, in a bad situation, and I'd like to get him, his mother, and his sister out of there. So, I might need to charge a year's worth of rent or something like that on a card."

"Chicago? Who do you even know in Chicago?"

I shook my head. "That's not important." I had a flash of Vince and me standing on the cliff at Red Rock Canyon. "And really, the less you know about it the better."

"So this is illegal?"

"Parts of it," I admitted.

She sat back in her chair and folded her arms across her chest. She wanted to hear it all.

"I can't tell you, Lor. This isn't my story to tell." As I'd said to Vince, I was just the middleman.

"Your friend in Chicago?"

"Yes."

"You're going to bring him, his mom and sister here, to Vegas."

"God, no. That's the last place he should go." Lorelei sat still, arms still folded, waiting. "He shouldn't be connected to anyone here. His sister's in drug rehab. Or at least she was. So I was thinking maybe someplace out of state, but near a good rehab facility. Maybe like Minnesota and Hazeltine? But maybe they'd like to get farther away than that. I'm going to leave it up to them."

She unfolded her arms. "Okay. I'll have the cards for you tomorrow morning. I'll have to check, but I think there's something like a fifty thousand dollar limit on each one."

"Fifty thousand?" I said, shocked.

"That's not enough? I can get more in cashier's checks or cash tomorrow if you want."

"No, that's not what I meant. I just didn't realize I had a limit that high."

She furrowed her brows at me. "Jo, you know you're filthy rich, right?"

I waved my arms around. "I know the house and everything in it is paid for. The cars. I know you have a stash to keep the house running for a few years if I hit a bad streak playing poker. I—"

"That's just the tip of the iceberg."

"Really?"

"I'm a very good investor, Jo."

"You invested for me?"

She snorted. "Well somebody had to think of the future."

"That's what the three-year cushion was for."

Another snort. "What happens after three years?"

"I've never had a dry spell longer than that. Not even close."

"What happens when you stop playing poker?"

I stared at her with a blank look. "Who says I'm going to stop playing poker?"

A long sigh escaped her. "I know. I know. But a girl can hope, can't she?"

"If this is going to launch into another intervention…" I started to rise from my seat, but she waved me down.

"It's not. I promise. I just want you to know that you don't have to gamble anymore. That you and Ben, and me if you want, will be okay for a long, long time on what you've earned."

"And you've invested."

She nodded.

"Even in this economy? You might want to check that balance again."

"I got it out of the risky stuff years ago. And when it looked like we were swinging back, I put it back in."

"You foresaw what the great economic minds of our time didn't?"

She shrugged. "A dancer I knew bought a house a few years ago that I knew she couldn't afford. She explained her mortgage to me, and I thought it all sounded kind of hinky. Then another dancer I knew got laid off, a whole bunch of dancers did. It hits the tourist places first, you know."

No, I didn't know. But apparently, Lorelei did. She started lapsing into talk of stocks, bonds, treasury bills, safe assets, and my head started spinning.

"Lor, Lor." I held up my hand cutting her off. "I'm never going to understand all that. I don't want to. Just…thank you." She nodded. "And what's the bottom line?"

"The bottom line is you cannot only afford the style to which we've all become accustomed, but you can afford it for another family of three as well. Two or three families of three if you don't buy Porsches for them all."

"Holy crap."

A satisfied smile crossed her face, but all I could think about were the missions JoJo had undertaken when all kinds of cash sat…somewhere.

As if reading my thoughts, she said, "It's not easily accessible. There are forms and things, and most of them need my signature as well as yours."

"But we can get some? By tomorrow?"

"Yes. I'll get it as well as the credit cards. How much?"

"As much cash as you can."

"Oh, Jo, that's not safe. Can't you just take some cash then use the cards?"

I was already shaking my head. "I was going to use the cards because I thought that was my only option, but I'd rather not have any kind of paper trail. Cash would be better. I'll take as much as I can to Chicago, but you better get some more freed up in case…" I didn't finish, didn't know how to.

"I hate to think of you carrying so much cash on you when you travel alone."

Good thing she didn't know about the under-the-clothes money belts that I had hidden in the back of my closet. Although, after this conversation, that fact might not surprise her all that much. I looked at my watch. I needed to leave now to meet Jack.

"It'll be okay, Lor," I said as I tapped my horseshoe pendant three times for luck. "And, depending on how the next couple of hours go, I might not be going to Chicago alone."

"**NO. NO WAY.** Absolutely not," Jack said a few hours later.

I started to rise from our table in the back of The Cheesecake Factory. "Yeah, it was a dumb idea. Sorry I—"

He yanked on my sleeve, and I sat back down. "Sit down," he said a bit harshly. "Jesus Christ, Johanna," he said a lot harshly.

I took a sip of my Diet Coke and another bite of my cheesecake, which was starting to taste like chalk in my mouth. But it was better than looking at Jack as he scrubbed his hands over his face and mumbled something I couldn't quite make out. Not that I wanted to.

We'd met and grabbed a table. I'd ordered cheesecake, he'd ordered nothing until I'd launched into my story. Then he'd held up a hand and ordered a bourbon before waving for me to continue.

I started with the statement that I wasn't going to lie to him, but I wasn't able to tell him everything, either. But that I'd gotten someone into trouble and I needed his help to go to Chicago's South Side with me and try to offer a way out.

I then told him that the person in Chicago was Raymond Joseph. Jack didn't know who that was, bless his non-gambling heart. I quickly explained Raymond's current circumstances and

Jack, no dummy, put most of the pieces together rather quickly.

Which is where we stood—or sat—now.

"How is Vince Santini involved in this?" he asked, taking his hands from his face and skewering me with his cop gaze.

"He's not," I said.

"You said you weren't going to lie to me."

"I'm not. Vince is not involved in Raymond soliciting this Bubba Kinney. This is all me."

"But he *was* invol—"

I raised a hand to stop him. "This is all me. From here on out, this is all me."

He stared at me for a long time, then gave a slight nod. "Go on. What's your plan?"

"I want to go to Chicago and find out what the hell is really going on. Jimmy's guys can only know so much. And, if possible, I want to get Raymond, his mother and his sister out of there."

"If the Feds are really investigating him, they're not going to let that happen."

"I don't want him to disappear. It's not about running. We'll let whoever needs to know in on our plans, give them forwarding addresses, whatever. If Raymond is truly under investigation, or if he decides he wants to…confess, they'll be able to find each other easily enough."

"Confess? So you know he's guilty?"

I shook my head. "I haven't spoken to Raymond about this Kinney guy. All I know is what the media is reporting and what Jimmy's guys know, which isn't much."

"But you think, given your…past history with this guy, that the accusations are probably true?"

I nodded once, but didn't say anything.

"Let's put aside the fact that the Feds aren't going to let him out of their sight if they don't want to, even if you give them a damned forwarding address." He snorted at that. "If it's not about running, why do you need to swoop in and get him out of Chicago?"

"From what I understand, he's fallen in with some bad guys. I'm actually afraid for his well-being in Chicago more than I am about his facing possible charges."

"And you said it was South Side?"

I nodded. "The Engelwood area. Know of it?"

"Shit," he said, confirming my fears. "Their homicide rate is the highest in the nation."

Now, unfortunately, we were talking Jack's language.

"That's what I've read online."

"I have a buddy from my Portland days that transferred to Chicago. I think he went to the South Side?"

"Willingly?"

Jack shrugged. "That's where he was from originally. When he and his wife split up, he decided to go back. He wanted to help his old neighborhood."

"Do you think he'd help me?" At his raised brow, I amended, "Us?"

"He was a good guy. I'll give him a call."

"Thank you. All I really need is someone to get me into that area to see Raymond. I'm sure I'm just being a chickenshit, but I don't want to face him and his…buddies…alone. I'd prefer to have someone with a badge and gun with me."

"That's smart, not wanting to be alone. But I don't know if the badge would help you or hurt you."

"That bad, hey?" I said, anguished again that Raymond was deep into the hell he'd worked so hard to avoid.

As if reading my mind, he said, "That's nothing for you to feel guilty about. South Side's a pretty violent place these days. If the kid grew up there, he knows his way around."

I was shaking my head before he'd even finished his sentence. "He doesn't. Not really. He spent his childhood staying out of trouble. Trying very hard to stay out of that life. All he concentrated on was basketball. It was his way out. For him and his mom and sister. He's been gone away to school for four years. He was going to get his mom and sister out of there as soon as he had some money from the pros. He never intended on going back."

Jack looked away from me, started to sit back in his seat, pulling away. I leaned forward and grabbed the sleeve of his blue chambray shirt. "He's not going to make it very long, Jack. Something bad is going to happen to him there," I said with absolute certainty.

He looked at me with his cop eyes that slowly, so slowly, turned into the Jack whose arms I'd laid in. "Okay, I'll go."

My hand, still on his arm, squeezed my gratitude. "Thanks, Jack. Can you leave tomorrow?"

He was already pulling out his phone while he nodded his head. "Yeah. I think so. I need to let Frank and our boss know, but I can take a couple of sick days." I nodded. "And one condition."

"Yes?"

"You're going to tell me the whole story, Johanna, on our way to Chicago."

"But—"

"But nothing. That's my condition. I want it all."

When I made to argue again, he held up a hand. "Don't worry, we'll be thirty-thousand feet up, way out of my jurisdiction. No repercussions."

I nodded. I owed him that, at the very least, for what he was about to do. I released his arm and watched as he dialed. "Thanks, Jack. I owe you."

He raised one brow at me as he raised the phone to his mouth. "Yes. You do. And Johanna, I mean to collect."

Seventeen
❖❖

JENNIFER WAS AGAIN at the front desk of the DNA testing place when I arrived Tuesday morning. Or, Day Ten without placing a bet, as I was now keeping track of time.

She remembered me, but still asked for two forms of identification before she'd release the results to me, which I guess is good that they're so diligent.

I'd brought the same NPR tote bag with me—this time empty. I wasn't sure if they gave the samples back or disposed of them, but I'd wanted to be prepared. Jennifer had the samples for me, but said they could get rid of them if I preferred. But I took them, placing the marked baggies in my tote. I didn't like the idea of Saul's ashes "out there". I'd pour him back into the urn when I got home.

I paid up, and Jennifer gave me a sealed, brown, legal-looking envelope. She watched me, waiting to see if I'd open it right then and there, but I didn't. I suppose she saw a lot of reactions from people in this reception area. I slipped the envelope in the tote bag, thanked her and left.

On the drive home I thought about Vince. He'd called me last night after I'd gotten home from meeting Jack. He asked if we could together tonight, but I told him I was going out of town for a couple of days.

He didn't ask where I was going, there was no need.

"What does this mean for you and me?" he asked.

"I'm not sure," I answered honestly.

"This—what you're doing—it's business, Anna. I wasn't able to help you in this business situation."

I hoped that meant that Raymond Joseph had no fear from Vince's corner, but I didn't ask for clarification. "I know. It's business, Vince. Not personal." Ha! How many times had he said that to me over the years as he'd calculated the vig on a loan?

"Can you keep the two separate?" he asked.

"*You* always have."

"Not always."

"No?"

"No. It was always hard to keep things separate with you."

"I have a limp on cold days that says you did just fine with that."

There was a long pause, and I started to apologize. I went to Vince—or Paulie on his behalf—for money. They never came to me. They never forced money on me with ungodly interest rates. I had no one to blame but myself.

For all of it.

"I'm sorry," I said at the same time Vince said, "Anna…"

"No. I'm really sorry, Vince."

He sighed. "Okay. Will you call me when you get back?"

I hesitated. I don't know why, but I did.

"At least to let me know you're okay," he said.

"Yes. I'll call when I get back."

Driving home now, I wondered if I'd need to. Hopefully, Vince wouldn't find out all he needed to know from the news. With my picture blasted across the front of the sports pages. He'd really regret not pushing that day at Red Rock.

Jack pulled to the curb in front of my house as I was getting out of the car.

"Good timing," he said as he got out of his and walked toward me.

I made sure the tops of the tote bag met and held it close together. I didn't think he'd look inside and magically recognize his strand of hair or drinking glass, but why take chances. "Yeah, good timing."

"We'll take my car to the airport," he said.

"That's fine."

"You packed?"

I nodded. "I just need to get some stuff from Lorelei, and grab my bag."

"I thought I'd come in and say hi to Ben, but if you'd rather I didn't..."

"Why would I not want you to do that?" I clutched the tote bag closer to my body.

He shrugged. "I didn't know if you wanted to explain us going away together."

"Oh. Yeah. But, I'm sure he'd love to see you. I'll just tell him it's none of his business."

Jack chuckled. "And that works with Ben?"

"Ben, yes. Well, sometimes. Lorelei, no. But she made all the flight, rental car and hotel arrangements, so I've already had to deal with her."

Which had been easier than I thought, explaining that, for reasons I couldn't go into, I needed a police officer with me and I'd chosen Jack. She wanted to pry, I could tell, but I shut her down with a look.

Which hardly ever works. She must be more worried about me than I'd realized.

We entered the house together. Lorelei appeared from the kitchen and walked down the hallway toward us. Her eyes went to the tote bag I held, and a question appeared in her eyes. I gave a tiny shake of my head, and she turned her attention to Jack. "Jack, it's good to see you. Thanks for doing this with Jo. It makes me feel a lot better."

"No problem," Jack said, "though I'm still not really sure

what I'll be doing."

Lorelei waved a hand of dismissal at him. "I don't either. Jo tells me nothing. But it eases my mind that you'll be with her."

"Oh, ye of little faith," I said as I took off my jacket and hung it, and Jack's, up in the foyer closet.

"You haven't really given us reason to have faith," Lor said softly. I froze in the middle of hanging Jack's jacket. "Sorry," she said quickly. "Totally uncalled for."

I closed the closet door, picked up the tote bag. And turned to her. "No. You're right."

She looked pained. "I'm so sorry. I never meant…"

I held up a hand. "Look, Lor, I'm the first to admit I fucked up. And now that's affecting you and the household. But I'm trying to…"

"Make amends," she finished for me, a triumphant glow in her eye, thinking some of her intervention bullshit might have seeped through.

"Right."

"Step Nine."

"That's what I understand."

"That's great, Jo, you should—"

But I was already walking past her. Unable to look at Jack, I called over my shoulder "Ben's probably in the book room, Jack. I need to get our travel stuff from Lor then grab my bag from my room."

I think Lor was doing a small clap behind me, but I headed down the hallway to the office. She entered soon after. "I know you don't want to talk about all of that twelve-step stuff, but—"

"That's right, I don't," I said as firmly as I could.

It must have worked because she let it drop and instead walked to her side of the desk. She picked up a large envelope and started pulling things out. "Here are the two credit cards. I was right, they both have limits of fifty thousand."

I took the credit cards from her and put them in my pants

pocket. She raised a brow at me. "My purse and stuff is in my bedroom. I'll organize all this stuff there."

She held out her hand. "Well, give them back then, and I'll put them back in the envelope so you can keep everything together."

I did and she dropped the cards into the envelope, which, coincidentally, was the same size, shape and color as the one containing the DNA results, which were still in the tote bag now resting against my leg.

Lorelei was pulling out papers from the envelope. "Your flight itineraries. I left the return date open, like you said, so you'll have to either call the airlines when you want to leave, or call me and I'll handle it for you."

"What if we're in a hurry? Can we just show up at the airport and get on the next flight?"

"Sure. It'll cost more, but you can do that."

I nodded for her to go on, and she pulled out another bunch of papers. "Your rental car reservation. MapQuest directions from O'Hare to your hotel. And directions from the hotel to your friend's mother's house."

Jimmy's guy had gotten Raymond's mother's address for me. He wasn't staying there anymore, but that was the first stop Jack and I were going to make. I was counting on his cop friend getting Raymond—and L'il Roy's—address for us.

I nodded my understanding, and she slid the pages back into the envelope. Then she pulled out the *pièce de rèsistance*. Three wads of cash, each with rubber bands around them. "Sixty thousand in cash. Will that be enough?"

I nodded, but I really didn't have any clue how this was all going to turn out. Would Mrs. Joseph accept my offer for her to take her kids out of Chicago? Would she see the offer for what it was? Guilt money? And if she did, would sixty K be enough?

Maybe not enough, but at least it was a start.

"Lor, this is great. Thanks so much. I really appreciate it."

My throat started closing up at the end, but I felt I had to go on. "I really don't know what I would do without you." My throat went to full-on choke up.

Lorelei's eyes got a little moist, and I had to look away from her. She came around to my side of the desk, handed me the envelope, then grabbed me up into a tight hug.

We stood that way for a long time, and then she suddenly sprung away from me. "Oh my God, I totally forgot about the DNA thing."

So had I, but I now reached for the tote bag. I slid the envelope out and put the tote bag into my bottom desk drawer. I'd deal with the samples later, after I got back from Chicago. I held the envelope up to show Lor. "Here it is."

"It's still sealed."

"Yeah."

"How could you stand not ripping it open the minute you got it?"

I shrugged. "First I wanted to just get out of there, you know? And then I didn't want to do it while I was driving. And then Jack pulled up to the house the same time I did. So, I really haven't had a chance."

"Should we open it now? Or do you have too much going on to think about this?"

I did, but I knew Lorelei wanted to know. I handed it to her. "Open it, but don't tell me anything."

"Really?" I nodded, and she didn't ask twice, nearly giving me a paper cut she took it from my hands so quickly. She ripped open the top of the envelope and took out the report. I could see that there were several pages, but apparently they summed up their findings on the top page, because Lor's eyes got big as saucers.

"Holy shit."

I almost grabbed it from her hands, but I halted mid-reach. Did I really want to know this now? As I was about to get on a plane with Jack where I'd promised him nothing but the truth.

"Jo, you're not going to believe—"

I took a step away from her. "Wait. Stop. Don't tell me."

"Really?"

I took a deep breath, let it out. "I'm sure. Only tell me this. Is Jack involved?"

"That's all you want to know? Really?"

"Yes."

"Yes."

"Yes, what?"

"Jack is most definitely involved."

I took another step back, which made the back of my legs knock against my desk chair. I lost my balance, tumbling down into the soft leather.

Well, crap. Now I needed to know it all. I had just opened my mouth to tell Lor to spill when there was a knock on the door and Jack poked his head in. "I don't mean to rush you, but we should probably get a move on."

There was no way Jack could have seen what Lorelei was holding, but she instinctively dropped her hand, lowering the report to her side, hidden by the desk.

He caught the movement of course, the man was a detective for goodness sake, but he didn't comment on it.

I stood up and took the cash and credit cards out of the envelope Lorelei had given me, then handed the envelope and its remaining documents to Jack, who had now come fully into the office and stood on Lor's side of the desk. He looked through them then said to Lorelei, "Nice work. Thanks."

She nodded, but didn't move from where she and I stood across the double desk from Jack. "Just take care of our girl."

Jack nodded and I started to object, but let it drop. That was kind of why I'd asked Jack to come with me, after all. Not that I needed taking care of, but I was smart enough to know that walking into L'il Roy's den and demanding Raymond leave with me was definitely a Too Stupid To Live move. I needed backup.

And I couldn't think of anyone I'd rather have at my back, but I hadn't wanted to put Jack in a bad position. A position that would surely be tested when I told him all about JoJo as I had promised.

Which is why I'd gone to Vince first.

I shoved the cash and cards in my pocket and moved around both Lorelei then Jack. "I'll go get my stuff."

"You're not going to get through security with all that cash," he said.

"Trust me," I said as I walked by him and out the door. I swear I heard him snort behind me, and I'm sure that one damn brow was raised, but I kept facing forward and went to my bedroom.

I shut the door and took the cash and credit cards out of my pants pockets and tossed the cash on the bed. I grabbed my seldom-used purse from my dresser and put the credit cards in my wallet, along with my license that was still in my pants pocket from my trip to the DNA place. I double checked that it was Anna Dawson's license. I would have loved to use a false identity for this trip so that I couldn't be traced back to Chicago and Raymond Joseph in any way, but with having Lorelei book the flights—obviously in my name—and Jack's accompaniment, that wasn't a possibility.

I put the wallet in my purse, zipped it up, set it on the bed and headed to my closet. My already packed duffel sat on my bed, but what I needed now was hidden in a different bag at the very back of my closet.

JoJo's bag.

I unearthed it from its hiding place and set it on my bed next to my packed bag. I unzipped it and almost had to take a step back as JoJo's overpowering perfume escaped. I dug through the gaudy, skimpy clothes, throwing some on the bed, pushing others aside, until I felt the leather money belts. I pulled them out. There were four of them, but I'd only need three. I put one back and unzipped the remaining three. A credit card and driver's license fell out of one. I picked them up, wishing again I could be Marie VanSipe for this trip.

Wishing I'd never done anything that would have made this trip necessary.

I pulled my knit Henley over my head, tossing it on the bed, then put the cash into the three money belts. I secured them around my waist, equally distributing them so there'd be no discernible bulge. I pushed them low and pulled the waist band of my pants up so they met.

"I'd ask if you needed help." Jack's voice came from behind me, and I spun around to face him as he stood in the doorway, "but it looks like you know what you're doing."

"I do," I answered as I grabbed for my Henley, tugging it back on. Jack had seen me in less that my bra before, but that was...before.

"In fact," he said as he stepped into the room and closed the door behind him, "you look like a pro at this."

I didn't take the bait, only arranged my shirt over the money and my pants. I was always extremely careful about wearing anything that would set off the sensors in an airport, anything that would make them need to pull me out of the line. Even if they did and ran one of those wands over me, there was nothing in the money belt that would set anything off.

That was the big selling point of these particular money belts.

Jack was beside me now, and he nudged me aside. "I came to get your bag for you," he explained. "Are both of these going?"

I turned, forgetting JoJo's bag was still on the bed, wide open, and Jack was now picking up a platinum blonde wig out of it. It dangled on one of his fingers as if it were something abhorrent, or a piece of evidence that he didn't want to contaminate.

I guess it was both.

"This one," I said, zipping up my duffel bag and handing it to him. But he didn't grab it, too busy digging into JoJo's life. He'd tossed the wig aside and pawed through the duffel, but all that was left in there were hooker clothes. Then he saw the remaining money belt. He opened it and pulled out the fake ID and credit card.

"Jack," I started, but what could I say?

He flipped the license over, rubbed his finger over it. "You know, it might be better if you were Marie for this one last trip."

I didn't comment on the "one last trip" part of his statement, but answered, "Flight's in my name."

He nodded. "Because Lorelei booked it?"

"Yes."

"You—or Marie—could have booked it."

"Yes, but when I knew you were going to come with me, I thought…"

"That keeping the felonies to a minimum might be a good idea?"

"Something like that."

I saw a small smile on his face, and then it grew a little bigger as he picked up one of the articles of clothing I'd tossed onto the bed when rummaging through the bag for the money belts. It was a red, sequined, tube top. He held it up, obviously seeing how tiny it was.

Way too tiny for Anna. Just right for JoJo.

He took my packed bag from my hand, set it on the bed, unzipped it and tucked the red top into it, then zipped it up again.

At my questioning look, he just smiled and said, "Who knows. Could be fun."

I tried to pull off an "as if" snort, but it stuck in my throat a little and I was terrified that it came out as a moan instead.

Yeah, judging from Jack's hungry look, it definitely came

out as a moan.

I threw the rest of JoJo's trampy clothes back into her bag, zipped it up and took it to my closet where I once again buried it deep, piling old sweatshirts and some shoes on top of it. As I backed out of the closet, I came up against Jack, who must have moved in right behind me and been watching every move.

He put his hands on my arms, turned me to face him. He nodded his head toward the hidden duffel bag.

"This is certainly going to be an interesting plane ride."

Eighteen
❖

I WENT IN TO SAY GOOD-BYE to Ben while Jack took my bag out to the car to wait for me. He started to get up, but I waved him back to his seat. He put his tablet on the table beside him to give me his full attention, waiting for me to speak first.

"I'm not sure how long I'll be away. Probably a couple of days. Three at the most."

He only nodded.

"Lorelei will take you and Gus to breakfast."

More nodding. The shame that I had come to this, become this woman, was the only emotion that seemed to take any bite out of the guilt I felt over Raymond.

"If you need anything, anything at all, let Lorelei know."

"I'll be fine."

Now I nodded. "I know I'll be back in time for your doctor's appointment at the end of the week."

"If you're not, Lorelei can take me."

I started to open my mouth to say I'd surely be home by then, but stopped. This could all go horribly wrong. Hell, Jack might arrest me mid-flight when I told him the whole story. Or if not, I could be under federal investigation just by coming within twenty feet of the Joseph family.

Or Vince could be. Which would be worse for not only Vince, but also for Raymond and me.

Orange had never been a good color on me—not to mention those shapeless jumpsuits.

"Okay. Well, then…"

Ben waved me over to him, and I bent down and received his hug, his frame feeling small and bony. Had he become frailer? Could he afford to?

"Hannah, darling, I love you," he whispered into my hair, then added, "Make this right."

I gulped, not able to speak, hugging him tighter, nodding my head into his shoulder. When I was able to gather myself, I pulled away from his embrace but couldn't meet his eye.

When I went outside, Jack was putting my bag into the back seat, where his sat, then went to the trunk and opened it. I came up beside him as he reached in and unlocked a steel attaché case. He removed his gun from his belt clip and placed it in the case in a custom spot in the foam obviously made for the gun. He took a clip of ammunition also from his belt and placed it in the case as well. Then he locked the case and closed the trunk.

"Why did you do that?"

"I didn't want to do it at the airport where someone might see."

I shook my head. "No. I mean, why did you take it off at all?"

He opened the passenger door, and I slid into the car. He shut the door behind me then crossed to the driver's side, got in, shut the door and started up the car. "I can't take a gun on a plane, Johanna."

"But you're a cop."

He pulled away from the curb. I probably should have felt like I had with Vince—like I should take a good look at my house in case I never got back there. But I didn't feel that way this time, even though the possibility was more likely now.

I decided not to question that feeling too much right now.

"Cops haven't been able to take a gun on an airplane for

years," he explained.

"Oh," I said, the disappointment in my voice. "Of course not. I guess I should have known that."

"Don't tell me you only want me for my gun," he teased.

"You mean you have other assets?"

"Oh, Johanna, you have no idea," he said, chuckling.

But that was the problem. I did have not only an idea, but proven fact of Jack's assets.

I was kind of hoping that the flight would be crowded, that we'd be surrounded, that there would be no way to tell Jack my story on the flight.

Dear God, why couldn't there have been a screaming baby?

But no. Lorelei had booked us into first class, which was utterly desolate with only Jack and me and two businessmen, rows away from us, who both put in earbuds and booted up their laptops as soon as we were given the all clear from the pilot.

We declined the initial offer of drinks from our flight attendant, but as soon as the businessmen had their earbuds in, Jack waved her over and ordered a bourbon. I asked for the same. Bourbon wasn't my favorite, but I figured I'd be talking more than drinking anyway, I might as well get something that Jack could finish for me.

She put down our drinks, asked if we needed anything else to which we said no, then disappeared to the front of the cabin.

Jack circled the top of his glass, slightly dipping his finger into the amber liquid. He put his finger to his mouth, barely wetting his lips. He raised the glass, took a small sip, savoring the taste in his closed mouth as he slowly lowered the glass to his tray table.

He turned his head to me. "Okay. I'm not only off duty and out of my jurisdiction, I am in no way a cop for the duration of this flight. Think of me as a priest hearing your confession in the safe confines of a confessional booth."

"Except with bourbon."

He smiled. "You can't be sure those guys don't have a bottle in there with them."

"They probably need a good stiff drink after most confessions."

"True." He took another sip, this one more like a gulp. "Let me just preface this with one question." I nodded. "Does your story in any way involve a homicide?"

"No. Not in—"

"Or possibly involve a homicide in the near future?"

Oh. Well. I didn't really think Vince would have Raymond taken out of the picture. Did I? And I didn't really fear there'd be some kind of shoot-out when faced with L'il Roy. Did I?

"Not in the past. Not even close. No plans for the future," I finally said.

Jack looked at me for a long time. His brown eyes almost the same shade as the bourbon in his glass, which was once again raised to his lips. He took a long drink. I watched the movement of his throat as the smooth liquor glided down. He set the glass back down. "Okay," he said, "let 'er rip."

I TOLD HIM EVERYTHING.

How I'd begun playing in back-room games so I could play better players, and play on credit if need be. That after playing poker for hours in a casino poker room and having won only a couple of hundred, or even lost, I'd find one of Vince's games to play on credit and win enough to make my bets for the next day's games.

"You were that broke? Living that close to the edge? Is that when you lived with Ben at his place?"

I shook my head. "No, I had money, I just gave it all to Lorelei. I'd just keep out enough to play for a couple of days then give her the rest."

"So why not ask her for some when you needed it?"

"That wasn't our agreement. I'd gotten into some… trouble…my first couple of years out here." Although we were probably over Utah or beyond by now, not "here". Maybe that's why it was easier to spill this whole sordid story. We were in no man's land. Space. The final frontier.

"I've seen the scar on your foot, Johanna," he said, "Paulie Gonads' signature. I know what kind of trouble you were in."

I nodded. "But I got out of it. With Ben's help. That's when we started living together. He—and the other boys—taught me to sink my money into things that couldn't easily be pawned for extra money. No easy temptations."

"The big house."

"Yes. After my first big win. My first final table. When all I wanted to do was take that fat check and plunk it down on the Giants."

"The Giants? Really?"

I shrugged, but continued to stare straight ahead at the back of the empty seat in front of me. "The Giants. The Lakers. USC. It didn't matter. It never really mattered what team."

He was silent, I suppose trying to understand. Good luck, I didn't understand it myself.

From the corner of my eye, I saw him run his finger up and down his glass, sitting empty on his fold-out tray. "Like it doesn't really matter if it's bourbon," he finally said, and I felt the first glimmer of hope that I might come out of this without losing Jack's help.

I knew I'd already lost his…respect?…trust?…whatever. It had been gone for awhile now.

And yet, he was here, right beside me, when I'd needed him.

"Yeah," I said, "like that." I took my untouched glass of bourbon and put it on his tray, taking his empty and putting it on mine.

The flight attendant entered the cabin from the front. She

asked the businessmen if they needed anything, then approached Jack and me. She eyed my empty glass. "Another bourbon?"

"Please," I said. "And a water, too."

I kept quiet until she came back with the drinks and disappeared once more behind the curtain.

"So," Jack said after taking a drink from his glass, "the house."

"Right. The house. The cars. The gourmet kitchen. The televisions—wall mounted so I'd have no idea of how to take them to a pawn shop."

"Were you ever tempted to? Get some quick cash by hocking your stuff?"

"Constantly. But that's where Lor came in." I explained to him our partnership, how I handed over my winnings and she kept the house running. "And it's worked great. Really great, I found out today. Apparently. I'm filthy rich."

"Terrific. Then what the fuck are you doing playing in backroom games with loan shark money?"

"Well, like I said, I'd hand over my money to Lor, keeping out my stake for the next day's play. But there'd be those times when I'd lose, or not win enough to place my bets, and so I'd go play on credit. It didn't really matter, because most nights I won or broke even. The times I lost, it wasn't too bad. I could usually win it back the next day or two playing poker, and I'd have it paid off before the week was out."

"But not always."

I took a drink of bourbon. It burned. I switched to the bottle of water, taking a long sip. "No, not always."

I could feel his body tense beside me. "Tell me, Johanna."

"Well, this is when JoJo came into existence."

"JoJo?"

I took a deep breath. "Yeah. And she's one bitch you do not want knocking on your door."

Two bourbons later, both drained by Jack, there were JoJo's

past escapades, lain bare, as if sitting on the table trays in front of us.

"Jesus Christ," Jack whispered.

"Yeah," was all I could say.

I didn't tell him that Vince had been the backer for Raymond Joseph, but he'd probably guessed that.

"So what's the deal with Raymond and this Bubba Kinney? Are you hooked up with this Kinney guy, too?"

"No. I cut Raymond off. He had no way to get ahold of me."

"So he went looking for a new stake."

"Probably."

"Greedy."

"No. Not really." Then I explained that all of Raymond's ill-gotten gains had gone to pay for his sister's drug rehab, and to help his mother so she could be there for the sister. "I told him the last time I saw him that he'd only have this opportunity a few more weeks. That CIU wouldn't be the favorites as soon as the tournament started. He knew his window was closing." I took a sip of water. "And then I cut him off."

"You didn't make him contact this Kinney character."

"Didn't I? I was like a drug dealer. Gave him a taste…"

"What's one of those damned steps? Take responsibility for your actions?"

"I'm not sure if that's exactly a step." What a pair we were. Between us we could probably cobble together a half-assed recovery program that would have us deep in rehab the first week.

He waved a hand in the air. "Whatever. It should be if it isn't. So, yeah, take responsibility for *your* actions. But you're not responsible for what this kid does after you."

"Aren't I?"

He didn't answer.

"I owe this kid, Jack."

"Jesus, Johanna. What a fucking mess."

I bristled. I had no reason to, he was absolutely right, but I still hit back. "You're no saint, either." I motioned to the empty glasses in front of us.

"At least my life is the only one I'm destroying. I haven't dragged some innocent kid into it."

"What about your son?

"Fuck," he said under his breath, and I felt instant regret.

"Jack, I'm sorry. I'm ashamed and embarrassed, and thinking you'll probably be slapping cuffs on me at any moment. I lashed out. It's none of my business. And I'm sure you're doing the best you can by your son."

A small snort escaped him. "Yeah. Right. Maybe I should come with an alter ego, too. Somebody sober and a dedicated father, and…" he trailed off.

"That was the easy way out. And you don't take the easy way, Jack."

"JoJo was the easy way?"

I shrugged. "I could have taken the beating. I didn't have to become JoJo."

"Why didn't you? Fear?"

"More than that. Shame. The shame of Lorelei and especially Ben finding out."

"Shame trumps fear?"

"Shame trumps everything."

He looked away, quiet for a moment as he stared as his empty glass. Then I heard him say more to himself than me, "Yeah, I guess it does."

JACK DIDN'T SLAP THE CUFFS on me when we landed, but we didn't say a whole lot either as we got our rental car and I drove us to the hotel. Jack called his contact with the Chicago police, but there was no news.

We checked in. Separate rooms, but adjoining. I didn't know if Lorelei had requested that when she'd made the reservation, or if it was standard with a couple checking in together but with two rooms, or if it was just the luck of the draw.

Jack came into my room with me, unlocked the adjoining door. "Keep that unlocked," he said then left through the hallway. I heard him in his room a moment later, and then he had his door open. I was still standing where he'd left me, in front of the two adjoining doors. He looked at me, nodded, then turned around to throw his duffel bag on his bed.

"Are you afraid I'm going to bolt the first chance I get? Now that I've told you everything?" I asked.

"Not while you still need my help."

"And after?"

He had his back to me. He pulled off his jacket, tossing it aside, his strong shoulders bunched as he grabbed clothes out of his bag, throwing them on the bed. He turned around, placed his hands on his hips. "No. Not after, either. You're the worst kind of criminal, Johanna. Well, actually the best kind, to a cop."

"How?" Was I actually insulted that I wasn't a better crook in Jack's eyes? Twisted.

"You have a conscience, and you have strong ties."

I put my hands on my hips. We looked like we were playing some kind of weird mirror game, same pose on our own sides of the double doors. "What do you mean?"

"You want to help this kid…conscience. And you'd never take a runner. You'd never leave Ben." He threw his hands up, grabbed his shaving kit from the bed and headed to the bathroom. "Pretty piss-poor mastermind criminal, Johanna."

He closed the bathroom door behind him. I stepped to grab my bag and noticed in the mirror that I was smiling.

Nineteen

❖❖

RIGHT NOW, SOUTH SIDE CHICAGO had the highest murder rate for school-age kids in the country. In the world, probably. Raymond was a bit above that average, age-wise, but I feared for him just the same. And not just because of the random violence. No, it was the non-random acts I was afraid of.

L'il Roy, to be exact. What that twisted mind would make of fallen hero Raymond Joseph, I had no idea. Maybe he'd make an example of him. Maybe he'd embrace him and raise him to second in command. I wasn't sure which scenario would be worse.

I'm no saint—obviously—but this killing of innocent bystanders—kids—in turf wars seemed inconceivable to me.

But it was the way of life here. Detested. Feared. But somehow resigned to the fact.

I was white, raised in an upper-middle-class household in Wisconsin. My parents were still married to each other, for goodness sake. I had no concept of what it was like to grow up wondering if you'd make it home from school alive. How you couldn't even send your kid out to the corner market to get a loaf of bread for fear they wouldn't make it home.

Totally out of my realm. Which is why I felt so much better having Jack beside me.

We found Mrs. Joseph's house—the house Raymond grew

up in—without much difficulty, thanks to Lorelei's MapQuest directions. It was early evening, but the night was already dark.

I don't know what I expected, but it seemed like any small, struggling, poverty-line neighborhood. The houses were small, some rundown, but most had a look of...I don't know...hope? about them. There were flowerpots on the porches. Though in Chicago, at this time of year, there was nothing growing in them. It had been a mild winter for the Midwest this year, but the snow was still around our ankles. Some of the front walks were just trampled down from the inhabitants, but most were shoveled clean.

Jack made a show of stretching when he got out of the car so that his badge, clipped to his belt, clearly showed for the kids that were gathered on the corner, huddling against the cold. He left the door open, so the dome light illuminated him. Cold air blasted through the door and I bundled into my jacket, much like the kids on the corner were doing.

You would think the winters alone would help bring the shooting rate down. Maybe it did, but on the other hand, grouped together like they were, the kids were that much more a target for a drive-by shooter.

When he was sure the kids knew who he was—though not close enough to see his badge was from Vegas, not Chicago—he zipped up his leather jacket and came around the car to meet me as I zipped up mine and rubbed my hands together.

"All those arrangements and Lorelei didn't send gloves or a scarf along?" he asked.

"She was raised in warm weather. It probably didn't occur to her," I said, jamming my hands into my pockets, watching my breath turn to near frost as I spoke.

"What's your excuse?" he asked, I assumed referring to my Wisconsin upbringing.

"Lapse in judgment?" I said, covering all bases.

He did a double take, saw the goofy smile on my face and

snorted. "Ya think?"

We made our way to the door. There were lights on so at least we knew she was home and still up.

"So, what's your game plan here?" Jack asked.

"I need to find out exactly where Raymond is, though between Jimmy's guy and your guy on the force I could probably get that anyway.

"I want to offer her a chance to take Raymond and her daughter and leave Chicago, either for just until this is all settled and Raymond has an option other than ending up being a bag man for L'il Roy, or indefinitely.

"If that doesn't work, at the very least I want word to get to Raymond, hopefully through her, that I'm here, in Chicago."

He nodded. "Any idea how she's going to react to your offer? To you?"

I shook my head. "Not a clue. I don't know how much she knows about how Raymond came up with the money for rehab. What he's told her since. If she knows about JoJo."

He scrubbed his hand across his face. "Don't you get a little schizo talking about yourself like that? Like another person?"

"Vince said kind of the same thing." I regretted it the moment it left my mouth. Even more after I saw the hard look on Jack's face.

"You know this has to stop, right?"

I looked up at him. "What do you mean?"

He waved an arm around, encompassing…well, everything. "This. You. Bets. Loan sharks." He dropped his voice to a mere whisper. "Point shaving. If you get out of this unscathed—and not indicted—it's over. It has to be."

"It's done. I'm done. That's why Raymond went out looking for a stake. 'Cuz I quit."

His brow rose. I cursed the Josephs' front porch light that let me see it so clearly. "Really. I haven't placed a bet in ten days, Jack."

"Seriously?"

I nodded. "Yeah. I know I can't do that anymore. I mean, look where it's gotten me." Much like him, I waved my arms around encompassing our current situation.

He stood for a long time watching me. I didn't flinch. Finally he turned to the front door. "Let's do this," he said as he knocked firmly.

The door opened fairly quickly—it was a small house. The woman took one look at us and started to shut the door in our faces. It caught me off guard, but Jack was prepared and had his body lodged somewhat in the doorframe.

"I'm not talking to any of you people. Nothing but vultures, all of you," she said.

"Ma'am, we're not the media," Jack said.

That didn't seem to stop her. "I don't care who you are or aren't. Get off my property."

Jack looked at me, his brows raised. He started to reach into his jacket, toward his belt, I figured to get his badge. I hadn't wanted to go that route if possible, in case I needed to use more strong-arm tactics later, but I didn't want to talk to Mrs. Joseph through a locked door, either.

"Mrs. Joseph," I said as softly as I could while still being heard. "I'm JoJo."

I half expected a repeat of "I don't care who you are…", but instead she looked closely at me then opened the door for Jack and me. She stepped several feet back, and Jack and I brushed our feet off on the front mat and entered her home, closing the door behind us. The foyer was tiny, not really an alcove even, just a mat on a floor and a table against one wall facing a closet with an accordion folding door that was off its track.

We stood on the small rug just inside the door, our shoes still wet from the shoveled sidewalk. She was a few feet away from us, squarely in the small living room. I took the majority of the tiny house in with one sweep of my head. Past where we stood was a hallway leading to the bedrooms and bathroom. A dining room to the right, and from there a galley kitchen. The dining room table was old and nicked, but sturdy. Like it had served many a family meal. The kitchen didn't have the myriad of gadgets that mine did, nor the expensive countertops and cabinets, but it looked homey and bright. And clean. As was the living room, with its small television, faded floral couch, coffee table and La-Z-Boy recliner that had seen better days. I'd seen one just like it in Raymond's Dubuque apartment the one time I'd been there. I absently wondered if they'd once upon a time been a set.

The house may have been tiny and its furniture out of date, but it was spotless. And no clutter, which was kind of weird in a home with a teenage daughter and a college-aged son, except neither of those two had been around here much lately.

Another thought occurred to me. Raymond hadn't used any of his money for upgrades on the house. The way he'd talked about his mother, so full of pride at the job she'd done raising him and his sister, I would have thought to see new furniture and a big-screen TV.

I'd warned him not to do that, of course, but I wouldn't have blamed him for wanting to help out his mother. But he hadn't. He'd been smart. That, and the money was probably all tied up in his sister's drug rehab.

"Is it all right if my friend and I talk with you for a little bit?"

I'm pretty bad at guessing people's ages, but I'd put her in her late thirties, early forties. She'd had her kids young. She had short hair that she wore in a shag cut, though one side looked a little flatter than the other, like maybe she'd been laying down when we'd arrived. But she was still dressed. She wore a simple, light-blue cardigan sweater set and navy slacks. Work clothes. I knew she worked as a receptionist in an office, and at various times in Raymond's life had taken second and sometimes third jobs when needed.

Bright pink, fuzzy socks that seemed so out of place in her neat appearance peeked out from the cuff of her pants. Had she worn those to work? Or put them on when she'd gotten home? I didn't know why I cared.

"You come from Raymond? He's okay?"

"No ma'am, I haven't spoken to Raymond in awhile." The woman seemed to deflate before my eyes, and I realized she'd had as much hope for this meeting as I did. Maybe she'd thought the mysterious JoJo would be some white knight that could ride in and save her son. Hardly.

"Come on in, then, but I don't know that I'm going to be able to tell you anything."

I kicked off my shoes, and Jack followed my lead. She held out her hands for our jackets, which we gave to her and she hung up in the closet, working the off-track door like she'd been doing it for years. She probably had.

She led us into the living room and sat on one side of the couch. I sat on the other, and Jack took his place on the recliner, leaning forward, his elbows on his thighs. I looked at his belt loop and his badge was gone. He must have taken it off when he'd removed his jacket. It didn't really matter. He'd shown those kids outside his badge, and that news would probably get back to Mrs. Joseph eventually, but he obviously didn't want to start this conversation with her knowing he was a cop.

I thought that was the right move. I also thought I should find out exactly how much Mrs. Joseph knew about what was going on.

"Mrs. Joseph, what has Raymond told you about me?"

She narrowed her eyes. "Unh-uh. You tell me about you and Raymond."

Smart woman, not giving anything away. But then, neither would I if I could help it. We could pussy-foot around all night, feeling each other out, dropping hints without saying anything.

I looked around the room. Every space on the wall and every surface of the end tables were covered with pictures of her kids at various ages. Some were the standard school pictures, some were various team shots of Raymond.

My eyes went to a picture of her daughter, now fifteen, in what was probably her third—or fourth—grade picture. I took a deep breath. That was as a good a place to start as any.

"How's your daughter doing, Mrs. Joseph?" I didn't say it with a menacing double entendre of a strong arm, but it hadn't been with real warmth and concern either. She could take it either way.

If she'd deflated before when I'd said I hadn't seen Raymond, she nearly crumbled when I brought up her daughter. Then, with the steel of a woman who's raised two kids alone in a shitty neighborhood with a low-paying job, she gathered herself, sitting up straight on the couch.

She looked at me with a calm exterior, but I'd been playing poker way too long to be taken in. "I don't know whether to thank you or wish you dead."

"A sentiment most of those in her acquaintance come to sooner or later," Jack piped in from his chair.

I ignored Jack, but Mrs. Joseph looked at him carefully, as if perhaps she'd written him off too quickly.

"So, she's doing better? Your daughter?" I asked, trying to get back on track.

She put her head down, and nodded. "Yes. Yes, she is." Her head came up. "She's almost ready to come home."

"That's good."

She made a sound that was somewhere between a gurgle and a chuckle, but I could hear pain, too. "Is it?" She shook her head. "Of course it is. My baby's coming home." She spread her arms wide. "And what a homecoming she's gonna have."

"Mrs. Joseph, what—"

"Halia," she interrupted.

"Excuse me?"

"Halia. Short for Mahalia. I think we're to a first-name basis, don't you? JoJo?"

"Yes, Halia, I do." She waved for me to go on. "What exactly has Raymond told you?"

"About you, you mean? Or what's happening now?"

"Both," Jack said before I could.

She looked at him again, then her gaze turned to mine. "I know my baby girl was not going to make it. That my insurance wouldn't cover a rehab stay, and for her to try and get clean living in this neighborhood wasn't going to work." Her voice turned defensive when she said, "I was a good mother. It wasn't easy alone. And living here with what all those children see even on the walk to school. I did the best I could by my babies."

I held my hand up. "Halia. I know Raymond. I know you raised him right. There's no way he would have done what he did if it wasn't to help his sister."

"DeeDee. D'eeandra, but Raymond couldn't say it when he was little, so she was DeeDee to him. It stuck."

"DeeDee," I said softly. I of course, had done my homework before even approaching Raymond with the first game weeks ago and knew his sister's name, but I'd never said it to him. It was a tactic that I hadn't wanted to use, making it too personal.

Well, there wasn't much less personal than sitting in a woman's living room, making her defend her mothering skills.

"Halia, lots of kids get mixed up in drugs. Rich people's kids. Poor. Single parents. Married. This wasn't all on you.

"I was raised in a great family, nice neighborhood, parents together, siblings that I got along with." I raised and dropped my hands in a helpless gesture. I swallowed hard then said, "And I'm a gambling addict. It's a crap shoot."

But she didn't seem to hear me. She was staring at a picture of Raymond and DeeDee that sat on the coffee table in front of us. Raymond was maybe seven or eight, and he held toddler

DeeDee's hand. His trademark smile had already developed, and he looked at his sister, not the camera, with adoring eyes.

"I didn't want nobody's money. I still don't. I just wanted my baby healthy. And safe."

"I know."

"And she is. Was."

"She will be, Halia. She will be."

She focused on me again. "All I want is my daughter clean and with me and my boy safe and out of reach of that L'il Roy. Can you make that happen?" There was dismissal and scorn in her voice.

"Yes. I can make that happen."

I saw Jack shift in his chair, but he wisely didn't say anything.

"How?" Halia said.

"I'm not sure yet. I have some ideas. But I need to know exactly what Raymond has told the authorities."

"Nothing."

"Nothing? I find that hard to believe."

"It's true. He wouldn't say anything. Not even to Coach Wayne, who he respects more than anyone in the world. But he wouldn't confirm or deny nothing. To nobody. That's why Coach Wayne said it'd be a good idea if Raymond left school for a bit."

"And since then?"

"Every time they came to question him, he said he had nothing to say, and if they wanted to formally charge him then he'd have his attorney meet them at the police station." She smiled grimly. "Kids in this neighborhood learn their rights early."

"Halia, did Raymond tell you I might contact you?"

She nodded. "He said you might call. Right before he left."

"I was told you kicked him out."

She shook her head. "No. After the second day of people parked on our front walk and calls—Lord, there were the phone calls—he left." Her voice cracked a bit at the last. She was used to him being gone, but there was a big difference between knowing your kid was safe on the campus of a major university and being cloistered with the neighborhood's worst gangster. "I begged him to stay. But he left."

"To protect you," I needlessly said.

She nodded. "He's always felt he had to take care of me. And DeeDee."

"Halia, you know if this doesn't go away soon, it's going to get worse. There's no paper trail, but sooner or later somebody's going to figure out your insurance didn't really cover DeeDee's rehab stay."

"That's exactly what Raymond said. That's when he said you might be trying to contact him here."

He'd probably thrown his phone away, smart kid, and knew that I'd have to resort to going through his mother. Or maybe he wanted to put his mother between us if I came looking for him?

"What did he tell you to tell me if I called you?"

"To find out what you can do to help him."

I took a deep breath and looked at Jack, who shrugged at me. Helping Raymond would help me. And Vince. That's what Raymond was counting on.

"All right. Let me give you my phone number. And the name of the hotel we're staying at. I'd like you to set up a meet with Raymond and me. Do you think you can do that?"

She'd jumped up and was bringing me paper and pen. I ripped the paper from the tablet and put it on the hard coffee table. I'd seen one too many cop shows where they'd etched on the pad and gotten the bad guy's phone number.

So, I guess that made me the bad guy?

"Yes. I can do that. He said if you contacted me, it would probably be better to go through me than for you to contact him directly."

"He was right. But there's some things he and I need to say

face to face." I handed her the paper with my phone number and our hotel name. "Obviously, you need to lose this after this is all over."

She nodded, looked at the paper and put it in her pants pocket.

"Halia, if you had the means, could you take DeeDee out of rehab and you, she and Raymond go somewhere else?"

"What do you mean?"

"If I were able to get you an apartment or rent a house for the three of you for awhile, until this all died down—"

"You mean run from the law?"

I looked over at Jack, who only waited for me to continue. "No. Nothing like that. I mean when we're sure that Raymond won't be arr...brought in for questioning. To get the three of you out of this neighborhood. Make a fresh start somewhere. Is DeeDee strong enough to leave rehab?"

Halia nodded. "She's supposed to come home soon. I think that's why—" She clamped her mouth shut.

"Why what?"

She looked from me to Jack and back again. "Raymond told me what JoJo looked like so I'd know it was you if you got ahold of me. But I don't know nothing about this man."

"He's...it's fine. He's a friend trying to help me out."

She looked back to Jack, who looked at Halia for a moment then gave a slight nod.

Apparently, that was enough for her. "DeeDee's well enough to come out of rehab and enter into some sort of treatment that she can do at home. But we—Raymond and I—were so worried about her coming right back into this area. Him at school, me having to work, nobody to keep an eye on her. I told Raymond it would be better if we could start new somewhere else. Get out of this place." She wrung her hands, looked down at her feet. "But I didn't have any money for that. The rehab took all the money Raymond...earned. I told him that." Her voice was cracking as she said, "I told him we could do it, leave here, with a little more money."

So that's why he'd gone to Bubba Kinney for a stake. One last time to get his mother and sister out of harm's way. And it had to be done fast as Central Iowa's window of being a favorite was closing. JoJo had told him that.

And then walked away.

An immense rush of relief went through me that this hadn't all been about greed for Raymond. He hadn't been entirely consumed by the voice. It had been waging war with genuine need. He'd just needed one more big score.

And yet, it was always that one last job that tripped you up.

I leaned forward and patted her knee. "It's okay, Halia. But maybe you should start making those arrangements for the three of you to find a place where DeeDee can continue treatment in a safer environment.

"I have a sister near Atlanta. In a real nice, safe area. I'd thought to go there. I'd even contacted her, and she got me some information on a place where DeeDee could see somebody."

"That sounds great."

"But there's no money for that, now."

"You let me worry about that. Just make your plans."

"But..."

I changed the subject back to our most important issue. "So Raymond really thinks that's all the authorities have? Still? Just this Bubba Kinney?"

She nodded again. "Yes. He seems pretty sure of it."

"Then Bubba Kinney has to go away."

"How does that happen?"

"Yeah, JoJo," Jack said, piping in for the first time. "How exactly does that happen?"

Twenty

❖❖

THE RIDE BACK TO THE MOTEL was deadly quiet. My mind was spun with how to make this all come out okay. Jack was…well, I didn't really know what Jack was thinking.

He pulled the car into a parking lot in front of a liquor store, jammed the car into park, and took the keys with him as he left, slamming the car door in the process.

Jack was apparently thinking about bourbon.

He took just a few steps then turned around, came around to my side of the car and opened my door. "Just some Diet Coke," I said, but he wasn't interested in my order.

He had his hand outstretched, palm up. "Give me your phone."

"What?"

"Your phone. Give it to me."

He was wearing his most stern cop face, and I knew better than to argue with him. I pulled my phone out of my jacket pocket and gave it to Jack. He started to rise, but then hunkered back down into my space. "This is it? No burner phones in those pockets?"

"That's it." He raised a brow at me. "You want to search me?" I said, holding my hands up from my sides.

He snorted. "Later." He shut my door and headed into the liquor store. His Mecca. His Sports Book.

I didn't blame him. I would have loved being taken over by the rush of the Hummer. But my addiction—compulsion, whatever—wasn't as easily assuaged.

Day Eleven without placing a bet was coming to a close. A bourbon sounded good.

Jack came out a few minutes later, putting the bag with his purchases on the back seat of the rental car. "Can I have my phone back now?" I said, holding out my hand.

"Not yet." We drove in silence the rest of the way to the hotel and stayed that way up to our rooms. Room—singular—for all intents and purposes, with Jack demanding the adjoining door be left open. Let's face it, I didn't really mind that.

After entering the room, Jack took an ice bucket and disappeared. I unpacked his booty—a bottle of bourbon, a six pack of Diet Coke and a can of nuts, which I opened right away. He came back in, flipping the key card on the bureau where I'd set up our make-shift cocktail bar. We were in what was ostensibly my room, though both had two queen beds and neither of us had settled in, our bags still by the doors where we'd dropped them earlier.

I put a couple of cubes in one of the hotel's glasses then filled half of it with Diet Coke before topping it off with bourbon. I motioned the bottle to him. "Not yet," he said, so I put the bottle down and, taking my drink and the can of nuts, settled into the upholstered side chair, placing my things on the round table next to it. I looked to my side, out the window. It was an amazing view of the Chicago skyline with Lake Michigan in the background. It would be spectacular in the morning, but the lights with the black lake beyond held a different type of beauty.

"Who do you think I'm going to call?" I asked, taking a sip of my drink.

"Somebody who can 'take care of'," he did his hands in air quotes, which was so not Jack's style, "Bubba Kinney."

"Oh, come on. Who do I even know who could..." I

stopped and took a sip of my drink.

He didn't say anything, just came over and set his untouched glass on the table next to mine. He stood behind me, looked out the window. "Great view. Tell Lor she picked well."

I nodded, taking another sip. I turned fully facing the window now, with the hallway light on behind us, it was like looking into a dull mirror, seeing our outlines, but not being able to see each other's faces clearly. Maybe that was just as well.

I held the can of nuts up to Jack, but he shook his head. "I figured we could order room service, but thought I'd get something to hold us over."

"Good thinking, I'm starving."

He went in search of a menu, brought it back and gave it to me. I gave it a quick look, but it was too dark on this side of the room. "Need more light?" Jack asked.

"Yes, but I like this, it's so pretty looking out." I handed the menu back to him. "Just get me a cheeseburger and fries."

He went back to the phone, placed the order then came back to stand behind me again. I held his glass up to him. "Not yet."

"You back on duty? Standing guard?"

He chuckled. "Hardly. But I do need to call Frank and check in."

"I need to call Lor and do the same," I said holding my hand up for my phone.

Jack took it out of his pants pocket, pulled up the contact info, then handed me the phone as it was ringing. "Unbelievable," I muttered just as Lor picked up. It was just past midnight here, ten Vegas time.

"Hey, it's me. Just checking in to make sure everything was okay there."

"Everything's fine. We're just watching TV. How's everything there?"

"Good, I guess." I wasn't in jail. Or dead. "Yeah, good."

"Do you still think you'll come home tomorrow?"

"I hope so."

She told me what mail had come that day, a couple of other mundane things, then handed the phone to Ben. He and I chatted for a little while, he carefully asking me nothing that I couldn't—or wouldn't—answer, then I hung up. At least the household was fine and not something I needed to worry about.

Jack held his hand open, and I put my phone in it. "Jack, you don't really think I'd have a hit put out on Bubba Kinney, do you?"

He put his phone in his pants pocket, stroked his face with his hand. "No."

"And even if I would, I wouldn't call Vince for it. I have no idea who I'd call, but certainly not Vince."

"Why not? 'Fraid it'd make for awkward pillow talk?"

I ignored his comment. "First of all, Vince isn't into murder for hire."

Jack snorted. "Don't be so sure."

"Oh come on, there's a huge leap between..." I chose to just let it all lie.

"He's ruthless," Jack said quietly after a moment.

"He's a businessman."

"He preys on the weak."

"Am I included in that category?"

"You're not who I picture when I think of Vince's usual clients."

"That's why I'm so good at what I do. Did. How JoJo was able to get away with it all. Nobody would ever picture Anna Dawson doing what JoJo did."

"Again with the third person?"

I waved that away. "Whatever. You're right. She's dead and buried anyway. But back to my calling in a hit."

He held up a hand, halting me, "I've looked the other way a lot today. *A lot*, Johanna."

"I know."

"There's no way I could do that if Bubba Kinney suddenly disappeared."

"I know that, too. I wouldn't want you to."

"If this shit hits the fan—and there's a good chance it might—I need to be able to protect you the best way I can. I need to be able to say I was with you all the time and there was no way you could have contacted anybody."

Well, when he put it that way. "What about the hotel phone when you're in the john?"

"They'd have a record of a call made. You wouldn't be that stupid."

I snorted. "Sure about that?"

"Not really. That's why I just mentioned they'd have records."

We both chuckled. He put his hand on my shoulder and gently squeezed. "I'm going to go next door and call Frank."

"I'm going to take a quick shower before the food gets here."

He went into the next room, leaving the doors open wide. I grabbed my bag and put it on one of the beds, unzipped it and found my toiletries, clean panties and a tee that hung to my knees that I used for pajamas.

The shower felt amazing. I stood with my head directly under the powerful stream for a very long time. Apparently, I'd been waterlogged in my ears too, because I'd never heard Jack enter the bathroom. But JoJo's red, sequined tube top sat front and center on the vanity. I mentally snorted. Yeah. Right.

And then I realized he'd probably just used it as an excuse to go through my stuff.

When I came out of the bathroom a while later, wet hair slicked back, long tee on, Jack took one look at me, shrugged and said, "Can't blame a guy for trying."

He was at the table in front of the window, a tray of food in front of him, eating a burger. His glass was half empty.

"You talked to Frank?" He nodded, taking a bite of his burger. "Everything okay?" Another nod. "Anything new in Paulie's case?"

By now he'd swallowed, wiped his mouth with his napkin, and taken a drink from his glass. "Nope."

"You'll probably never solve this one," I said. "There's just too many suspects. And you'll never know all the fires Paulie had irons in. Men like him dabble."

"Yeah, you're probably right," he admitted.

"And you're okay with that?" I knew Vince wouldn't be. I couldn't really see Jack letting it go, either.

"Hell no, I'm not okay with that. Do you have any idea how many murders go unsolved? This isn't fucking *CSI*. It's not going to be neatly wrapped up by the end of the episode."

"That's what I'm saying." I sat in the chair opposite him and started in on my dinner. The fries were kind of mushy and only slightly warm by now, but I still scarfed them down.

"Maybe I should switch to Vice. Seems like I could bring in some heavy hitters in that department."

"Very funny." I took another bite of burger, savored, chewed, swallowed. "Why *are* you homicide, anyway?"

He leaned forward, his arms on the table. "I speak for the dead that are no longer able to."

My mind reached for something. "Wait a minute. That was from the opening of some cop show."

He leaned back, smiled. "Yeah. Good line. Wish I'd thought of it."

We ate in silence for awhile longer. "No, really," I finally said. "Why homicide? There's justice to be had in other departments. And you wouldn't have to see the things you must see on a daily basis."

I sat my plate back onto the room service tray. Jack had brought the ice, bourbon and pop over to the table, and I cracked myself a new Diet Coke, pouring it into my glass. He picked up the bottle, but I shook my head. "I'm good."

He put his dishes on the tray also, covering it. He poured another splash of booze into his glass. I leaned back in my chair, glass in hand, stretching out my legs under the table.

He leaned forward, put his hand under the table, took one of my legs in his hand and lifted it so my foot lay across his thigh. He absently cupped the underside of my calf, his fingers a feather-light stroke. He used his other to hold his glass, but he didn't drink. He looked out the windows while I watched him in silence.

And waited.

"Homicide is the best. But besides that, it's the ultimate puzzle. I like puzzles." He looked at me when he said that. I would have expected his cop face, but no, it was the soft Jack that watched me. Well, as soft as Jack can get.

I didn't say anything, and after a moment he looked back at the dark night in front of us. "But it's more than that. It's trying to understand why somebody would hurt someone else."

"You told me when Danny was killed. Revenge or money."

He nodded. "Yeah, most of the time it is. Those are the easy ones. The ones I can understand."

"You understand murder?"

He shrugged, took a small sip of his drink. "I can understand it for those reasons. I don't like it, and I'll still try like hell to get 'em behind bars. But I understand it." He put his glass down, reached under the table and took my other leg. His hand was cold from the cool glass, and my leg jumped a tiny bit.

"Easy," he whispered like he was gentling a skittish colt.

I wasn't skittish. I probably should have been, but I wasn't. I knew exactly what I wanted. What I'd always wanted since meeting Jack Schiller on the steps of a twelve-steps program.

"It's those fuckers who beat their kids to death. Or psychos who kill for the thrill of it. That I don't get. I want to. I try to. I figure it'd be that much easier to catch them. But I don't. I don't understand." His voice was soft. I wasn't sure he was even talking to me anymore.

"Nobody can understand that," I said, drawing his gaze back to me. He looked at me like I'd just come into the room, surprising him. There were ghosts in his eyes that took a moment to clear. I came back into focus for him, and his face softened all the more.

His hands ran up and down the back of my calves. His eyes dipped to my neck. To my horseshoe necklace, and stayed there. "When I dream...sometimes..."

"Jack?" I whispered.

His brown, sad eyes moved up my neck to meet my gaze. "When I dream of naked women, I—"

"You dream of naked women a lot?"

He shrugged. "I'm a guy."

"Go on."

"Whenever there's a naked woman in my dreams, no matter who she is..."

I nudged his thigh with my foot for him to go on.

"They're wearing that necklace."

I looked at him for a long time, then slid my legs through his hands and off his lap. I stood up, pushed my chair in, and turned away from him and the table.

"Hey, I'm sorry, I—"

His next words died in his mouth, and I peeled my T-shirt over my head, revealing the red top underneath. I peeked at him over my shoulder. He was already out of his chair and headed toward me. He stopped, and for a second I thought he'd start spouting all the reasons why he and I wouldn't work. That nothing had really changed since he'd dumped me. And that he'd spent most of the day looking the other way as I'd tried to cover up my crimes. That I was sort of seeing Vince Santini.

All true (although I wasn't really sure of my status with Vince since that night on the cliff, and I certainly wasn't thinking about him right now). All valid. All things for which I had no comeback.

But instead of saying any of those things, Jack reached behind him, grabbed a few cubes out of the ice bucket and started toward me, a huge grin covering his rugged face.

And one brow raised.

Twenty-One

❖❖

"YEAH?" I HEARD JACK SAY in the morning. Really early in the morning if the dusty Chicago skyline was any indication.

"She's here," he said, and I pulled my head out from under the covers to see who the hell he was talking to so early. And why the hell he'd left our bed to talk to anybody? "It doesn't matter who I am. I'm nobody."

Yeah? Well, my body was humming in a pretty serious way for having spent it with nobody. I tried to shake the good sex hangover from my head. To whom was Jack a nobody?

I flipped the covers away from my body. The red tube top was now being worn as a belt and I pulled it down and over my hips and tossed it to the floor as I sat up on the edge of the bed and reached for my shirt, which was on the floor next to the bed where I'd dropped it last night.

Jack was standing in the doorway of the adjoining room, sliding his jeans up his legs, his phone cradled between his ear and shoulder. No, wait. He was cradling *my* phone.

I made a motion and drew his attention. He finished getting his pants up and walked to the bed. "Here she is," he said, handing me my phone. I'd never even heard it ring.

"Hello?"

"JoJo," Raymond Joseph said.

"Where are you?"

"It doesn't matter. Nowhere."

"Are you okay?" He snorted. Yeah, okay, stupid question. "I mean…well, shit."

"Yeah, that about sums it up…shit."

"What were you thinking going to Bubba Kinney?" I waited for him to explain his need to help get DeeDee and Halia somewhere safe. Or, if not, to ream me for disappearing on him, forcing him to go elsewhere.

"Stupid move. No excuses."

"How'd you even find him?"

"He's known around town. The locals know him. He's a dirtbag, but brags about the killing he makes gambling. I figured he was either a bookie, knew of one, or would be interested in staking a can't-lose bet. I just didn't count on him having a conscience where CIU was concerned."

"Oh, Raymond," I said softly, which promptly pissed him off.

"Fuck that. I'm not about to turn you."

"I know that." Jack had his jeans buttoned up the fly, but the top remained undone. He crossed his arms over his bare, hairy chest and leaned against the wall in front of me. "What are you calling me on, anyway?" I asked Raymond, remembering Jack's warning about phone records, and how careful JoJo had always been about using a disposable phone.

Until I'd given Halia this number last night. Couldn't have been helped.

"A hot cell phone. The number that called you can't be traced back to me."

"No, but the call can be traced to the tower that your phone is using." Jack gave me a look that he was impressed I'd known that (no need to tell him I hadn't until Lor had explained it to me a few days ago). Then, he seemed to remember how I would have gained and used that knowledge, and a frown crept across his rough face.

I wasn't sure, but I think he cast an eye toward where the bourbon bottle sat on the table where he'd left it last night to join me. Sheesh, I sure drove the men in my world to real healthy choices.

"I'm calling from the neighborhood that the phone was lifted from. Mr. and Mrs. Suburb and their cell tower."

"Oh," I said, but I was impressed. "A trick you learned from L'il Roy?"

"Fuck you."

"Where'd you get the phone, then, if not L'il Roy? Or are you now lifting cell phones in the food court at suburban malls?"

"Listen. Just back off, all right? You ain't got nothing to worry about on my end. Get the hell out of Chicago."

"If I had nothing to worry about, why'd you tell your mother about JoJo? What I looked like? Warn her that I might be showing up?"

"I was right, wasn't I? You did show up. And why exactly is that? You here to threaten me, JoJo?"

"No. I'm just looking for a happy ending here." I heard a soft snort from Jack, but when I looked at him, he was looking beyond me, out to the windows and the lightening skyline. "For me, yeah, but also for you, Halia and DeeDee."

There was a long sigh on the other end of the line. "All right. Let me make some calls. I'll call you back later."

"No. No more calls. Let's pick a time and place right now to meet."

Another long sigh. "Fine. Where are you staying?" I told him, and he let out a low whistle. "Nice place. Guess crime pays, after all." I peeked at Jack, but he didn't seem to hear that. I wasn't really sure how much on Raymond's end he could hear, but he was certainly staying on my side of the room.

He gave me directions to a meeting place, and we agreed on eleven this morning. Which was good because I wanted to check in with Jimmy myself and see if his people knew anything new.

Vince too, but I didn't think Jack would go for that.

"Hey, Raymond, just so you don't think I'm pulling anything, I won't be alone when I meet you. The guy who answered my phone will be with me. I just don't want you to think I'm trying anything when he shows up with me."

"'Fraid of me, JoJo?" There was a bit of a taunt in his voice.

"Nope. It's in both of our best interests to stick together on this, you know that, too, or you wouldn't be calling me now."

"Best interest for each of us would be for the other one to disappear."

It certainly would be in mine. And I hadn't thought about it, but I guess it would be for Raymond, too. "That may be true, but it's not something I'm...capable of." I took a deep breath. "And neither are you."

"No," he said quickly. "But L'il Roy is." The line went dead.

I put the phone on the table next to the unopened can of pop. I looked up at Jack. "You get most of that?"

He nodded. "So, we meet him at eleven?"

I nodded. Jack was already unbuttoning his jeans, a smile creeping across his beard-stubbled cheeks. "That gives us several hours," he said.

"I need a monster breakfast, and when it's a little later Vegas time, I want to call Jimmy," I warned, but I was already scooching back on the bed, making room.

"Plenty of time," he said, stepping out of his pants.

"JIMMY? HEY, I'M SORRY to call so early," I said two hours later. Two glorious hours later.

"That's okay, Anna. I'm up. In fact, I was just about to call you, but I was waiting 'cuz I didn't want to wake up the whole house."

"I'm not in Vegas."

"Dubuque?"

"No. Chicago."

"Good. That's good. Might even be better. You ain't done nothing, yet, have you? Nothing you can't undo?"

Did everyone think I was capable of murdering Raymond Joseph, either myself or by making a phone call?

Which led me to the thought I'd been avoiding. If exposure for myself—and Vince—was truly at stake, what *was* I capable of doing?

"No," I answered, and thought I heard Jimmy sigh in relief.

"Well, you need to sit tight, this thing is about to blow up."

"What do you mean?" There must have been something in my voice, because Jack, freshly showered and shaven, who had started dressing after dialing my phone and handing it to me, now stopped and watched me.

"I'm hearing that the whole Bubba Kinney story is falling apart. The cops in Dubuque have been talking to three different people for the last seven hours, pretty much all through the night."

"What three people?" My God, how many people had this domino affected?

"Don't know."

"What did they say?"

"Not sure of that either, but my guy says things are starting to move."

"Move? Which way? Will they be arresting Raymond? Do they know about…anything beyond what Bubba Kinney told them?"

"I don't know. Can you hold tight for a couple of hours? I should know more then."

I looked at the alarm clock on the bedside table. "I'll be with Raymond in a couple of hours."

"That might be good. Depending on what shakes out. I'll call you as soon as I know anything. Hopefully it will be before or after meeting the boys."

"Okay. Thanks, Jimmy."

"Sure thing, Anna."

I replayed Jimmy's story for Jack. "What do you think is happening?" I asked him.

Jack shrugged as he buttoned up his white, cotton shirt. "They could be corroborating Bubba's statement. They could be refuting it. They could have other information about Raymond."

"What other information?"

"You'd know that better than I would."

I didn't know what to think anymore. Was whatever was happening in Dubuque going to affect my meeting with Raymond? Did Raymond know what was happening? Would I be walking into some kind of trap?

"Maybe you should stay here," I said to Jack.

He looked up from his shirt. "Yeah, right. That's gonna happen."

I sighed. Yeah, that wasn't going to fly. "Okay, now what?"

He looked at the clock. "Monster...*monster* breakfast."

HE ENDED UP NOT EATING nearly as much as I did. Not much of a breakfast eater, Jack. Was that true of all drinkers? Or was I just used to daily breakfast with the boys as my big meal of the day?

"So, how are you able to help me out with this all and not feel compelled to arrest me?"

He almost choked on his coffee. "What?"

I looked around, but the diner we'd found wasn't very busy, and the customers that were there sat well away from us. "You heard me."

"Who says I don't want to arrest you?"

"You haven't so far."

He raised his eyebrow. "Maybe I just wanted one last night with you."

I knew he was joking, but the word 'last' resonated a little too deeply with me.

"Hey, I'm just kidding," he said, reaching for my hand, but I picked up my coffee cup instead and nodded my understanding while taking a gulp.

He sat back, straightened along the back of the booth. "Okay. Yeah, I should have put cuffs on you the minute we stepped off that plane. Hell, I should have had you in for questioning in Vegas once I'd seen those clothes."

I took another sip of coffee, sat back myself, putting space between us, and nodded for him to continue.

"I'm a cop. In theory, there should be no difference between levels and kinds of law breaking."

"But there is?"

"For me, yeah, I guess there is." He scrubbed his hand down his face. "There probably is for every cop. There is for everybody, isn't there? I mean, you wouldn't think the same about someone who stole a loaf of bread to feed his family as a man who cheated people out of their life savings."

"I didn't need to feed my family."

He waved a hand of dismissal. "I don't really give a shit about point shaving. Is it a crime? Yeah. Who's hurt? Gamblers. Did you know that ninety percent of sports gambling is done illegally? Either through bookies or online accounts, which are done offshore because it's illegal to sports bet anywhere in the U.S. except for Nevada."

"And Delaware," I corrected.

"What?"

"Delaware, too. Actually it's legal in Delaware, Nevada, Montana and Oregon, though only Nevada and Delaware currently allow it. But the NCAA has threatened to ban any kind of playoff games in the state if Delaware allows college sports betting, so they don't. Same with New Jersey, who's been looking into sports gambling for years."

"Trust you to know all that," he said, no amusement in his voice.

"I can spout the tenets of the Professional and Amateur Sports Protection Act of 1992 if you want."

"Thank you, but no."

"So really, the victims are other criminals. You can justify it that way?"

"Maybe." He took another sip from his cup then set it back on the table. "And yes, the innocent teammates of the perp are affected. Win/loss records. Bids to tournaments. And that can all add up to revenue for schools that may be gained or lost based on fixed games. But usually point shaving doesn't affect the outcome of the game, just the point spread."

"Geez, Jack, you sound like the rationalizing voice in my head. How about the integrity of the game?"

"Integrity? In professional sports? How many steroid scandals will crop up in baseball this year? Care to make an over/under bet on that? How many NFL players are going to get caught with guns at nightclubs this season? How many hockey players were taking Sudafed for a high on the ice? Don't talk to me about the integrity of the game."

"That's the pros. Well, most of that stuff, anyway." I'm sure steroid abuse happened in college sports too, but I let it lie for now. Jack was making my point for me, I'd let him.

"The integrity of college sports? The purity of the game should not be corrupted? What about all those recruiting violations? SUVs put in players' parents' names? Cushy, no-show jobs for players in the off-season? Overzealous alumni wanting to help out the program? These kids—some of them, at certain schools—are being paid to play. Maybe they should be, I don't know. But I do know it's an uneven playing field for a kid like Raymond, whose family desperately needs the money, but chooses to go to a clean school...for that *very* reason." His voice was louder, more forceful, but he quickly pulled himself in check. He looked around, saw nobody had noticed, then leaned forward, putting his elbows on the table, his white shirt sleeve coming dangerously close to a displaced drop of syrup.

"So yeah, I should probably be making phone calls to the Dubuque police right now. But for whatever reason, I'm here, having breakfast, and about to go meet Raymond Joseph. That okay with you?"

I leaned forward too, took my napkin and dabbed up the syrup drop, brushing his arm as I did. "Yeah, it's okay. More than okay."

Twenty-Two

❖

IT WASN'T RAYMOND who met us at the designated spot. He'd sold me out. Sent L'il Roy, or someone just as scary, to make sure I was no threat to him or his family.

We were in the right place, a deserted part of the Chicago railway system on the South Side. There were tracks crisscrossing around us, and several train cars stood empty. The faded Air Jordan billboard—many years old, I don't even think they make that particular shoe anymore—that Raymond had given me as a marker was a few feet away.

I also knew we were where we were supposed to be because the thug walking toward us showed no surprise at our presence. He even put his hands into his sweatshirt front pocket, probably wrapping his hands around a gun handle.

He wore a ratty hoodie sweatshirt—not nearly enough warmth for mid-winter Chicago—jeans that hung down his hips, and black boots, untied, with the tongue hanging forward. He was a kid, probably not much older than Raymond, but this kid was used to the streets, not campus life.

"I'm so sorry I got you into this," I whispered to Jack.

He snorted. "A little late for that now. Besides, I didn't give you much choice." He directed his next comment to the hood nearing us. "Raymond."

"No," I whispered, "That's just it, that's not—"

"Who the hell are you?" Raymond's voice came out of the man's body.

I stared. Hard. It took a while for me to make it out, but it was indeed Raymond. Gone were his trademark braids. Instead his hair stood straight up, a good six or seven inches high, in an unshaped pile of frizz.

But it wasn't just the hair that had thrown me. His face wasn't even the same shape. When he got a few feet away he stopped, still eyeing Jack, and I was able to put it together. He'd lost weight—a lot of weight—in the short time since I'd last seen him. But on top of the shrunken effect, there were odd-shaped bumps, which I now realized were the aftereffects of somebody beating the shit out of him. His beautiful mocha skin was a rainbow of ugly yellows and purples. There were two scabbed slices running down his cheeks.

"Jesus, Raymond, what the hell happened to you?"

He turned his gaze from Jack to me, and I almost took a step back. He'd looked at me—at JoJo—with hatred before, and I would have expected that, but this look was something more. Mixed with hatred was defeat.

A look I'd never seen from a competitor like Raymond Joseph.

He only shrugged. Tough guy. But I knew better. This was a kid who, yes, had grown up in this neighborhood, but had spent his nights playing basketball, not standing on street corners.

"L'il Roy did this to you?" Another shrug. "But I thought he was your friend?"

"Price of admission," he said.

I'm no innocent, I'd taken a good beating—though Paulie had tried hard not to mar my face—but I didn't understand this kind of violence. In my world, you can't pay up, you get hurt. Simple. Fair, in its own way.

"Why did you need to be admitted?"

He looked at Jack again, then back to me. "It's okay, you

can talk in front of Jack," I said then regretted it. What if part of this "admission" process involved murder, or something else that wouldn't fit with Jack's sense of justice. Raymond should know that Jack was a cop, but I was afraid he'd turn around and I'd never see him again.

As if sensing my indecision, Jack said, "I'll wait in the car."

"Thanks," I said.

He stepped to Raymond. "Mind if I pat you down? I can't leave her alone with you otherwise."

"Jack, there's no—"

"Whatever," Raymond said, holding out his hands, spreading his legs. He took the stance way too naturally, and my heart ached that this might be Raymond's future.

Jack patted him down quickly. Raymond didn't seem to notice the practiced efficiency that Jack possessed. Or if he did, he didn't say anything. He would have to think I wasn't stupid enough to bring a cop with me, as much as I had to lose in all of this.

He'd be wrong about my stupid factor.

"Give a wave if you need me," Jack said to me, then left us. I heard the car door close behind me. We'd parked about thirty yards away from where Raymond and I now stood.

He motioned with his chin to the car behind me. "That your bodyguard?"

A flash of Jack guarding my body—several times—last night whisked through me. "Something like that."

"You that high up you need a bodyguard? Shit, JoJo, what exactly am I dealing with?"

"No, it's not like that. Jack is a friend. He's just with me for this trip, in case I needed backup."

"To take me out?"

I looked squarely at him. "No. I'm not here to do that. And I think you know that or you never would have agreed to meet me."

"Maybe I just wanted to get the whole thing over with."

"No. You're not a quitter, Raymond."

He looked down at his feet, but didn't comment. I decided to get back to where we'd left off when Jack went to the car. "Why did you need to be admitted to L'il Roy's gang?" Nothing. "Why hold out now? I'm in this as deep as you are—deeper really. It's in our best interest to work together."

"Your best interest," he said. "My best interest would be to tell them all about you."

"Why haven't you?"

He looked away, down the train tracks, took a deep breath, then turned back to me. "Who says I haven't?"

"You haven't," I bluffed. It paid off. I knew from the flicker of his eyes away and then back to me, that I was right. Oldest tell in the books. Raymond would not make a great poker player. "I know that as surely as you know I didn't come here to get rid of you."

Vince's words rang through my ears, but I pushed them away. There were many ways I could clean up this mess without having to hurt Raymond. Hell, another week with L'il Roy's crowd and it might be taken care of for me.

But I knew I didn't want that. Not really. "Come on, Raymond, cards on the table. Why did you leave your mom's and go to L'il Roy's?"

"Things got crazy at my momma's house. Reporters, neighbors, it was a zoo. I figured it'd be better if I left."

"So why not take her with you and go somewhere else? Why did you go alone to L'il Roy's? Why did you take the price of admission if this was all until the reporters stopped coming around?"

"It wasn't. Not really. I had to plan for the future."

"And L'il Roy's your future?"

"If things go bad with the Bubba Kinney thing and I get sent away, it's better on the inside to be connected. Plus, L'il Roy said if I joined up and then got sent up, he'd take care of my mom and DeeDee."

"You believe that?"

He shrugged. "I want to believe it. And, look, my life is over anyway, even if they don't press any charges."

"How do you figure?"

"Ain't nobody going to touch me to play. Or coach."

"But you could go back to school and get your degree. You had to be close to it."

He nodded. "I woulda made it in four years. Heavy load spring term, but I would have graduated."

"That's great. You can still do that. What was your major?"

"Physical rehabilitation. I figured when I was done playing, if I didn't coach, I could get on with a college or maybe even the pros as a trainer." He stooped, picked up a rock and hurled it at one of the empty train cars. The hollow noise the stone made sent a shiver down me. "I just wanted to be involved in the game, you know?"

"Yeah, I know."

"There's no way any team would let me even tape a player's ankles with point-shaving accusations. Even if they don't stick."

He was right. He was finished with basketball, in any form.

"So, if I came out of this without jail time, and no way to be near the game…" He threw another rock. "I figured I better cement myself with the powers that be in my backyard."

"Okay. I get it. In a way, it's a good plan, Raymond, but it's not necessary. We can figure something else out."

"We?" He raised his eyebrows, then narrowed his eyes. "There's no we in this."

"We. I'm here to help find a way so you don't end up like L'il Roy?"

His hand twitched mid-throw, the rock going off in a helter-skelter direction. He turned to me. "No. You don't belong here. You don't need to be involved anymore."

"Why? I can see you not wanting me involved because of further charges, but I'm the one who dragged you into all of this."

"True. And it sucks. But…DeeDee's clean."

"Yeah."

"And, what you did that last time. In that parking lot?"

"You mean putting my phone in your pocket?"

He nodded. "You know how I found it? When I found it?"

"No, how?"

"I went home and threw that jacket somewhere. It's not one I usually wear. And then, just two days later, I called you. And I heard a ringing coming from my jacket, thrown over a chair in my apartment. I didn't get it for a minute. And then I did."

What could I say? Nothing, so I kept my mouth shut.

"I was so royally pissed at you. At myself…"

"That's usually how it works," I said, knowing that feeling well. Or at least I used to.

Day Twelve.

"Yeah."

"You forgot one part in there, Raymond."

"What?"

"Your mother calling and saying DeeDee was ready to come home. And how she was afraid about what that could mean."

He hung his head. "She told you about that?"

I put my hand on his shoulder. I hadn't touched him much—if at all—as JoJo, but somehow he was able to accept Anna's comfort. "Yeah, she told me. It wasn't a very smart thing you did, Raymond, going to Bubba Kinney."

He snorted. "Ya think?"

I squeezed his shoulder. "But you did it for the right reasons. And believe me, compulsive gamblers—people with a real problem—do lots more stupid stuff all the time."

"You trying to make me feel better by ranking my stupidity?"

I chuckled. "Raymond, I could tell you stories of stupid

things gamblers do that you wouldn't believe…that's why it's called gambling."

He looked at me again, not touching me, but neither pulling away from my hand on his shoulder. "We have to figure out how to deal with this Bubba Kinney guy," I said.

"That may have already been done for you," Jack said behind me.

I whirled around to find he was about three steps away, which he closed quickly. The car door was open, which is why I hadn't heard him. He was holding out my phone to me. "Jimmy for you."

I took the phone from him and took a couple of steps away from Jack, who was now standing next to Raymond. "Jimmy? What's up?"

"It's your lucky day, Anna," Jimmy said. I could hear the telltale sounds of a casino behind him. I looked at my watch, which I'd kept on Vegas time.

"Are you at breakfast?"

"Yeah, well I was. I just left Ben and Gus."

I relaxed a little. Things were normal in Vegas, anyway. "What's happened?"

"The cops in Dubuque are throwing in the towel. The feds have packed up and gone back to D.C."

"What? Why?"

"Three different people came forward and totally blew this Bubba Kinney's story all ta hell."

I looked at Raymond, who was watching me. "But, Bubba's story is right."

"Not according to these three guys."

"What did they say?"

"I don't know everything. My guy in Dubuque is just now getting all the details. But it looks like these three—I don't know, witnesses, I guess—all came forward and said that Bubba Kinney was pissed 'cuz he'd lost a lot of money on the Hogs recently and so he was going to make the players pay. He was starting with the Joseph kid."

"But...but..."

I could almost hear Jimmy's shrug, his hefty shoulders raising and lowering. "Yeah, I know, but I guess all three stories mesh."

Vince. It had to be. Vince, not able to help me in Chicago, and knowing that I ultimately wouldn't be able to hurt Raymond, had arranged for this. I don't know how he did it, but I was deeply grateful.

I hadn't called for a hit on Bubba. I hadn't needed to because this was so much better. If Bubba Kinney had turned up dead, there'd be even more suspicion on Raymond. By making him out to be some crackpot disgruntled gambler, Raymond would look like the victim.

My God, might he even be able to play basketball again?

"Anna, I got to go," Jimmy said to me. "I'll call when I know any more, but it looks like your boy will be in the clear."

"Thanks so much," I said to Jimmy, my voice cracking, which caused Raymond and Jack both to take a step toward me, Jack even outstretching a hand to me.

I hung up the phone and explained the situation to Jack and Raymond. They both looked at me with disbelief. Raymond's mixed with hesitant relief, Jack's with suspicion.

"Well, that was awfully neat and tidy," Jack said, causing Raymond to look at him then follow Jack's accusing glance to me.

"Did you do this?" Raymond asked. There was almost... respect in his voice.

"No. It didn't even occur to me," I admitted. I wished I'd been the mastermind for this, but it had come from somebody much more used to this sort of thing.

"But it's because of her that it looks like you're off the hook," Jack said. No respect in his voice.

"Really?" Raymond turned back to me.

"I don't know," I said honestly. Jack raised a brow at me. "Probably," I said.

"Well, whether you did it or had someone do it, or whatever," Raymond cleared his throat before he went on, "thank you."

I couldn't very well say you're welcome, so I was grateful when Jack said, "Let's get out of here."

"I need to see my mom."

"We'll take you," I said. I hadn't forgotten my promise to Halia to help out her and DeeDee. "Do you have a car or anything we need to get?" I asked.

"No, I came on foot."

"Come on, then," Jack said, and we headed to the car.

When we were out of the railway area and headed toward Raymond's home, he said, "JoJo, really, I want to say—"

I put a hand up, turned my body in the passenger seat so I could face him in the back. "JoJo's dead. Gone. She doesn't exist anymore."

Raymond looked at me for only a second before he got it. He nodded once.

I put my hand over the seat and held it out to him. "Anna Dawson, nice to meet you."

Twenty-Three

❖❖

WORD HAD ALREADY REACHED Halia by the time we did. Coach Wayne had tried twice to reach Raymond with the news that the investigation was being dropped. Raymond took the phone and went into a bedroom to return the call. Halia was bursting at the seams with relief and happiness, and there was an awkward moment where she started to hug me and then, as if remembering that I was not quite friend but not quite enemy, stopped herself.

I stepped to her, took her arms and pulled her to me, hugging her tight. Her weight shifted over to me, and her arms came around my back. After only a second, I felt her body racking with silent sobs.

Jack stood behind Halia, I could see him from where I was. He watched Halia's relief then turned away, walking toward the living room, pulling out his phone and quietly making a call. It was a scene he witnessed a lot, but usually the sobs were of grief. It probably sounded about the same.

We stood like that, Halia slowly gaining control, me patting her back, Jack finding a box of tissues and handing them to me while still on the phone, until Raymond came out of the bedroom. He hurried his steps when he saw me comforting Halia.

"Momma?" he said, but I held up a hand and nodded my

head, letting him know she was fine.

When she heard his voice, Halia left my arms. I handed her several tissues, which she used to sop up her excess tears. "What did he say?"

"Pretty much what Jo—Anna—told me. Three different people came forward and said that Bubba Kinney was pissed he'd lost money on us, so he hatched this plan to say I'd come to him looking to shave points."

"So, you didn't go to him, Raymond? This was all a big misunderstanding?" There was hope in her voice. I watched Raymond as he struggled with his answer.

"I went to him, Momma," he finally said.

"Oh," Halia said, nodding. She'd known that he had, of course, but I guess somewhere along the line she'd tricked herself into believing something different. Denial could be a potent thing.

"So you can go back to school?" Halia asked the question that was on my lips.

He shook his head. For the first time since I'd met Raymond Joseph, and all the shit he and I had gone through, I saw him tear up. "Coach said he didn't think it was a good idea."

"So he doesn't think it's over?"

"No. He does. He just…"

Halia stepped over to her son, put her arm around him. "What is it, baby?"

Raymond's voice was choked. "He said he'd looked at the tape of the last few games and thought maybe it was better if I didn't come back to the team."

Shit. Coach Wayne knew. He hadn't seen it in the heat of the game, but when looking for it…The authorities hadn't seen it—or we wouldn't be sitting here now—but the one person who would know Raymond's game inside and out had watched the tapes looking for Raymond's slips.

And found them.

"Is he going to say anything to anybody?" I asked, but I knew the answer. Coach Wayne was an honest guy, ran a clean program, and I imagined would hate to cover something like this up. But he also had a career to protect, and something like this happening on his watch? He'd be gone in a heartbeat.

It wouldn't be fair to him, he'd had no part in this. Or the rest of the team, who had a conference championship in front of them.

"No. He didn't even say he found anything. He just said, 'I watched the Penn State game three times.'"

I imagine hurting his coach bothered Raymond more than the thought of life with L'il Roy or possible jail time did. It was that way for me with Ben.

"He said I could come back to school, that they'd honor my scholarship through the spring so I could get my degree."

"Oh, thank the lord," Halia said.

"How are they going to explain that? If you didn't do anything wrong, why wouldn't the coach put you back on the team?" I asked.

He was nodding. "Coach thought of that. We're going to say that the stress of this was too much for my family. That I needed to be with them. The term's almost over, and I should be able to take exams, or whatever I need to do from here. And then I show up for spring term and get my degree. He even said if the team was still in the tournaments that maybe I should wait and finish up summer term."

Maybe I'd been hanging around Vince too much, but him saying all these things out loud, in something as buggable as his own home...I started looking around, waiting for a SWAT team to come crashing through the door. Jack had just hung up his call, and must have noticed my unease.

"It's okay, Anna. Raymond, Jimmy, they're all right. I just got off the phone with my buddy on the Chicago force. Dubuque called and said it was being dropped."

"Why did they call Chicago police?"

"They've been keeping an eye on Raymond's whereabouts. In case he decided to run."

"I wasn't going to run," Raymond said defensively.

"They didn't know that."

Raymond eyed Jack again. "And how do you know a Chicago cop?"

"I'm a Vegas cop."

I felt Halia tense next to me. Raymond turned to me. "What the fuck?"

"Raymond," Halia chastised. "Watch your language."

"Sorry, Momma," he said, but his eyes were boring into me. "He's not...it's not..."

"I'm not here as a cop. I'm only here as Anna's...friend." His pause, and emphasis on "friend" gave Raymond either the right or wrong idea about us, but he definitely got that we were sleeping together, as Jack had obviously intended.

And it worked. Raymond looked back at me, then Jack, then shrugged and walked into the living room. Halia and I followed, and we all sat down except for Jack.

A thought occurred to me. "So, this morning, was Raymond being followed?"

"No. They got the call late last night, early this morning. They'd pulled off his tail about two hours before we met with him." Jack looked at me to see if I got the significance of that timing. I did. Boy, did I. Another couple of hours and seeing Raymond meeting furtively with two unknown people in a deserted setting would likely be enough to warrant further investigation.

Not to mention possible surveillance pictures taken of Jack and me. I could just imagine Vince's reaction if something like that surfaced.

But it didn't look like that would happen now. Good timing, and Vince's intervening with some low-lifes in Dubuque had closed the chapter on this whole sordid mess.

The fear. The shame. It all caught up to me then, and I started to shake. Just a little, but Jack noticed and came over, sitting next to me on the arm of the couch and placing his hand on my shoulder. "It's okay. It's all over."

I nodded, but I couldn't keep my hands from trembling. Halia, sitting next to me, reached over and put her hand on my knee. I took some deep breaths. I felt stupid, really. Here I was the calm, collected, criminal mastermind who set this whole thing in motion, and now that it was all over I was ready to dissolve into the same type of sobs as Halia.

Maybe not so stupid. Maybe just human.

A phone rang, and Jack pulled it out of his pocket. It was my iPhone. "Here," he said, handing it to me. "You might as well take it back anyway."

A part of me didn't want to. A part of me liked handing some of this off onto somebody else, having options taken away, just being told what to do.

But the other part of me took the phone. "Hello?"

"Anna, it's Jimmy."

"Hey, Jimmy, what's up?"

"Where are you?"

"Chicago."

"Where in Chicago?"

"At…friends."

"Okay. You might want to have your friends relocate for a while. And your other friend, you might want to tell him not to head back to Iowa anytime soon."

"Why? What's going on? I thought everything was dropped."

"By the cops, yeah. But Bubba Kinney was made to look like an idiot, and he ain't too happy about it."

Shit, would this thing never end? I took a deep breath in and out, desperately thinking of options. "What kind of clout does he have?"

"Not a lot. A couple of bums working for him have some muscle. It ain't on Vegas level, but you probably don't want to piss him off."

"And we did."

"Oh yeah, big time."

"Does he have any reach in Chicago?"

"I haven't been able to find that out."

"Okay, thanks Jimmy. Holler if you hear anything else."

"Will do. Time to get your ass back home, Anna."

"Hopefully soon." We hung up and I turned to Jack. "We may have a problem." I explained Jimmy's news, then looked at Raymond. "You can't go back there. Not right now. Not anytime soon."

"Fuck," he said. Then, before Halia even said a word, "Sorry, Momma." He started to rub his face, but as soon as he touched one of his bruises, his hands came down. "Maybe this Bubba thing will be worked out by summer term?" His voice tried to sound hopeful, but in his face, I knew he knew that wasn't likely.

But for Halia's sake, I said, "Maybe. Maybe by summer he'll have forgotten."

That seemed to do the trick for her, and she looked happy for a moment. But then she seemed to remember something, and that haunted look came back to her face. "So we're right back where we were two weeks ago. DeeDee coming home to this neighborhood."

"But I'll be here now, Momma. At least for a while, until it's okay to go back to school. I can take care of DeeDee while you're at work."

She stood up, crossed the small room to him and softly put her hands on his bruised face. "And who's going to take care of you, baby boy? Who's going to keep L'il Roy away from you?"

I cleared my throat. "This is where I can help out, I think." Halia turned toward me, but kept her hand on Raymond, standing behind him. It kind of mirrored the way Jack half stood, half sat behind me, his hand still on my shoulder.

"I'd like to get you all to the place near Atlanta that you were thinking of. As soon as you're able to get DeeDee."

"We were supposed to pick her up tomorrow, but it was on hold until we saw what was going on with…" Nobody finished the thought. It was like now that the investigation was over, we were all complicit in pretending it had never happened.

"Well, you could still get her tomorrow, then keep on going, the three of you, out of town. Raymond, you can get your mom and sister settled, and hang out until you're able to go back to school. Or who knows, you might like Atlanta and want to stay. I'm sure you could finish up your credits somehow. Online. Correspondence. Maybe even at a school down there?"

"We don't have the kind of money to just pick up and start up all over. Every bit of savings I had went into DeeDee's care, before…"

Before JoJo. No matter how it turned out, Raymond's life would forever be divided into two categories—before and after JoJo.

"Do you own a car?"

"No. I took the bus and the El to work."

"Okay. So, you'll fly to Atlanta. Get yourself a good used car when you get there. You said you'd been looking at places already?"

"But I can't—"

I held up a hand. "Halia, please. I've got the money for this. For as long as it takes until you're settled, and DeeDee's doing well. You don't even need to work if you feel you should be with her. Just get the three of you to a place that you feel safe in and is near a rehab center for DeeDee to keep up with her treatment."

"You got the kind of money to do that?"

"Yes."

"But—"

I raised my hand higher. "I need to do this for you, Halia.

DeeDee's clean, yes, and that's a good thing. But Raymond's done with basketball. I'm the one who set everything in motion. Let me…" The words stuck, and I cleared my throat. "Let me make amends."

Jack's hand moved from my shoulder, under the collar of my coat that I was still wearing, under my hair, and stroked my neck. I desperately wanted to lean into him, to hide my ashamed face in his lap and let him comfort me, but I didn't.

But I didn't pull away from his hand, either.

Halia nodded slowly. "Thank you," was all she said.

"Momma, why don't you go into the bedroom and call DeeDee's doctor and see if he still feels that it'd be alright to take her away from here. Ask him about the place Auntie Ree told you about."

"Okay. That's a good idea." Given a task, Halia seemed more composed than she had since we arrived. She smoothed her hands down her pants and stood a little straighter. "I've got those pamphlets from apartment complexes Ree sent me, too."

"Yeah. Good. Grab those."

She took the cordless phone that Raymond had sat down after his call with Coach Wayne and walked down the hallway to the bedroom, closing the door behind her.

Raymond leaned forward in his seat and said quietly, "Okay. No bullshit. Do you think this guy would come after my momma and DeeDee?"

"I don't know." I turned to Jack. "What do you think?"

He took his hand away from me and rubbed it up and down his tired-looking face. Neither of us had gotten much sleep last night. I probably looked like hell, too. "I don't know. Depends on how nasty this guy is. Most thugs have some code of ethics and don't involve civilians."

We both looked at Raymond.

"I don't know. I can't take the chance that I'd lead him to my family."

"You okay letting them go to Atlanta alone?"

He shrugged. "I don't like it, but my momma's been alone with DeeDee the four years I've been at school."

"We'd make sure she was in a real safe place," I added.

"My Auntie Ree would be a help. She's done real well for herself."

"Okay. So, they go to Atlanta tomorrow. We could put them on a bus, even, instead of flying so there'd be no records of where they went."

He was nodding. "Yeah, that would be good."

"I've got enough cash with me now that she wouldn't have to use any cards or anything. Maybe your aunt could put the apartment in her name?" He nodded again.

"You're both assuming that she'd leave Raymond here," Jack said. Raymond and I looked at each other. He was right. No way would Halia leave Raymond in Chicago, so close to L'il Roy, without her.

"I'll go somewhere else. Throw the scent off of Atlanta if Bubba is pissed enough or powerful enough to search for me out of Dubuque."

"Where?" Jack asked.

The three of us sat in silence. But I knew what I had to do. How to make this right. Make my amends and move on to another step—not that I totally believed in that stuff.

"Ever been to Vegas, Raymond?"

Twenty-Four
❖

IT TOOK AWHILE TO CONVINCE Halia that this was the best way, while trying not to scare her with the threat of Bubba Kinney. She didn't want to go to Atlanta without Raymond. She definitely didn't want him to stay in Chicago without her. She asked me lots of questions about my place in Vegas.

The presence of an octogenarian made her feel a little better. The presence of a showgirl did not.

We also knew that if anyone was looking closely, Raymond Joseph moving to Vegas and living with a professional poker player might raise some eyebrows. We were going to have to be low key, with him staying close to home while he stayed with us.

If anybody like the feds went looking for him, his name would be on a flight roster to Vegas, but I'd pay with cash or my credit card, so hopefully there'd be no red flags for a bit. None at all if the investigation were truly dead as it seemed to be. And we all were hoping this would be a short stay, that we'd all feel confident that Raymond could return to school, or at the very least, join his mother and sister in Atlanta and finish up his degree there.

All this was discussed while we packed up the Joseph family. The essentials went into luggage, which she and DeeDee could take with them on the bus. We boxed up some other things that we would ship to Halia's sister in Atlanta. Halia went and spoke with a neighbor that she trusted and gave her the keys to the place. Then she called her boss and told him about her change in plans.

By late evening our plan was in place for the next day, and Jack and I left to go back to the hotel. He and I would head back to the Joseph household tomorrow morning. I'd drive Halia to pick up DeeDee while Jack and Raymond finished up stuff at the house. Then we'd take the women to the bus station and see them on their way.

I called Lorelei on the way to the hotel and she found some flights for all three of us for the next evening.

I couldn't wait to get the hell out of Chicago.

"Wanna do room service again?" Jack said to me as we pulled into the hotel valet area, his voice low and seductive. It reminded me of where room service had led to last night.

Maybe one more night in Chicago would be all right.

IT HAD TAKEN HALIA two busses and the El to see her daughter at the rehab center. And she'd gone nearly every day once they'd allowed visitors. After working all day. In the dead of winter. My admiration for her—and all single parents hovering at the poverty line—grew even more.

DeeDee looked small and frail, and I wondered if she'd make the long bus ride, but she perked up in the car when Halia told her of their plans. I realized that the thought of going away with her mother was a welcome one to her.

She wore her hair in braids, and at fifteen years old, she had the eyes of someone who'd lived a lot longer.

Having been through several of Lor's interventions, I knew that part of recovery was breaking habits and changing environments that could lead to relapse. Which is why Halia wanted to get DeeDee out of that neighborhood.

I wondered if I could ever not be around casinos? They were my place of business after all, and I needed to play poker to support my family.

Which was now expanding.

Then I remembered this was Day Thirteen without placing a bet. And the way today was planned out to the last minute, there was every hope that I'd easily get to Day Fourteen. Maybe I could change my patterns and habits too, but without leaving my neighborhood.

When we entered the house, Raymond was at the door in seconds, scooping his younger sister into his arms. DeeDee seemed to relax even more, and I thought for the first time that maybe this was all going to work out okay.

They clung together, and then Halia joined them both. The scene was so touching, and yet so private, that I had to look away. I sought out Jack, but he had turned his back to the reunion and stared out the living room window.

Was he thinking about his own family? His son? The biological parents he never knew? Would I, in a few short hours, be able to tell him about his natural father?

I moved to him. He must have heard me approach him because he raised an arm for me, which I moved under. He dropped it across my shoulder as I burrowed into his side. It was unusual for us, this posture, and yet with the outpouring of emotion behind us, it felt right.

Very right.

"What are you going to tell Vince when we get back?" he said quietly.

Suddenly, all was not right. I didn't pull away, not physically, but there was a definite shift.

"I'm not sure," I said.

"You're not going to keep seeing him, are you?"

"Well, we—he and I—we weren't, we hadn't..." He didn't move, but I felt a slight release of breath.

It was true, what I couldn't seem to articulate. Vince and I weren't exclusive, hadn't even broached the subject. Hell, we'd only shared a few kisses. But juggling men had never been my style, and it didn't feel real good right now. "But I'm not...I can't..."

"End it," Jack said.

I wanted to protest, to tell him he didn't have any say in the matter, that he was the one who had dumped me. But, if I were honest, he'd just said exactly what I was thinking.

"But you can't want to keep on with..." I stepped away from him, motioning between us. I took a quick glance over my shoulder, but the Josephs had moved into the kitchen area.

"Yes," he said, taking his eyes from the window and looking at me. "Yes."

I was happy, believe me, and I certainly didn't want to talk Jack out of continuing on with this line of thinking, but it had stung—badly—when he'd ended it before, and I didn't want to set myself up for that again.

That's what we in the biz called a sucker bet.

"Jack, you couldn't handle all of this before. What makes you think you can now?"

He looked behind us, saw that the Josephs were indeed out of earshot, then turned back to me. "That's when I didn't know what I was dealing with. I could only imagine what you were doing, what kind of trouble you were getting yourself into."

"And knowing for sure is so much better?"

"Oh, yeah. My imagination, with what I've seen? Yeah, reality is much easier to handle."

"But—"

"Besides, you said you were done. That JoJo is dead and buried, right? Or was that just to keep me from calling the feds?"

"No, I meant it. Mean it."

"Then, we should have smooth sailing." He grinned. "Except for my two ex-wives, son I barely know, your poker playing, and living with a houseful of codgers."

"Oh yeah, except for all that."

"Right. Smooth sailing." He smiled. It took years off his face.

"And you love those codgers," I pointed out.

"Yeah, I do," he admitted. The smile faded from his face. He looked out the window, took a deep breath and looked at me. "And, I love—"

"Anna?" Halia said behind us.

I held my hand up to her. Rude, but I wasn't about to interrupt Jack.

He swallowed his words, with an actual gulp, most likely of relief, and turned to Halia. "Are we ready?" he asked her.

She looked at me with curiosity as she nodded to Jack. I can only imagine what she saw on my face, still frozen at Jack's almost words. Shock? Hope? Fear? All of the above?

Most definitely all of the above.

"We're ready. DeeDee's gone through her room to make sure there wasn't something she absolutely needed that we'd forgotten."

Jack brought his and my bags in from the car to allow more trunk space for Halia and DeeDee's luggage, then he and Raymond started loading up the car.

Halia and I stepped into her bedroom, and I helped her put on the money belts for safe traveling. There weren't the restrictions on bus travel about cash declarations that there was on airplanes, but the cash would still be safer tucked under Halia's clothes than in her purse or luggage.

As she pulled down her sweater, I started to step out of the room, but she put a hand on my arm. "Like I said before, I don't know whether to thank you or curse you."

I nodded. "I know. It's all—"

"Thank you," she said, squeezing my arm. I looked into her eyes and saw, for the first time in the past three days, hope.

I just nodded again, not able to speak. JoJo had been a total fuck up, but at the very least, she was ending her reign by helping out a worthy family.

We all crammed into the rental car, and Halia directed us to the bus station. Jack and Raymond dealt with the luggage while Halia and I took DeeDee with us to the ticket counter. We waited for the bus and tried to give them some time for good-byes, but just before the women got on, Halia called me over, took my hand and whispered, "Take care of my baby boy."

"I will," I promised. I didn't have a lot of faith in my maternal instincts, but I figured I couldn't do much worse than if Raymond was left to L'il Roy's gang.

We watched the bus pull away, Jack on one side of Raymond, me on the other. I put my hand lightly on his shoulder, not knowing if he'd brush it away, or start crying, but he did neither, just stood and followed the bus out of the station with his eyes. Neither Jack nor I made a move, waiting for Raymond.

Long after the bus had disappeared, he turned, and the three of us walked back to the parking lot, got in the car and drove back to Raymond's house.

We had plenty of time before our flight, but I wanted to get all of our stuff and head to the airport right away. I don't know why, I just didn't like the idea of sitting around Halia's house, empty of her personal belongings.

We entered the house, stamping the snow off our shoes, pulling jackets off. Raymond froze first, and I bumped into his back. Jack, on my side, slowly slid his hand to his belt, only to realize that his gun was back in Vegas.

A young, black man, still wearing a parka sat on Halia's couch, his eyes moving from Raymond, to Jack, to me, then back to Raymond.

"Where you been, Raymond?" the man asked. His tone was light, but there was menace in his eyes.

"I been looking after my momma, L'il Roy," Raymond said.

L'il Roy rose from the couch and walked toward us. Jack took my arm and started to pull me behind him.

"You know we had a deal," L'il Roy said to Raymond, coming closer. He didn't have any weapon in his hands, but who knew what was hidden in that huge parka or under the baggy sweatshirt he wore over droopy jeans.

"Situation's changed."

L'il Roy was just about to answer Raymond, and it didn't look like a "Really? Okay, then!" type of answer, when he looked at me again, more closely. His eyes narrowed then flashed with some sort of recognition.

"Holy shit," he said, "you're the Black Widow. Bitch, I *love* you."

It wasn't the declaration of love I thought I'd hear today, but I'd take it.

"The who?" Raymond asked.

"The Black Widow. Damn, man, don't you know who's in your own house?"

Raymond looked over his shoulder at me. I stepped past Jack, even though he tried to pull me back, and brushed past Raymond, holding my hand out to L'il Roy, using all my poker bravado I'd learned over the years to simply not shake like a leaf in front of him. A man who'd killed his own brother.

"Anna Dawson," I said. No sense trying to hide anything. If he knew I was the Black Widow, he knew my real name. The only time I was called by that nickname was for televised poker tournaments.

Lots of pros played in made-for-television tournaments, and had lots of sponsors that they did advertising spots for. And I'd been offered them. A lot. But I'd never done them. For one thing, the specter of JoJo always loomed over me. I couldn't take a sponsor's money knowing I could very well be unmasked one day.

And I didn't do the extra TV tournaments because I just

didn't want to be recognized more than necessary. That wouldn't help when JoJo made an appearance.

But, I have had a few televised final tables. And when I make a final table in a big tourney, I wear my black suit—though it's been getting much more use at funerals these past few weeks than poker tournaments. At my first final table I dominated, and one of the announcers said I was like a black widow, chomping the heads off of my competitors.

The name stuck. And in a small—but growing—circle, I was a celebrity. A novelty, really.

And apparently that small circle included L'il Roy.

"L'il Roy," he said, taking my hand. His hand was cool and smooth, but what did I expect? Blood to be dripping off of it? "Holy shit," he said, "what are you doing here? Do you live in Chicago?"

"No. We're just here…my friend, Jack and me," I pointed to Jack behind me. L'il Roy looked past me, sized Jack up, and looked back to me. He did seem to realize that Jack was not someone to just dismiss out of hand. "We're here for Raymond. He's going to come and stay with me for a bit."

"Izzat right?" L'il Roy said, looking at Raymond.

I stepped in front of Raymond. "I know you and he have made…arrangements…but we all think it might be better if Raymond gets out of Chicago for awhile." L'il Roy didn't say a word, but I could tell he wasn't happy about losing his newest recruit.

I played my ace. "Surely it would be in your best interest not to have someone so…high-profile…as Raymond is right now in your midst. Who needs the scrutiny?"

His brown eyes narrowed on me. I don't know if he took it as a helpful hint or a threat, and I'm not really sure how I meant it. His eyes left me and went behind me to Jack. I turned slightly and saw that Jack had put his badge back on his belt loop, and was holding his coat open for L'il Roy to see.

"I'm not looking for any trouble," L'il Roy said. But he didn't back away, either.

"Neither are we. We just have a couple of bags to pick up and then we'll all be on our way."

"But Raymond, he came to me. I didn't go looking for him. He *came to me* for protection."

"And I'm sure he appreciates *all* you did for him." I couldn't keep all the sarcasm out of my voice. Raymond's face was still all kinds of ugly from the bruises.

"That ain't even a Chicago badge," he said to Jack.

"You that familiar with a Chicago badge?" Jack asked.

L'il Roy grinned, but it wasn't the happy, joyful grin of Raymond Joseph. It was the smile of a man who was looking for a fight.

And I didn't want to give him one.

"L'il Roy, you're obviously a poker player. Let's lay our cards on the table. What's it going to take for the three of us to walk out that door, take Raymond with us, and keep you from... pursuing the situation?"

"I don't know, I've made an investment in Raymond. I had big plans for his future."

"Are we talking money?" I had a chunk of cash left that Halia didn't feel she'd need at this point, but not the kind of money L'il Roy was probably talking about.

"Hard to estimate future earnings and all..."

"Then what?"

"I'll play you for him."

"What?"

"Heads up poker. You and me. Winner takes Raymond home with him." He had a cocksure smile that rubbed me the wrong way. Like every punk I saw at cash games that wanted to take down a pro.

"That's crazy, we need to—" Jack said, but I cut him off.

"Shuffle up and deal."

Twenty-Five
❖❖

RAYMOND FOUND SOME PLAYING CARDS in a junk drawer, and the four of us pulled up chairs to the kitchen table.

"You got any chips?" L'il Roy asked Raymond, who shook his head.

"How about toothpicks?" I asked, remembering my early days playing with The Corporation when Ben didn't want to play for money. Raymond went to a cupboard and grabbed a box. I counted out twenty for L'il Roy and twenty for myself. The thug had the audacity to count them behind me.

"Hold 'Em?" I asked.

"Definitely," L'il Roy answered. "Raymond can deal."

"I don't know how to do all that flop and river shit."

L'il Roy let out a grunt of disgust, then lifted his chin to Jack. "You know how to deal Hold 'Em?"

Jack nodded and took the cards from Raymond.

"No limit?" I asked L'il Roy. He seemed to be setting the rules for this game.

"Of course."

I tapped my horseshoe pendant three times and sat forward in my seat. "Let's do this."

It went back and forth for an hour and a half. He won a couple of hands, I won a few more. The chip count—toothpick count—was slightly in my favor. I had three more than he did.

"We have a flight to catch soon," I said.

"Maybe. Maybe not," L'il Roy answered. I shrugged, which seemed to piss him off. Which had been my strategy all along, to appear as if I was humoring him, letting him play with a pro. That this could all be over the minute I started playing seriously. It worked a little bit, he'd bet one hand way more aggressively than he should have, and when he lost it, he lost his cool, slamming his hand down on the kitchen table. I hadn't shown any sign of emotion, just calmly collected the winning pot, slowly sliding the toothpicks across the table. Away from him and toward me, even letting a few of them trickle through my hands, like there were so many I simply couldn't handle them all.

I was definitely in his head.

A few more hands and I had three more of his toothpicks. He wanted to go all in, I could tell. It was a showy move and L'il Roy was a showy guy. Who else would kill his own brother to make a point? He was just busting to say it. To push his toothpicks in and say the words to a pro player—one he had apparently watched quite a bit.

"All in," he said on the very next hand, proving my point. I had a pair of fours. Not a bad hand, but not a hand I'd typically go all in with. But I didn't think he had anything, that he was bluffing. And I covered him in chips, meaning if he won, I'd still have chips—toothpicks—left, although I'd be down. Whereas if I won, it would be over.

And we'd be on our way to the airport with no more bruises for Raymond, and no shots fired. Always a good thing, no shots being fired.

"I call," I said and put my toothpicks into the pot, and tossing over my fours for everyone to see.

He sneered as he showed his pair of tens.

Shit. This game was going to keep going, with me severely handicapped, unless I got a four somewhere in the five community cards that were to come. And if it kept going, and I was seriously down in chip count, anything could happen.

Jack discarded the burn card then dealt the three flop cards, placing them face up on the table. An ace, a seven and a ten.

"Fuck," Raymond said, pretty much summing up my sentiments.

"Looks like you'll be coming home with me, Raymond," L'il Roy said.

"She's got more picks than you, she can keep playing," Raymond pointed out.

"Limping is more like it than playing." He looked squarely at me. "Or bleeding."

It was a poker term, bleeding chips, but I didn't think he meant it like that.

"Hey, L'il Roy," Jack said, causing us all to turn our heads toward him. He hadn't said a word during the whole game, which was typical for the dealer, and also for Jack. "How did you know Anna? She wasn't on TV that much. You must watch a lot of poker." He turned to me before L'il Roy could answer him. "What did you tell me? Three final tables? Four?"

"Six," L'il Roy and I said at the same time. He looked over at me, a tiny bit sheepish if a cold-blooded killer had the capacity to look sheepish. "I got 'em all on my DVR," he explained. "You and Vanessa Rousso. I save both of you. She plays a lot more than you do, though."

"She travels, like the other players. I stay in Vegas." He looked at me like he didn't understand, but I wasn't about to go into my makeshift family with L'il Roy. The less he knew about them all, the better. "There's other good female players," I said.

"Yeah, but I don't want to picture them naked when I watch them play."

"Ewww," I said while L'il Roy laughed and dropped his eyes to my chest.

It was a light moment in a very tense day, and I tried to draw it out a little. "When did you first start to play poker?"

His laugh died on his face. "My brother taught me when I was little."

So much for light banter across the table.

"Let's get this fucking thing over with," he said sharply as he motioned for Jack to continue.

Jack dealt the burn card to the side then placed the turn card next to the flop cards. A four. I had a three of a kind, which was an awesome hand. But they were fours, and L'il Roy had three tens.

"I kept your room nice and ready for you Raymond," he gloated.

"This game isn't over yet," I reminded him, even though it probably was. Only a four would win this hand for me, and the chances of getting a four of a kind against a three of a kind were astronomical. Yeah, I'd still have some chips, but L'il Roy would be in a much more dominate position. Which was probably what he pictured when he watched tape of Vanessa Rousso and myself.

He only laughed at me and motioned for Jack to get on with it. Jack buried the burn card and turned up the river card. A four.

Silence. Complete silence while the fact that I'd drawn a four of a kind to win the game crept over all of us.

Finally, I pushed my chair back and stood up. I held my hand out to L'il Roy. "Good game," I said with my Black Widow persona.

I think that's what did it. It wasn't a personal sense of honor, but I'd held my hand out to him, like I would any pro I'd beaten, and he seemed to know that.

He stood up, shook my hand, and said, "That was one hell of a hand."

"It was a bad beat, we both know it, but that happens in professional poker all the time." I'd slipped the professional part in there, and even smoothed my hands down my hips, like I did to my black suit when I took out a good player and was trying not to show relief.

And man, was there relief.

L'il Roy turned to Raymond, but there was no losing with grace where Raymond was concerned. "Don't show your face around here again," he said and walked out of the house before Raymond could even answer him.

WE LOADED UP THE CAR and closed down the house in record time. Just before we left the house, Jack walked back to the table and took the two jokers from the deck we'd played with. He folded them up and jammed them in the top of the track of the accordion door in the hallway. He tested it a few times, made sure it now worked properly, then motioned for us to hit the road.

We were still okay time-wise, but nobody wanted to stick around the house after L'il Roy left. While Jack drove, I called Lorelei from the car and told her we'd be having a houseguest for awhile.

"Is everything…okay…in Saul's room?" I asked. I hadn't gone back into that room after it had been cleared by the police. I'd assumed Lorelei had cleaned Saul's personal belongings out and had the cleaning woman do a thorough cleansing.

"It is, but I thought I'd put him in the other guest room."

"But Gus is in the other guest room," I said before I thought about it. Oh, Gus was not sleeping in that room. Okay.

"Gus moved back to his apartment today," she said, not elaborating, which was weird.

"Oh. Okay. Are you…did you…"

"So that room will be ready by the time you get here," she said very matter-of-factly. "But maybe you're right, he'd have more privacy in the wing with you." I could tell she was figuring this all out in her head—what would be best for all of us.

"Whatever you think. Thanks."

"No problem," she said, but there was just a tiny quiver in her voice.

"Lor?"

"So, I'll see you later, then?"

She obviously didn't want to discuss what did or didn't happen between Gus and herself, so I let it go. "You don't have to wait up."

"I'll probably still be up. It won't be that late with the time change."

We said our good-byes then hung up.

"Did she know I was coming?" Raymond asked from the backseat.

"No."

"'Cause you didn't even tell her who was coming or how long I was staying."

"So?" I looked over the seat to his puzzled face.

"Your roommate don't care that you're bringing an angry young black man home?"

"You'll be right at home with the angry old Jewish man," Jack said, and I swatted him on the arm.

"Ben is not angry."

"He might be tomorrow," Raymond and Jack said at the same time.

"Ben will love having another male around, especially now that Gus has moved out. All Ben likes to do is go out to breakfast with his friends, and then watch sports all day, then a friendly game of cards at night. Think you can handle him?"

"If your idea of a friendly card game was what we just went through, no, I think you'd better let me out right now." He smiled. Not his trademark, wide-as-his-whole-face smile, but it was a grin just the same and I quickly returned it.

There was—finally—a sense of lightness, now that we were

so close to getting out of this whole thing, both physically and legally. I studied him for a moment, thinking of the three of us walking through the airport, then grabbed a knit hat that I'd bought earlier for myself or Jack, from the well of the console, and tossed it back to Raymond.

"Put that on. Your bruises are noticeable enough without that scary, frizzed-out hair."

"Racist," he teased, but put the hat on.

I pushed the console top back into place, jerking into Jack's right arm as I did so. Something slid out of the cuff of his shirt, peeking beyond it and his leather jacket. He started to move that arm to the steering wheel, but I pulled it back toward me. I pulled the object out, already knowing it was a playing card, but not understanding.

And then I did.

"What is this?" I asked, turning the jack of spades over in my hands, although I knew what it was. I only wondered if Jack would tell me the truth.

He looked in the rearview mirror to see if Raymond was listening. He was not only listening, he'd also propped himself up so he could see what I was holding. He was also looking at Jack with a questioning gaze.

"That," Jack finally said, a resignation in his voice, "was supposed to be the river card."

Raymond blinked, trying to process it, but I was way ahead of him. "How'd you get the four?"

"When I was shuffling, I saw it was on the bottom of the deck. When you went all in and I saw you had fours, I thought maybe it would come in handy." He shrugged. "And it did."

"But how?" Raymond asked, but I'd already figured it out.

"That's why you asked about my final tables, you knew that would get L'il Roy talking."

"It did."

We all sat in silence for awhile, letting Jack wind us through the Chicago traffic and on to the airport.

"Huh," Raymond finally said.

"Yeah," I agreed.

"So, you cheated?" Raymond asked, just for clarification, but there was disbelief in his voice. And he didn't even know Jack the way I did.

"Well," Jack said, looking pointedly at first Raymond in the rearview mirror, and then a sideways, meaningful look at me. "I was just trying to keep up with the company I was keeping."

Ouch. But we deserved it, Raymond and I both. I watched as the city disappeared behind us and our labyrinth of freeways became wider and more expansive as we approached O'Hare.

Something about Jack and cards was playing at the back of my head. Something just out of ... "Hey," I said to him, grasping it. "The other night at the house when we were playing cards?"

"Yeah?"

"The night Vince was there?"

"I know which night you mean, Johanna." There was an impatience in his voice.

"That last hand? What did you have?"

"Deuces. You saw. Ben beat me with a flush."

"Not that hand. The last big hand. The one you mucked."

"Yeah?"

"What did you have?"

"What does it matter? Vince won the hand."

"Did he?"

"Why would I muck a winning hand?"

"I guess that's what I'm asking."

"That would be stupid."

"Would it? Or was it some mind game you were playing to let him think he had the upper hand."

"The upper hand with what?"

"I'm not sure. The investigation into Paulie's murder? Or me?"

"I don't need the upper hand in a murder investigation. I'm the one wearing a badge."

"And the other?" I asked.

But he didn't answer.

"Come on, Jack, did you have kings or aces?" I gave him the out of just naming his winning hand, not even having to admit he'd done it. But still he didn't say anything.

I shrugged, but I kept my face on Jack's as he stared straight ahead, out onto the road. Finally, finally, there was just a tiny, infinitesimal movement of his mouth, and I knew as surely as I sat across from him at a poker table that I was right.

I just wasn't sure which one of those two motives I was right about. Knowing Jack, I'd probably never know.

I sat back in my seat, hands crossed against my chest, a smile on my face, my satisfaction that I'd read him apparent. He looked over, read my body language, and knew that he'd given up some kind of tell.

"Kings," he finally said as we pulled into the rental car lot, "I had kings."

Twenty-Six

❖❖

"HANNAH, DARLING," Ben said as the waitress cleared away our dishes after breakfast the next morning, "are you going to tell me who is staying in Gus' room, or do I have to guess?"

It was Friday morning. Day Fourteen without placing a bet. But it was early, and I wasn't feeling all that strong. And really, didn't I deserve some kind of treat for successfully avoiding bloodshed and legal prosecution in Chicago?

I'd proven I could go without placing a bet. Wasn't that what it was all about, knowing I could control it? Now that I'd shown that I could, what would be the harm in placing a couple of bets? I had the money, it's not like I'd have to go out on a marker to Vince to rustle up the cash. That's really when the trouble began, and I wouldn't be doing that.

Yeah, I could—

"Hannah?"

I broke away from the thought of a possible Hummer today to focus on what Ben had asked.

"I didn't think you'd realized he was there," I said. Ben had been asleep last night when we'd arrived at home, and Raymond was still asleep this morning when Ben and I had left for breakfast.

"Lorelei was fluttering around last night getting that room cleaned out, and there was a strange jacket in the closet this morning."

"Out with the old and in with the new, kiddo?" Gus jokingly said. At least I think he was joking. He almost always had that devilish look in his eyes, so it was hard to tell for sure.

"You know you were welcome to stay Gus. Anytime. We've got plenty of room."

"I know, I'm just yanking your chain."

"Besides, from the way I understand it, you'd left before I gave the word to Lorelei about Raymond staying with us."

It was a question for more information, and he knew it, but only murmured, "Yes, that's right, I did."

Hmmm, neither he nor Lor were talking. I didn't know if there was trouble in paradise or if their playful flirting was only that and had reached an end. I kept my mouth shut and turned to Ben instead. "Raymond Joseph is going to be staying with us for awhile, until some things get straightened out with his family."

Jimmy, of course, wasn't shocked by the news that I was involved with Raymond Joseph, but he did raise a brow at, I assumed, Raymond's coming to Vegas with me. I didn't blame him because it wasn't my first choice, either.

"You mean that kid that was shaving points at Central Iowa?" Gus asked, clearly confused.

"It's a long story," I said.

The three men looked at each other. Finally Ben said, "Is this what you were talking about the other day? The thing that you said you weren't proud of?"

I nodded. "Mostly."

Ben took a sip of his coffee. The others waited to see what he'd say. He took a deep breath, then let it out. "And are you making it right, Hannah?"

I let out a combination sigh and chuckle. "Mostly."

That seemed to be enough for Ben, and Jimmy and Gus followed his lead, saying nothing else. We paid for breakfast and walked toward the book room to get today's betting sheets.

Jimmy pulled on my jacket sleeve, and I hung back with him.

"You okay?" he asked.

"Yeah."

"You know, if you need to stash the kid away somewhere, I could probably take him in for awhile."

I placed my hand on his shoulder as we slowly walked a ways behind Ben and Gus. "Thanks, Jimmy, but I think he's okay with us. Unless somebody was tracking him last night,—and if the investigation really is over, I can't imagine why anybody would,—then he can just hang out here for awhile. He's not really recognizable right now, so he should be okay. Hopefully it won't be for too long."

"Offer stands," he said and lumbered off to join Ben and Gus.

I stuck my hand in my pocket, looking for my wad of cash, already thinking ahead to the games being played tonight and tomorrow morning. And the Hummer about to wash over me.

But Ben stayed at the entrance of the book room, while Jimmy and Gus made their way to the end of the cash cages where the rows of sheets with the day's odds on them resided.

"Is something wrong?" I asked Ben when I drew up alongside him.

"No, but I think I just want to go home today."

Ben never bet on games, but he always took home a betting sheet. He loved to compare the odds he set in his little tablet with what the casinos posted each day. "That's fine. Let me just grab you an odds sheet."

He put his hand out, stopping me from entering the book area. "Gus is bringing me one." Sure enough, Gus was returning to where Ben and I stood, a sheet of paper in his hand.

"Here you go." He handed the sheet to Ben, but didn't meet my eye when I looked at him questioningly.

"See you tomorrow, Gus," Ben said, already maneuvering his walker around in a circle and heading toward the exit.

"What's up?" I said to Ben, catching up to him.

"Nothing, I just thought it would be nice to go home and meet Raymond. Should we stop and pick up something for him for breakfast?"

"Knowing Lorelei, I'm sure she has it well in hand."

"That's true," he said, then proceeded to prattle about the dinners Lorelei had made while I was gone and other mundane things until we were in the car and halfway home.

And I realized I hadn't made a bet.

I slid a suspicious glance at Ben, but he was staring out the passenger window, the picture of innocence. I didn't say a word, just drove home in silence.

When we walked into the house, we could hear a low buzzing noise that neither of us recognized. We followed the sound to the guest bathroom where Lorelei stood over a half-bald Raymond, electric hair clippers in hand, buzzing right down the center of his scalp.

I didn't ask. I didn't want to know what had preceded this change. But it made a dramatic change in his appearance, and I realized that could only be a good thing while he was staying in Vegas.

I made the introductions between Raymond and Ben then left them all there in the bathroom while I made my way to my bedroom.

I'd slept alone last night, Jack going home after dropping off Raymond and me. I should have caught up on the sleep lost in Chicago, but I hadn't, my mind wouldn't turn off. Now I slipped off my jacket, toed off my shoes and crawled back under my covers, trying not to think about what Day Fourteen and beyond would hold.

I EMERGED FROM MY ROOM and instantly smelled

the most tantalizing aromas coming from the kitchen. I made my way there to discover Lorelei handing a steaming platter to Raymond, which he then carried past me toward the dining room.

"We thought we'd have to go in and wake you," he said as he walked by me. It was odd seeing him not only bald, his black scalp gleaming, but so at home in my kitchen. Well, Lor's kitchen.

"I was trying to catch up on some sleep," I justified. "Aren't you exhausted? With everything you've been through?"

He shrugged, and I was able to see that the platter held large Italian sausages smothered in a tomato sauce. "Jimmy coming for dinner?" I asked Lorelei.

"He's already here. We were going to give you ten more minutes of sleep while we got dinner on the table."

"What can I do?" She handed me another platter, this one loaded down with her ziti, and directed me to the dining room. Where Ben, Jimmy, and Raymond were sitting at the table.

"Hey, sleepyhead," came a voice from the corner behind me.

I turned so quickly the ziti almost slid off the platter, but Jack was there to right it for me at the last minute. Good thing, too, if Jimmy's gasp was any indication.

"Hi," I said, inexplicably nervous.

"Lor invited me for dinner. I hope that's okay."

"Of course." I could feel Ben, Jimmy and Raymond's interested eyes on Jack and me. Well, Jimmy was probably just interested in the ziti.

Lorelei came in then with a basket of crusty rolls, and we all sat down to a delicious dinner. Nobody mentioned Gus' absence, so I didn't bring it up. I wasn't sure when Jimmy had arrived, or how Raymond had spent his first day here, but they'd apparently spent some time together because they all seemed to be getting along fine, even arguing about who would win the upcoming basketball games.

After we'd filled ourselves to the gills, Raymond helped Lorelei and me clear the table even though she tried to shoo him back to the table to wait for coffee and dessert. "No, I'll help," he said, so Lor put him to work.

As we settled in for coffee and dessert, Ben said to Jack, "Are you staying for cards, Jack? We're going to teach Raymond the finer points of poker."

"Don't let them take your money, Raymond. They may look like harmless old men, but they're ruthless when it comes to cards," Jack warned. Ben chuckled and Jimmy tried to look innocent.

"So, you're staying?" Ben again asked Jack.

Jack was sitting next to me. He put his arm across the back of my chair, his hand, warm from holding his coffee mug, slipping under my bedraggled ponytail to rest on my nape. "Am I? Staying?" he said softly to me.

He wasn't asking about cards.

I was just about to say yes when I remembered Vince. Chicago was one thing, like a free space in this whole game, but to have Jack stay here before I'd talked with Vince? Like I said, there was nothing declared between Vince and me, but it didn't feel right for Jack to be in my bed while Vince was still thinking that we'd be seeing each other again.

Not my style.

"You're welcome to stay," I started and saw Jack's mouth turn up in a slow smile. "For cards," I added pointedly and saw the smile disappear. "But I have something I have to do tonight, so I won't be able to join all of you."

You'd think I'd admitted I wanted to spend the evening out shooting heroin the way the table came to a complete standstill. Jack drew his hand away from my neck.

"You going to play somewhere, Anna?" Jimmy asked. "Maybe I could join you. I been meaning to play in some cash games lately."

I looked at him like he'd lost his mind. Jimmy never played in cash games with me. For one thing, when you're playing like that at a casino, you don't *want* to be on a table with friends, or people who know your game. Makes winning tougher.

"Um, no, that's okay Jimmy. We can play a cash game together some other night. Tomorrow?"

He looked at Ben and shrugged, like "I tried". Ben nodded slightly then looked toward Jack.

Oh, I got it. They thought I was going out to place bets. "I'm not going out to place bets."

They all looked at each other, even Raymond, which told me there'd been some kind of conversation between them all, probably when I'd been sleeping just now. I should have been touched, but I was kind of pissed. I'd gone fourteen days without placing a bet, by far the longest I'd ever gone. And I'd done that all on my own. And now they were going to swoop in and shadow my every movement? Get me quickly out of the casinos after breakfast so I wouldn't place a bet?

"Is this how it's going to be?" I asked the entire table as I stood up and pushed my chair in. Nobody answered me. When I tried to step away from the table, Jack gently grasped my hand. I looked down at him. "Is this how it's going to be?" I asked again, quietly this time, and to Jack alone.

"Why don't I come with you," he said.

"You can't."

"Then how about me?" Lorelei said.

"No."

"Hannah, darling, maybe if you just told us where you have to go so late?"

I looked around the table at my ragtag family—two retired book makers, a close to washed-up showgirl, an alcoholic cop, and our newest member, a point-shaving point guard.

And *I* was answering to *them*?

"I'm going to tell Vince that I won't be seeing him anymore. I want to do it tonight, because I don't want to sleep with Jack again until I do it. And I really want to sleep with Jack again."

Ha. The look on poor Ben's face. Jimmy snorted. Raymond whispered, "Who's Vince?" to Lorelei, and Lorelei gave me a huge smile.

"See you when you get home," was all Jack said.

Twenty-Seven

❖❖

I CALLED CARLA ON MY PHONE after I couldn't reach Vince. I'd left the house and was driving, headed toward the Strip. "I'm trying to reach Vince, do you know if he's around tonight?"

"He's due here pretty soon. We have a new, big-shot player tonight, and he wanted to stop and say a personal hello."

My hand left the steering wheel and dug in my pocket to see if I still had a wad of cash. I was already tabulating how much I'd have for buy-in and if I'd have to go on Carla's books to get in the game.

No. I quickly put my hand back on the steering wheel, the cash undisturbed. JoJo was what became of going on Carla's books, and JoJo was dead.

"You want to play?" Carla asked.

"No. But I need to talk to Vince."

"Why don't you swing by. He might even be here by the time you get here."

I didn't really want to say what I needed to say to Vince in some hotel suite with a table full of poker players nearby, but I felt this sense of urgency that I really needed to do this tonight. "Okay, I'll do that. Where are you?"

They were playing at Bellagio tonight, and I said a silent thanks that my route from the parking deck to the guest rooms would not take me past the Sports Book. Now, I just needed to say my piece to Vince and walk away from the table.

Who knows, after tonight—and what I had to say to him— maybe I would be banned from Vince's tables. The thought was both freeing and terrifying.

Vince had indeed beaten me to the suite where tonight's game was being played. Carla must have let him know I was on my way and wanted to talk with him, because he greeted me with a small nod then picked up Carla's ledger and led the way to one of the bedrooms of the suite, closing the door behind us.

I looked puzzled at the ledger in his arms and he put it aside, on the table next to me. It flipped open to a page about a third in, and I tensed when I saw my name and signature from money I'd borrowed in the past.

That was done, over, I told myself. That book was closed. As if to make my point, I shut the ledger.

Vince pointed to it. "I wanted the players to think that we were discussing business. I didn't want them to know about us, at least not without your permission."

"Oh, that was thoughtful."

He lifted his hands in a "no problem" gesture. "Protection for you, yes. But also I don't want them to think I give preferential treatment to anyone." He moved toward me, put his hands on my hips. "So, we obviously can't stay in here as long as I'd like to, and do the things I'd want to do in a hotel suite. At least not this one."

His smile was warm, and of course handsome, and part of me, a small part, wanted to return his smile and sink into his body. But I stepped away from him and crossed to the other side of the room. "Vince…" I began, now suddenly wondering why all the urgency that this needed to be done tonight. I knew we had just started dating, that there was no way Vince had really deep feelings for me yet. But I truly liked Vince, cared for him. And I'd been on the receiving end of this little speech enough times to know that however deep or not deep you'd fallen, it was a bitch to hear.

He held a hand up for me to stop, which I gladly did. Let him be the one to do the talking. "Schiller," is all he said.

I looked into his eyes, careful not to show pity—he'd hate that, and I didn't really feel it for him—but I tried to look resolved, yet understanding. "Yes."

Vince's face dropped into a professional mask. If it had been Jack, I would have called it his cop face, but it was different with Vince. Beyond stern and professional, but not quite all the way to scary. "He hurt you before," he said.

"Things are different this time," I said. It sounded weak even to my ears.

"Do you know how many times a day that sentence is said in this town?"

He had me there.

"Even so," I said. I wasn't going to make the case for Jack and me being together. I couldn't really even make it to myself. There were definitely still issues between us, but he wanted to try. So did I.

He waited for me to go on, and when I didn't he smiled softly at me. "One of the things I like about you, Anna, is you never made excuses. You always took responsibility for your actions. You have accountability, that's different from gamblers with a problem."

See, even Vince seemed to think that I was different from compulsive gamblers. And Lord knows he'd seen his share of them.

"I am sorry, though, if it feels like a sucker punch," I said. "I know you didn't see this coming."

"Oh, I don't know. I suspected it might come to this. I guess I'd hoped it wouldn't happen so soon, that perhaps we'd have a chance to have something a little more solid."

"I'm not sure if that would be possible for us, Vince. Seems like we have too much between us on a…professional level. I don't know if we could ever really see our way past that."

"I could. I did."

I put my hands in my pants pockets. "I guess I couldn't."

"So, where do we stand then? Professionally?"

"I'm assuming you're aware of the investigation being dropped." He was nodding his head and starting to speak as I continued. "Thank you for that." He stilled, his eyes narrowed on me, and I could have kicked myself. I guess I'd thought that this being a random hotel suite that there'd be no concern for listening devices. He was hosting a high-stakes, illegal poker game in the next room, for goodness sake. "I'm sorry. I thought it would be okay to speak freely here."

"It is. Sorry, it was just a gut reaction. We're fine here." He waved a hand. "Go on."

"I came by tonight, not only to tell you that I couldn't see you anymore, but to thank you for what you did. Getting those men to discredit Bubba Kinney was a stroke of genius."

He was quiet for a few moments, and I almost thought he was about to search me for a wire or something the way he was looking at me, with such a studied countenance. Finally, he said, "I wanted to help in some way. I couldn't go with you to Chicago."

"I know that," I said softly.

"I'm glad it helped."

"It did."

"Where does it all stand now?"

I gave him a brief rundown of the Joseph family's exodus from Chicago, the relative assurance that it was over, and the fact that JoJo had never been mentioned by Raymond to anyone.

"He's staying with you? Is that smart?"

I shrugged. "We didn't have many options given that we wanted to get Halia and her daughter squared away as soon as possible."

"Still…"

"He's going to lay low. His appearance has already drastically changed, and he's just been hanging out at the house, playing cards with the boys. And let's face it, if *you* didn't know he arrived in Vegas, nobody does."

"I didn't say I didn't know he was here."

"Did you?"

A small, reluctant smile graced his face. "No."

A look passed between us. One of what might have been. I took my hands from my pockets and walked toward him, holding my arms out. He opened his, and I gave him a quick hug. "Thanks, Vince."

"You're welcome."

"I'd say I owed you one, but I'm afraid what you might charge me," I said jokingly, but it wasn't really funny. Too close to the truth. But I knew I owed him for this. And so did he.

"I guess I'd better get going," I said as I stepped away from his warm body.

"Not playing tonight?"

I shook my head. "No, I'm trying to limit my games to casinos. I don't want to be on anybody's books."

"Not even mine?"

"Especially yours."

"Fair enough, but you know a seat is always open for you at a table of mine, Anna."

"I know," I said. I didn't add that I hoped I would never again take him up on it. "I appreciate it." He picked up the ledger, and we headed toward the door to the rest of the suite. "Would you like me to look appropriately chastised? Be an example to the players out there?"

His mouth twitched up. "Too bad we don't have any ketchup or something we could dribble down you to look like blood. No one out there would owe me again."

"But that's not what you want, not really."

"True."

I waved to two of the players at the table when I walked by and demurred their offer to join them, and then I stopped and chatted with Carla for a moment. Vince handed her the ledger back and she put it on the floor beside her chair, then looked closely at me.

On the drive home, I thought about how I could repay Vince for siccing the dogs on Bubba Kinney. I didn't like owing him, but I needed to think of a repayment that was still on a professional level and didn't involve a resurrection of JoJo.

Obviously, it was in Vince's best interest that the investigation into Raymond was dropped, but he'd done it for me, too, and I'd like to repay that if I could. Partly as a thank you, and partly because I didn't want to have Vince hanging over my head in anyway if I was going to be with Jack.

And judging by the sleeping body waiting in my bed for me when I got home, I was definitely going to be with Jack.

I hurriedly threw my clothes off and went to the bed wearing only my bra and panties. He turned over when I crawled in beside him. "You have too many clothes on," he whispered. "Let me take care of that for you."

And he did.

Later, lying in the darkness, he asked, "How'd it go?"

"Okay. Better than I thought, I guess."

He turned my very pliant and sated body over, then pulled me to him, spooning me. "Any regrets?"

I snorted. "You ask me that *now*? After everything we just did?"

He placed a kiss on my shoulder. "That's why I waited until now to ask."

"No," I whispered, taking his hand from my hip and bringing it to my front, holding it between both of mine. "No regrets."

♠ ♥ ♦ ♣

IT WAS AN ODD SATURDAY, my second one of watching games all day with Ben at home and not having money on any of them. Raymond, much impressed by our TV room, barely left his seat all day. Pretty much only for the john and food.

Which is how it should be on college basketball Saturdays.

There was no Hummer, but the promise of another night with Jack awaited me and it was a good replacement.

He'd gotten a call early in the morning—scaring the crap out of me—and had to go to a crime scene, but had promised to come by tonight after he was done.

Lor had announced that morning to Ben—before I got up—that she was going out for the day and then had a date that evening, so we were on our own for meals. Ben and Raymond had already had breakfast, and I got by on coffee and a bagel. I offered to either call out for delivery or heat up leftovers later on, and that seemed to work for Raymond and Ben.

We ended up, the three of us, calling out for pizza when we discovered that all the ziti leftovers were gone, sent home with Jimmy last night, no doubt. Jimmy called about the time we finished up our pizza to see if anybody was up for cards. Which, of course, we were.

Jack came in as we were just shuffling up the deck, and I heated him some pizza, which he ate as we played.

Nice, quiet, Saturday night playing cards with the gang.

Jimmy asked if we knew the score of the final west coast games played that afternoon, and I went into our office to call it up on the Internet. As I rounded my desk, I saw the NPR tote bag sitting on the floor, leaning against the leg well of the desk.

I had totally forgotten about the DNA testing. Well, not forgotten, but had certainly shoved it from my mind during the trip to Chicago, and the two days we'd been back. The results were waiting for me in a brown envelope in my desk drawer. Did I want to know this information right now, with Jack and Ben down the hallway?

Fate intervened and Jack walked into the office. "Never mind, I got the score for Jimmy off of my phone."

Not that he could see it from where he stood, and it in itself wouldn't divulge anything, but I nudged the tote bag a little farther under my desk with my foot. A little farther away from having to deal with it.

"Oh, great, thanks," I said and walked past Jack and back down the hallway.

"You know, you can get those on your phone."

"I know. Lor set that all up for me. Got all the apps on it she thought I'd want. But I still like a larger screen." Neither of us mentioned my other phone, the JoJo phone, that was much more simplistic. And long gone.

As we came back into the living room, Jimmy was writing down something in his little tablet that he kept scores and results in. It was the size of Ben's, but whereas Ben's tablets were cheap ones with spiral wiring at the top, Jimmy's were small, leather-covered ones that opened like a book. The leather was navy and had a red piping stripe across the top third. A red, satin marking ribbon dangled from the top.

I looked at the ledger closely as cogs and wheels fell into place.

"Oh, my God," I said to Jack. "I know who killed Paulie."

Twenty-Eight
❖❖

JACK LED ME OUT OF THE ROOM amidst the hubbub of Jimmy and Ben shouting, "Who?" and Raymond questioning who was Paulie. "Keep quiet," Jack said and steered me down the hallway. I thought he might be headed to the office—he was definitely wearing his cop face, not his bedroom one—but we passed the office, and he gently pushed me by the lower back into the bedroom, shutting the door behind us.

"What do you think you know?"

"Not what. Who."

He waved his hands in a get on with it motion. "Who?"

"Carla."

His body tensed, and I knew that I'd hit on something. Maybe Jack already knew that Carla had done it—or had it done—and just didn't have enough for an arrest. Maybe I could help him with that.

"Why do you think Carla did it?"

"The ledgers."

He crossed the room and sat down on the edge of the bed. He motioned to the floral, upholstered chair that sat in the corner of the room, and I moved to it and sat down, casting aside a pair of pants and a top that I'd thrown there the previous night. He pulled a small notebook out of his back pocket and grabbed a pen from my bedside table.

It seemed all the men in my life carried around tablets, notebooks, or ledgers of some kind. Whether it was full of borrowed money and interest rates, betting odds and sports scores, or information on a murder investigation, depended on which man. And which type of ledger.

"Spill," Jack said, pen poised over paper.

"Whenever I play in one of Vince's games, I sign in for money borrowed in a ledger that Carla keeps."

"Vince Santini allows that stuff to be written down?"

"I don't know if Vince ever even has contact with the ledger. Carla usually keeps it. I don't know that it could ever be connected to Vince if it came down to that. I'm sure it would be destroyed long before it got to that point." He looked at me skeptically. "There's a lot of players involved here, Jack. Too many and too big of numbers to go solely by memory. Plus, when you borrow, you sign the ledger."

"Which in no way could be legally binding if you're talking about extortion," he pointed out.

"Right, and we—the players—know that, but there's something about signing that ledger in front of Carla—and Paulie—that, I don't know, makes it feel a little less seedy. Like we were just going to a cash cage at a casino and getting a line of credit or something. Cashing a check at a bank." I leaned forward, my arms resting on my thighs, trying to understand it myself, why signing that ledger lent a sense of...honor to something so dishonorable. "I'm sure it started as old school, just a way to keep track of it all. Obviously, it could now all be entered into something electronic that could be easily erased, but they must have known that the ledger would be more influential for a borrower. More...binding somehow."

"Honor amongst thieves?"

I leaned back in the chair, crossed my arms over my chest, not really liking Jack's summation. But not able to disagree with it either.

"Okay," he said, sensing my mood change, "let's get back to this ledger. The one Carla kept."

I uncrossed my arms, leaned forward once again, fully engaged now. "It's a blue leather one, with a red piping stripe across the front and down the binding. Jimmy's smaller one reminded me of it, that's what triggered this."

He wrote something in his notebook and motioned for me to go on. "But when I went to talk to Vince last night, he brought a ledger into the bedroom with us." Jack looked up sharply at me. "At a hotel suite," I tried to clarify, but that didn't seem to help. "Where a poker game was being played. With lots of other people there." Jack studied me for a second, then put his head down, writing and motioning for me to continue. "He wanted to talk in the bedroom of the suite for some privacy, but he brought Carla's ledger in with us because he didn't want the other players to think there was anything other than business going on between us."

"Which is true, right?"

"I wouldn't have crawled into bed with you last night if it wasn't."

He nodded. "So, the ledger last night?"

"The one he took from Carla and brought into the bedroom with us was a black leather one, with a gold piping stripe."

"So? They started a new ledger."

"No, I saw this one. It was half full with really recent dates in it. It had my signature in it from past games."

"So?"

"I never signed a black ledger. Always blue."

"You can be sure of that?"

"Yes. I'm absolutely sure of that."

"Double books."

"Yep."

"No way are there going to be two sets of something so incriminating. One is bad enough, but necessary."

"Exactly," I said. He was with me now.

"She cooked the books on Vince. When she ran a game alone, she used the one ledger then showed Vince the other one."

"Right."

"She would have had to forge the players' signatures."

I shrugged. "Not so hard to do if they're right in front of you. I'm sure Vince wasn't studying the signatures too closely. He'd be looking at amounts borrowed and start figuring how much he'd make in interest. He's seldom at the games. In fact never when Paulie was alive, so he wouldn't have noticed the different books."

"So, somebody borrows 20 K, signs for it in Carla's ledger. Then she writes 18 K in Vince's ledger. When they collect, she pockets the difference."

"Right, but she couldn't do it alone. She had to have the cooperation of the collector, the enforcer."

"Paulie," we both said at the same time, Jack scribbling away.

"So they were skimming off the top from Vince Santini."

"Probably little amounts, but who knows for how long. I'm sure it added up."

"So, why would she kill the only man who can keep their scam going?"

I shrugged. "Maybe Paulie was skimming off of her share? Or she was on to him? Maybe he was going to rat her out to Vince? The way she spoke about him at his funeral, I don't think there was ever any love lost between the two of them. Something probably came to a breaking point."

"That's a long leap to murder," Jack said calmly, but I noticed there was no skepticism in his voice.

"That leap is made every day, you know that."

"Yes, it is."

"There could have been all kinds of other things going on, too. You've said yourself you never really know what's going to make people snap. Look at Saul."

"That's true."

"It makes sense, Jack. I don't know all the whys, and the hows, but it makes sense."

He was nodding and folding up his notebook. "I need to go," he said, rising from the bed and coming to stand in front of me. He knelt down onto his haunches, putting himself level with me. "I probably won't be back tonight. We'll want to move on this."

"So you think there's something there?"

"I think you're on to something, yes."

I let out a long breath. I was glad I could help out Jack, and in a way, Vince. But I liked Carla and didn't want to be the one to cause her downfall. Though I guess she did that herself the moment she decided to get rid of Paulie.

"I'll call you tomorrow," he said, rising.

I got up from my chair and put my arms around his neck, kissed his strong jaw. "Be careful," I whispered.

"Always."

"Call me as soon as you know anything." He looked down at his feet, avoiding my gaze. "Please," I added. He slowly looked up, met my eyes, and gave a small nod of consent. He kissed me and left the room.

SUNDAY WAS DAY SIXTEEN, and I desperately wanted to place a bet. Not so much for the bet itself, but for the distraction a Hummer would create. I hadn't heard from Jack by noon, so I called and left him a message asking him to call me back.

By two, I'd almost gotten in my car and gone to a casino, but Ben, sensing my agitation, asked me to help him set up a new jigsaw puzzle in his bedroom. I spent a few hours with him, turning pieces over, separating the edge pieces.

I'd told Jimmy and Ben (and Raymond, but he didn't know any of the players) about my suspicion of Carla last night after Jack left. After I laid out my case, they seemed to think I was on to something. Not hearing a word from Jack was, I thought, confirming my suspicions.

Was Carla right now being interrogated in that dreaded room at the station? Were Jack and Frank Botz searching her apartment for the murder weapon? I couldn't see Carla shooting Paulie in cold blood, but recently I'd seen a lot of stuff happen that I wouldn't have believed from people I thought I knew well.

And really, did I know Carla all that well? Sure, I'd seen her a few nights a week, talked with her as I got my chips and cashed out. She always had a magazine with her at the poker games, and we'd often chat about the celebrities on the cover or an article she was reading.

I liked her, but it was more the type of relationship you might have with a waiter at a restaurant you frequented a few nights a week.

Except for the extortion part.

Finally, around eight, and after three voice mails, Jack called me back.

"I can't talk long," he said. "I just wanted to let you know I wouldn't be coming over tonight. I think it's going to take all night."

"What will, exactly?"

There was a lot of noise in the background, men shouting, so he must have been at the station. "I can't tell you exactly, you know that. But it's all coming to a head."

"So, it was Carla? Were you able to find her?"

There was a hesitation. "Come on, Jack, I'm the one who turned you on to her."

He let out a long breath. "She's here now."

"Did she confess?"

"She's uh…being cooperative, that's all I can say." He

sounded distracted, and I knew I wasn't going to get much out of him.

"But she's in custody?"

I heard someone in the background shouting for Jack. "What? Yeah," he said, then to the background person he yelled, "Coming." And then softer, to me, "Listen, I have to go."

"Oh, okay. Thanks for keeping me up to speed."

"I'll call you when I can," he said and hung up.

So, it was over. Paulie's murder solved. Well, if not completely over, it was well on its way. I'd been questioned by Frank and Jack myself. Those guys knew how to work it.

It had been wrapped up at the end of the episode, much as Jack—and I—thought it wouldn't be. I guess I should have felt something more than I did—pride that I'd helped, satisfaction that justice would be served. But I didn't.

I felt bad for Carla and what was going to happen to her. I felt worse for Vince, who not only lost his best friend but would now also lose another piece of his past. And would find out he'd been betrayed by both.

God, it would kill him to know that Paulie and Carla had cooked the books and stolen from him. As loyal as he'd been to those two on his climb up the loan shark ladder? It would be devastating. And to find it out from Frank Botz, or worse, Jack? Cruel, cruel salt in his wound.

As if I'd conjured him up, my phone rang and my caller ID showed Vince. Would he have known about Carla already?

"Hi," I said when I answered.

"Anna, are you busy?"

"No."

"I need to see you."

"Vince, I thought we kind of decided…"

"This isn't about that. About us. It's about Carla."

Did he know about her being questioned? Possibly arrested.

"What about her?"

"I'd rather not talk about it on the phone. I could come there if—"

"No," I said quickly. I did not want him here with Raymond in the house. I didn't want Raymond to ever see Vince if at all possible. Vince wouldn't want that either. "I'll come to you. Where are you?"

"I'm at home. At my condo."

"I'll be right over."

"Thanks," he said and hung up.

On one hand I would have rather met somewhere public so that there were no misinterpretations of me going to Vince's condo. From either Vince or Jack. But on the other hand, anywhere else would probably be a casino and after the last twenty-four hours of being on edge about Carla, Jack and this whole damn thing, I wasn't feeling particularly strong.

I went into the book room to tell Ben I was going out for awhile and saw a flash of concern in his eyes. "I'm not going to a casino," I added. "Just to see a friend for a couple of hours."

His brown eyes narrowed. He knew all my friends.

"I'm going to talk to Vince."

"You're not going to tell him about Carla, are you?"

I shook my head. "I'm not going to tell him anything. But I think he already knows. I'm guessing that's why he called."

"Oh." He looked away for a moment, toward the televisions, but I knew he wasn't watching the game. "You don't need to meet him, you know. You could stay right out of it. Let Jack handle it."

"I know. But it sounded kind of important and I owe him. He was...he got..." I looked at Raymond, who sat in a chair next to Ben and had been silently taking this all in. "He's the reason Raymond—and I—are safe and out from under an investigation."

Ben looked from me to Raymond, who remained silent, then back to me and began reluctantly nodding. "If you owe him, this would be a good payback. You're right, he probably already knows and just wants to talk about it with somebody who knows all the players. It's awful to be betrayed by a friend. It's easier if they're with someone they trust and…love."

I knew Ben wasn't just talking about Vince, but also about the news I'd had to break to him after Saul had died.

"I won't be long," I said softly and left.

I put on my jacket, left the house, fired up the Porsche and drove toward Palms Place.

Twenty-Nine

❖

"COME IN, ANNA," Vince said, holding the door open wide for me. "Thanks for seeing me."

"No problem."

He closed the door behind me and held his hand out for my jacket, which I handed him and he hung up in the closet. His voice dropped a bit lower, softer, as he added, "I wish we were in the same place we were the last time you were here."

Thinking about our near miss that night, I avoided his gaze and turned toward the living room, following Vince as he walked past me, led me to the couch and sat down, motioning me to sit next to him. Instead, I sat in the chair opposite him, prompting a small, sad smile from him.

"What can I do for you, Vince? Or should we maybe step out onto the balcony? It's a cool evening, but..."

He held up a hand. "No. I can ask you what I need to in here." Either this didn't concern his loan sharking business, or Vince was certain his room was not being listened in on. Maybe he swept on a regular basis? Maybe it was just his car he was concerned about? "When you signed for money borrowed, do you remember much about the ledger?"

So he'd figured it out. I nodded. "Yes, it was blue with red piping."

His head dropped as if he'd taken a blow. In a way he had.

"Are you sure?"

I nodded. "I'm sure. Blue with red. Every time."

He let out a large sigh. "That's what I was afraid of." He looked at me. "You know, don't you?"

I nodded.

"How long have you known?"

"I just figured it out the other night, when you had that other ledger with you."

"The ledger she gave me each week."

I didn't say anything more, just nodded. I didn't tell him I'd told Jack about it, or even that Carla was right now possibly being charged for Paulie's murder.

His cool demeanor completely slipped off his face. Actually seemed to slide down his strong features, leaving a look of bewilderment and hurt. Oh, you could see the hurt there, raw and undisguised, for a few seconds. Then he gathered himself, took several deep breaths, looked at me and said, "Thank you for telling me." His shoulders slumped as he sat back into the deep cushions of the couch. "Christ, I don't believe it. After all we'd been through together? They'd steal from me?"

"Maybe they knew you were changing, Vince. Maybe they thought you'd grow out of them, that they'd be cut out."

"I'd never do that. I never *did* do that. And I could have." His voice had a bruised defensiveness in it, which made me ache for him.

"I know. And they probably figured that out at some point—your loyalty to them. But by then they'd probably gotten a taste and..." I didn't need to finish the thought. He and I both knew what happened to people when they got a taste for something. He made a living off of those people.

JoJo had been born because of it.

"Would you have told me about this if I hadn't called you? Hadn't asked you?"

I leaned forward, touched his knee. "Yes, I would have." It

was true, I would have, but not until it had all played out and Carla was arrested.

He put his hand over mine. I patted his, and then, not wanting him to read more into my motives than were there, I removed my hand and sat back in my chair. He studied me for a moment. "Because you owed me?" he said, hitting the nail on the head.

"Yes," I whispered. "But I do think of you as a friend, Vince, and I want to be a friend to you."

He nodded but didn't look at me. "I know. Thank you."

I was wondering if I should leave him alone now or just stay quietly in my chair in case he needed me when the buzzer in the hallway went off, signaling a visitor.

"Were you expecting someone? I can leave—"

He waved for me to stay in my seat as he rose and strode to the hallway. "No. Stay. I don't know who this could be." He reached the intercom, pressed the button and said, "Yes?"

"Vince," came Carla's voice through the speaker. "Thank God, you're home. I need to speak with you."

I could see Vince's hand, frozen near the buttons as he looked back at me. I sat, stunned, then lifted my hands in a "I don't know what's going on" manner. He was watching me, thinking. I could see his wheels turning, but I wasn't sure what was adding up. Had he known that Carla had been picked up and was wondering what she was doing free? Or was he thinking how fortuitous that Carla had come to him just as he'd figured out she was stealing from him? Had he already made the jump that I had, that Carla was involved with Paulie's death?

Something clicked for him, and a look of steely resignation came over him as he buzzed Carla in then walked over to me. "I need you to get out of sight."

"Why is she here?" I asked, knowing Vince didn't have the answers any more than I did.

"I'm not sure, but I think I have an idea." Oh, maybe he did have the answers.

He started to lead me to the balcony. The kitchen was an open space, so there was no place to hide there, and I didn't really want to go to his bedroom. The balcony was dark now, and I'd be able to see in but would be unnoticeable to anyone inside. In case Vince…what? I put my hand on his arm. "What are you going to do to her?" I could understand his fury with Carla, but I certainly couldn't stand by while he hurt her.

"I'm not going to do anything. I just want to see what she's up to."

I couldn't argue with that—I wanted to know what was going on, too. I stepped out onto the balcony, and Vince slid the door shut behind me. But I stuck my foot in the crack just as the doorbell rang and he turned to go to the door, leaving myself enough space to be able to hear. I knew that wasn't what Vince had intended, but I wanted to be able to help if needed.

Though I wasn't really sure whether it was Vince or Carla that would need the help.

I crouched down low, so that I wouldn't be in anyone's line of sight in case they were able to see into the darkness better than I thought, or if the lights of the city behind me would outline me in some way. I inched my way to the crack in the door. There were a couple of blind spots in the sunken living room, but for the most part I could see most of the living area.

Vince answered the door and Carla stormed into the room, her short, straight bob of hair swinging wildly against her chin. Vince tried to corral her into the space in the foyer, but she blew past him and came into the living room, then turned to face him as he slowly made his way down the two steps from the foyer to the living area. I thought he took a quick peek over Carla's shoulder in my direction, but I wasn't sure.

"You set me up, you son of a bitch," Carla said to Vince. She was pointing at him, her hand shaking.

"I don't know what you're talking about." He was calm,

cool, giving nothing away. Trying to draw her out, see what cards she was holding. Almost like a poker game.

With a murder rap as ante.

"When did you find out about me and Paulie? When did you find out about the skimming? How long have you been planning this whole thing you sick fuck?"

"I don't know what you're talking about," he repeated.

He could have just told her, I suppose, that he'd just figured it out, but he was playing some sort of game, and I just waited to see where it was going. He certainly didn't seem like he was about to pull out a gun and blow her away, so I didn't think there was any need for me to announce myself.

She really paused this time, as if she didn't know which direction to head next. Finally, she said, "Is this how you're going to play it? You kill a man who has been nothing but good to you for twenty years, set me up to take the fall, and you just stand there like you've never seen me before."

"I don't know what you're talking about," was all he said. All he'd said since she came in the door, and all in a total, icy monotone.

I didn't know what the hell she was talking about either. First of all, what was she even doing out of police custody? No way could they have arraigned her and she make bail all since I talked with Jack.

I replayed my conversation with Jack. He didn't actually say they'd charged her. Being cooperative, that's how he'd put it. I took that to mean she was confessing, or at least answering the questions they asked. But it could have meant something else. This was all bubbling around me, trying to make some kind of sense.

No way would they let her out of there if they had enough evidence to hold her. Maybe that was it, they had to let her go because there wasn't enough evidence. "All coming to a head" —that was the other phrase Jack had used. That didn't seem likely to happen if they were just letting her walk away after questioning.

And here she was, accusing Vince of murdering Paulie. Trying to deflect the blame from herself? Had she done that when she'd been with Jack, try to set up Vince?

"How long before you took me out, too, Vince?" Carla had seemed to find her footing once again, though this time her voice was clearer, calmer. Trying to match her opponent's game, a good poker tactic. "Or did you just need to get rid of Paulie because the skim wouldn't work without the collector in on it? Did you think that it was all Paulie's idea and that he was the one that deserved the punishment? Well, it was me, Vince. I was the brains behind it all. Paulie just went along with it."

I could have figured that out. With those two, Carla had definitely been the brains and Paulie the muscle.

"I don't know what you're talking about," Vince said once again. Wow, the man should play more poker, as cool as he kept with Carla taunting him like this. I started to wonder about Carla being the brains if she was stupid enough to come here and beard the lion in his own den.

And it seemed as if that's exactly what she was trying to do. Make the lion roar.

But why? Did she think to provoke him into admitting to a murder he didn't commit, that she herself had?

Thoughts started whirling around again, not adding up in the direction I had thought but possibly in another?

I saw Vince dart his eyes toward the balcony again, and I crouched lower. Stupid, he knew I was out here, and I obviously hadn't gone anywhere, nor could I, twenty-five stories up. Was he trying to gauge if I could hear Carla and him?

Or was he already thinking about what to do with a witness? Me.

Because now I was starting to believe that Carla hadn't killed Paulie. And that Vince had.

I grabbed for my phone, which was in my coat pocket. In the hall closet. Suddenly, I realized how freezing I was in the brisk air. I looked around the balcony for something that could be useful in some way. A random cell phone would be nice. But no, just your run-of-the-mill balcony stuff. Furniture, a potted plant, that blanket that he'd so gently wrapped around my shoulders not so long ago.

Carla had taken a step away from Vince, but she still had her back to the balcony. "Were you planning on taking me out too until you got cozy with Anna Dawson? Was that the plan, Vince? I suppose I was the next target until you found a way you could frame Paulie's murder on me. Nobody would find out you did it, and I'd be doing fifteen to twenty. Win, win for you.

"It really was a stroke of genius though, Vince, showing her the ledger the other night. It was a risk though, that she'd put it together and run to her boyfriend, but I guess you know her better than I thought."

I guess he did. I had been well and truly played.

Whatever she and Jack had hatched up—and now I was guessing she was wearing a wire and Jack was listening in—had no chance in hell of working with me on the balcony listening in. No confessions would be forthcoming.

As if proving my point, Vince said yet again, but this time staring beyond Carla and out into the dark night, in my general direction, "I have no idea what you're talking about."

Carla knew something was up. She knew Vince was on to her and wasn't going to spill anything, let alone make any kind of blanket confession. She shook her head, called Vince a really bad name, then headed toward the door, having given up.

I thought of my options. If I came through the door now and spoke up, whoever was listening in would know I was there. That would make it harder for Vince to stop me from leaving with Carla. *If* Carla was wearing a wire. And *if* those listening in were nearby in case something went wrong.

It could also force Vince into making some kind of move against Carla. He was letting her walk out the door now. Why shouldn't he? She'd learned nothing new from her visit. But if I popped into the room, after what I'd heard, would he willingly let Carla walk out the door? I couldn't take the risk. I'd already accused the poor woman of murder. Could I put her in harm's way on the off chance that somebody might come charging to the rescue?

I needed to get her out of the room, and yet let her backup know I was here.

I crawled my way across the balcony, emptying my pockets as I went for anything I could use. Nothing but money and odds sheets. Nothing that would help me right now, but if something happened to me...if I didn't get out of this. I touched and re-touched the odds sheets, leaving my fingerprints all over them and slid them into any nook and cranny I could find. Under the legs of the table, along the walls where they met the cement slab, jamming them in. I wasn't sure how old they were, hopefully they were dated for games that happened after the other night I'd been here so, if found, Vince couldn't say I'd left them here that night.

I went to the blanket and shook my head, letting stray hairs fall on it. I scraped my hand against the privacy wall between Vince's unit and the one to his side, letting my skin peel off, not even feeling the pain.

If I disappeared, there'd be DNA traces of me all over this balcony, and skin samples and blood would be pretty hard to explain away. As would hidden odds slips with dates after the night I'd been kissing Vince on this very balcony.

The thought of DNA reminded me that I'd never found out about Jack's parentage. Surely Lor would see to it that Jack found out about whom his father was if I didn't make it.

The seriousness of this—that I may never see Jack, or Lor, or Ben again—suddenly rushed through me. I went through all of that shit to make sure Raymond was okay, that I wouldn't be found out. Confessed to Jack about JoJo. And I now…no, no way was I going to have gone through all that and not make it now.

I made my way to the balcony railing then stood up and leaned over and out. "Is anyone on their balcony?" I asked. I didn't yell, but was as loud as I thought I could be without tipping off Vince inside. I took a quick glance inside. He was shutting the door behind Carla and now turned toward the balcony.

"Can anyone hear me?" I said more loudly now that Carla was gone. "Anyone? I need help!"

Nothing. Too cold for the normal glass of wine on the balcony crowd. I stood as tall as I could and faced the city. I looked down but nobody was walking in the parking lot. I'm not sure they would have heard me anyway with all the regular city traffic. There was even a siren blaring in the near distance, a regular Vegas backdrop.

If Carla had been wearing a wire, would there be a sound truck nearby, like in the movies? Would they be watching? If they had been, would they still be now that Carla had left the condo? I didn't know, but on the off chance, I started waving my hands frantically, jumping up and down.

I looked below me. A chair, one of the chairs. I'd throw it over the side, hoping that it hit a lower balcony, drew attention or just went crashing to the ground. I started to turn to the table and chairs when I stopped cold.

"So, Anna," I heard Vince say behind me.

I slowly turned around to face him. I moved up against the railing, trying to put as much space between him and myself as possible.

He made a motion with his hands toward me. "I assume from your actions that you heard all that?"

I nodded.

He took a step closer to me, a genuine look of sadness on his face. "Oh, Anna, what am I going to do with you?"

Thirty

"**YOU DON'T HAVE TO DO** anything, Vince. What I heard tonight doesn't prove anything. I don't *know* anything."

"No, nobody was going to find out anything on that little fishing expedition. I thought your boyfriend was a bit more subtle than that."

"It might have worked if I hadn't been here."

He just nodded his head; he'd already known that. Trying to get Vince to talk on wire was a long shot at best, but it had no shot whatsoever the minute I stepped into Vince's condo.

"Come on in from the cold, Anna. Let's talk about this," he said softly, holding his hand out to me.

Everything I learned in a women's self-defense class that Lor dragged me to came flooding back to me. First and foremost, never go anywhere with an abductor. You're much better to stand and fight in a parking lot than to get into a car with anyone. I didn't know if that applied to moving from a balcony to a—warm—living room, but at least out here there was nothing hidden.

I knew Vince was unarmed, that there were no weapons of any kind out here—Lord knows I'd looked—and if by chance it came time to scream, I had a much better chance of someone hearing me out here. "We can talk about it right here," I said.

"You must be freezing," he said. He walked over to the table.

I edged further down the balcony rail, but he only grabbed the blanket placed on the back of a chair and tossed it to me. I held my hands out to grab it when I belatedly wondered if he'd rush me, or do something, if the blanket was just a decoy. But no, he didn't move. I caught the blanket and wrapped it around my shoulders. I leaned against the railing of the balcony, its metal bars pressing into the backs of my legs.

We looked at each other for a moment when I finally tried to bluff my way out of this. "Look, Vince, like I said, I didn't hear anything that the cops didn't on a wire—if that's what they're doing."

"I'm sure they were."

"Yeah, probably. But you obviously didn't give them anything."

"What if I told you there was nothing to give?"

I didn't miss a beat. "I'd believe you."

He watched me for a long time, but I didn't flinch or look away. I just kept my normal look. Jack always said I had a tell, but no professional poker player I'd ever played had found it, and I didn't think Vince would either.

He looked away, then quickly back at me. "God, you're good. I can see why you've won all that you have."

"I'm telling the truth, Vince." He scoffed at that, but I could tell he was unsure. "And besides, what if I did believe Carla, that you killed Paulie and tried to set her up? The cops obviously can't prove it or we wouldn't be out here in the fresh air talking. You'd be in some holding cell."

"Because, Anna, in your own way, you're as tenacious as Schiller. If you believed it, you'd..."

"What? What could I do that the cops couldn't?"

He didn't have an answer because there wasn't one. I was right. The cops had a ton of crime-fighting stuff at their disposal. If they couldn't get the goods on Vince, how could I?

But he was right, too. I was tenacious. You didn't survive—

thrive—in this town for as long as I have if you weren't. I wouldn't let it go, and not because I felt the need to seek justice for Paulie. He and Carla had worked for a loan shark. Paulie had beaten the shit out of too many people to count, had probably even offed a couple over the years. And they'd both been stupid enough to steal from Vince. It was the world they chose, and Paulie had received what was his due in that world.

But him setting up Carla to take the fall for something he did—and most importantly, using me to do it—that would never allow me to drop it.

But he didn't need to have that confirmed.

"Vince, this is silly. And between you and Carla and the cops. I'm not involved, I have no intention of becoming involved. And I don't think you have much to worry about. The cops believe Carla's story that she was set up, they have nothing on you, so this has all the makings of a very cold case."

"Until they find the gun that killed Paulie hidden in Carla's air-conditioning unit with her prints all over it." He let out a deep breath after he said it, knowing by admitting it he had just sealed both of our fates.

One of us wasn't walking out of here.

My shoulders slumped, the blanket slid down my arms and to the concrete floor of the balcony. "I'm not leaving this balcony with you," I said softly.

"I'm sorry it has to be this way Anna. I know you thought you were doing me a favor by breaking the news about Carla to me, but you only…"

"I owed you, Vince. And I didn't think I was telling you anything you didn't already know. Besides, you were only asking me about the ledgers in case I hadn't figured it out by myself. You *wanted* me to take that information to Jack."

He chuckled. "The hell of it is, you *didn't* owe me. I didn't do it. I didn't arrange for those men to refute Bubba Kinney. I have no idea who did, but it wasn't me. You didn't owe me anything. You could have said no to coming over and been home playing cards right now."

After my initial, "Oh, fuck," my mind raced with this new information and what it could mean. And then landed on a big, fat, answer. "Jimmy."

"That's what I figured, too," Vince said. I hadn't even known I'd said it out loud. "Who knew he still had those kinds of connections?"

"I knew," I said, "I just thought yours were stronger."

"They probably are, but I wasn't going to call in any favors for Raymond Joseph. He's a big boy, he knew what he was doing."

"And if he'd ratted?"

"He never would have had a chance."

"Quite the night for true confessions, Vince."

A small smile quirked on his lips. "They say it's good for the soul."

He took a step toward me, and I inched closer to the corner where the waist-high balcony railing met dividing wall. "I told Ben this is where I was coming tonight."

"And you did. You stopped in, we had a nice chat, and then you left. Carla can verify that no one else was here when she stopped in later."

"Security cameras," I offered up. I didn't even know if his building had security cameras. It must. Vegas was the home of security cameras.

"There are blind spots. I made sure of that before I bought."

Of course he did. What self-respecting criminal wouldn't? "My car…," I started, but I was running out of cards to play and he knew it. He had much more experience at this than I did.

Not that I wanted to beef up my résumé on the topic of having my life threatened. But this was my second time in just a month or so. You'd think I'd be getting a little bit better.

"Your car will be gone. As will you. Come on, Anna, we've

played this game long enough."

He held his hand out to me. He had maneuvered himself—and I had stupidly inched my way into a corner—between me and the door to the condo.

"I'm not leaving with you, Vince," I tried to sound solid and confident and I thought I did, but he only smiled at me, a tiny touch of pity mixed with patronization.

He walked the steps between us and grabbed my arm. "I'm with Vince Santini and I'm in danger. Call the police," I yelled as loudly as I could. "I'm with Vince Santini and I—" I felt Vince's warm hand go across my mouth, and his other one grab my arm as he swung me around, my back to his chest, and tried to drag me toward the glass doors.

And you know what went through my mind? Not thoughts of Jack and never seeing him again, or of what would happen to Raymond now, or even my beloved Ben.

What I thought about was how could Vince's hands be so warm when it was so cold?

Then he started to move with me, and I sprung into action. Better to have this out, now, where someone might hear my, albeit muffled, cries than in my Porsche in the desert right before I got a bullet in the head and my baby was torched.

I struggled, I tried to wrench my mouth free to yell. I went for the windpipe, the throat, the arch of his foot, the groin, all the places I'd learned to attack first in that self-defense class.

But Vince could have taught that class, because he seemed to know exactly where his vulnerable spots lay and protected them, pushing me this way and that so that I never got a clear blow.

He tried to pull me with him, but I looped my leg around one of the vertical bars that connected the railing to the floor. There was just enough room for me to slide my foot in and hook it around the back of the steel bar. I stayed in place, but had given up any kind of leverage with that side of my body.

I started to reach for his hands, his face, anything I could scratch. I'd get his skin under my nails in case…well, if it got to that, they'd probably never find my body. But at least I'd leave marks on Vince. Marks that hadn't been on his face when Carla had come by. Let him explain that.

I got a good swipe at his face and heard his groan of pain. He probably wanted to call me all sorts of names, but he was trying to be as quiet as possible outdoors like this. I tried to hear any sounds around me, wondering if anybody would be able to hear my cries if I could just get my mouth free for a good yell.

I heard traffic, of course, but it was distant, and the sounds of Vince and me breathing heavily, and the sounds of our struggle. But I heard something else. A ringing? Buzzing? I couldn't quite make it out, or even where it was coming from. The street? A condo nearby?

My head as I started to lose the battle?

He wrenched me hard, and I felt my ankle pop as he tore me away from the bars. Shit, my bad foot. That was going to be a bitch to rehab. And yes, even though I was elbowing and gouging and trying to fight off a man six inches taller and a good seventy pounds heavier, the irony of the situation fled over me.

My first real brush with Vegas, all those years ago, started with my foot being mangled courtesy of Vince Santini. And now it looked like my last hurrah was going to end the same way.

Unless I could start screaming again and hope that whatever—and whomever—had produced that buzzing sound would be able to hear me. I tried to wedge my mouth open a tiny bit through Vince's iron grip. Just enough to…there. I bit down with everything I had, catching mostly my own bottom lip, but enough of Vince's hand to make him yelp and pull his hand away from my mouth.

"Help," I screamed. We were standing about a yard from the railing, facing one of the divider walls, our back to the other. I opened my mouth to scream again and from the corner of my eye I saw Vince's arm reach high—very high—a wind-up for a blow that would surely knock me senseless and end this whole thing.

I pushed back with my butt, trying to gain as much space as possible between our bodies, thinking that would lessen the blow. Vince's other hand was still firmly grasped around my arm, on the railing side of our bodies. His arm started to descend, it seemed as if in slow motion.

But then my brain speeded up as I saw a flash of white coming from the condo. I heard a "No," screamed very loudly, and not from me. And then the flash of white—a person—was flying at Vince, catching him with his arm up high, and just a bit off kilter from where I'd pushed back with my butt.

It was enough. The white blob's momentum, Vince's position and my last effort push was enough to send Vince back with a force that took him over the side of the railing. He fell, and I felt a rush of relief, until I was jolted by my arm…that Vince still held on to.

I tried to drop to the ground, to create as much leverage as possible, but I couldn't, my arm was already, due to Vince's momentum and body weight, over the side of the railing. He hung on to me, my knit Henley stretching as his grip slid down my arm. I thought for a moment he might just slide down and away, but he grabbed my hand with his. And, with a reflex so basic I didn't have time to understand it, I grabbed back.

"Hang on," I said. "We'll get help."

I looked to my savior. Carla. "Call for help," I said to her. My arm felt like it could pull out of its socket at any second. I tried to brace my body as well as I could against the bars, sticking my legs in between the bars, turning to my side to ease the pressure, but I couldn't seem to put much weight on my bad foot, and my hold on Vince was tenuous at best. At least the railing seemed to be solid enough to hold the weight.

Carla looked over the railing to Vince, who looked back

at her. Years and years passed between them in that one look. Carla's face turned up into a smile, but there was no joy there, only hatred. "We need backup," she said with a sneer, confirming to both Vince and I that she had indeed been wearing a wire.

Vince looked at her, knowing that cops were seconds away. They would easily be able to pull him to safety. And then the cops would take him away. He looked at me.

"I always liked you, Anna," he said to me, repeating the words he'd said to me ten years ago, the first time he'd sent Paulie my way to bash my foot.

I'd believed he meant it then. I believed he meant it now.

He let go of my hand and plunged twenty-five stories.

I turned away, not able to look. Carla had no problem, leaning over the railing to see Vince's body. I think I even heard her spit in his general direction.

I slid down to the cement floor, my foot having taken all it could. I wrapped my arms around myself, finally allowing myself to shiver from the cold. "Thank you," I said to Carla, but it came out rough. I cleared my throat and tried again. "Thank you." I heard a bustle in the condo and saw people, led by Jack, rushing toward us.

Carla didn't take her eyes off of Vince's body. "Don't thank me. I didn't do it for you." She took a deep breath, let it out. Just a lovely night on the balcony, getting a spot of fresh air.

"I did it for Paulie."

Thirty-One

❖❖

MY ARM TURNED OUT TO BE FINE. Wrenched, and sore as hell, but basically no damage. My foot didn't turn out as bad as I thought, either. Well, it was bad, but I'd been through two surgeries and months of rehab with it before, so walking out on crutches with a boot felt like I was getting off pretty lightly.

Certainly in better shape than Vince.

The buzzing/ringing I'd heard was Carla at Vince's door. She'd come back to try again. Jack and Frank were in an empty condo on the same floor, and when she'd left Vince she'd gone there and talked them into letting her have another go. They'd gotten nothing, so they had nothing to lose.

She'd rung the bell and when Vince hadn't answered she should have turned around and gone back to the cops, but she had a set of keys that Vince had given her to drop off the ledger when he wasn't around and she figured this was her chance to snoop around and maybe find something that the cops wouldn't be able to without a warrant.

Thank God she was so determined.

Although, it might have been funny if things had played out and Vince was trying to get rid of my body by sneaking it past the condo two doors down where Jack and Frank were holed up.

Well, not funny, of course. Ironic? Comedic?

Okay, it would have been horrific. And it didn't happen, and I figured it was the pain meds they'd given me that took my mind there in the first place.

Jack could barely speak to me through his fury, and after making sure I was basically okay, he stayed as far away from me as possible as Frank took my statement and other investigators scurried about. It was Frank who'd ridden with me in the ambulance to the hospital. And now, twelve hours later, it was Frank who was holding my crutches as a nurse wheeled me to the hospital doors to be released.

But it was Jack who pulled up to the curb driving my Porsche.

All my years of poker training were shot to hell as I started sobbing, so relieved that this was all over, that Raymond was out of trouble, I was alive, and Jack...

Jack was giving me the evil eye as he snatched the crutches from Frank, who then helped get me settled in the passenger seat. I saw my jacket, the one I'd left in Vince's closet, strewn over the headrest and dangling down the back.

We ended up having to stick the crutches out of my window a bit, and then Jack roared us out of the hospital lot.

"Christ, will you stop crying," he said as he stopped at a red light. He dug in his back pocket, pulled out a handkerchief and dumped it in my lap. "It's hard to stay pissed at you when you cry like that."

I sniffled and sort of snorted a laugh as I brought the handkerchief to my nose. It smelled of Jack, and I breathed in deeply. Jack was the only man I knew, besides the men of The Corporation, who still carried a handkerchief. The thought that'd I almost lost the chance to ever see Jack again—to see anyone again—hit me once more, and I hiccupped tears for the rest of the drive.

He pulled into my driveway and turned the ignition off, and we just sat there until I was once again back under control.

I didn't want Ben to see me like this. The crutches and bruises were going to be bad enough to explain.

As if reading my mind, Jack said, "I called the house, talked to Ben. I told him what happened, so he won't be shocked when he sees you."

"Thank you."

He stared straight ahead, at the garage door in front of the car. "This has to be the end of it, Johanna, if we're going to be together." I started to say something, but he held up his hand, stopping me, though he still stared straight ahead. "And I do. Want us to be together. But I can't spend more time working the shit you're into up to your neck than I do my homicide cases."

"You won't. It's all over. It all died with Vince. JoJo. Raymond's point shaving. My sports betting. It all went over the side of that railing."

"He could have killed you. He *would* have killed you."

"I know. I think he would have hated to, but there was no doubt he was going to." I rubbed my hands through my hair. My ponytail had come undone hours ago, and my fingers got tangled in a mass of snarls. "He played me so well," I said.

Jack shrugged. "He knew how sharp you are, knew you'd put the pieces together. The pieces he used to set up Carla."

"Did you know it was him all along?"

"We suspected so, but we didn't have anything solid. And due to our—your and my—past history, I needed to be very sure before we could move on it. It had to be very by the book."

"So you knew he was using me?"

"Not entirely. We figured he was trying to set Carla up, and would need a way to do that. And by keeping you close, dating you, he could watch the progress of his plan play out."

"And here I thought he just wanted to sleep with me."

Jack snorted, then leaned close and placed his index finger on my horseshoe pendant. "Well, that's a given."

And then he finally looked me in the eye, his warm, brown

eyes searching mine, pleading with mine. "Honestly, Johanna? This is done? I mean, I know with my drinking I have no room to cast judgment, and I'm not, it's just that I can't handle…"

I put a finger to his lips. "Honestly," I whispered.

I don't know who moved first, but our mouths met in the sweetest kiss I could ever remember giving. And receiving.

"Come on," he said all too soon. "I think I see Ben poking his head through the curtains. We better go in."

He came around to my side of the car, helped me out, then handed me the crutches. "You're a pro on those things," he said after my first few steps.

I gave him a wry smile. "I learned the hard way."

We were almost to the front steps when he put his hand gently on my arm, and I turned to face him, leaning on my crutches.

"So, am I about to visit my father, or my father's best friend?"

I gasped, stunned. "How did you know?"

"Lorelei was none too subtle when taking my hair from my jacket."

"She said you never noticed."

"Please. And then, that same night? You being so careful when you took my drinking glass from the table. CSI people with tweezers in their hands and magnifying glasses aren't that obvious."

I was insulted. I thought I'd been so smooth.

"And then you take a bag into a DNA testing place a few days later."

"You were following me?"

"You, Vince, Carla, and anyone else involved in the case."

"I wasn't involved in the case."

"You were involved in Vince."

I looked away, to the front yard, so perfectly manicured by some lawn service Lor had hired. "How did you make the leap from you to Ben and Saul?"

"I am a detective, you know." I looked back to him, and he shrugged. "I remembered something Saul said when he died about Ben having a son. It made it all click."

"I'm sorry, Jack. I should have told you right away, but I wasn't sure there was anything to tell. I wanted to know more before talking to you. Or Ben."

"And are you sure now?"

I nodded. "The results were conclusive."

He took a deep breath, rubbed his hand along his cheeks. "Tell me."

I shook my head. "I don't know. Only Lorelei knows. We got the results back right when we were leaving for Chicago. I didn't have time to look at them."

"Are you shitting me? You really don't know?"

"Nope."

He gave me a quick kiss, opened the door for me and said, "Let's go find out."

Acknowledgments

I have been incredibly blessed to have two best friends, Kelly Campbell and Amy Pellizzaro, for well over 30 years. They know all my secrets…which is okay, 'cuz I know theirs.

A big thank you to critique partners extraordinaire, Holli Bertram and Colleen Gleason. As well as Kelly Young, a tremendous motivator!

Tanner Kearly was an early reader and helped me stay on track to finish—much appreciated. Ted Kearly shared his poker expertise and helped me out on winning hands. Any poker inaccuracies are my own.

And a special thank you to my agent, Jodi Reamer, for her advice, her confidence, and her belief.

The intervention information about compulsive gambling was gathered from various online sources, most notably www.psychologyinfo.com.

The Anna Dawson Series continues with

AGAINST THE RULES
ANNA DAWSON BOOK 3

Try Mara Jacobs's romantic mystery

BROKEN WINGS

Try Mara Jacobs's *New York Times* bestselling Worth series

Worth The Weight

Worth The Drive

Worth The Fall

Worth The Effort

Totally Worth Christmas

Worth The Price

Worth The Lies

Worth The Flight

Worth The Burn

Find out more at
www.MaraJacobs.com

Mara Jacobs is the *New York Times* and *USA Today* bestselling author of The Worth Series

After graduating from Michigan State University with a degree in advertising, Mara spent several years working at daily newspapers in Advertising sales and production. This certainly prepared her for the world of deadlines!

Mara writes mysteries with romance, thrillers with romance, and romances with...well, you get it.

Forever a Yooper (someone who hails from Michigan's glorious Upper Peninsula), Mara now splits her time between the U.P. and Las Vegas.

You can find out more about her books at **www.marajacobs.com**